THE PERFECT MARRIAGE?

I0691270

JYOTI GUPTA & VARUNA GUPTA

WORDIT ART FUND

This book has been fully funded by the Wordit Art Fund. Wordit Art Fund helps deserving authors publish their work by providing monetary support. To apply for funding, please visit us at www.BecomeShakespeare.com

First published in 2017 by

Becomeshakespeare.com
Wordit Content Design & Editing Services Pvt Ltd
Unit - 26, Building A-1, Nr Wadala RTO, Wadala (East),
Mumbai 400037, India
T:+91 8080226699

©
ISBN 978-93-86487-59-9

True happiness lies in the natural harmony of physical, mental and spiritual and without this one can never attain happiness which is the only goal of human life.

To two strongest women in our lives
Our late grandmother Smt.Uma,
And
Our sister Shilpa
Plus
Our two wonderful nieces Shivika and Kritika
who bring joy in our lives
And
Last but not the least
Our pillar of strength
Our father Shri.M.K. Gupta.

The Perfect Marriage?

Dear Friends,

We are so delighted to share with you our novel, The Perfect marriage?

Like one of the girls in the book, every girl lives the fondest memories of her childhood after her marriage.

In our novel, our character Smita is a young woman. The idea of marriage is what she wishes, but going to a new environment is a feeling we think all girls understand. The new faces in life play hide and seek with her and she learns to win the game.

This story would touch all of you as it shows the original emotions of an Indian married woman. This book gives you a chance to escape to a whole new world and makes you wish you were a part of it.

We have had a lot of friends, family members, sisters and cousins who are close to us and have inspired us.

Now please turn the page and meet one of the strongest heroines we've written. Smita is eager to tell her story, and we hope you are just eager to read it.

With warmest regards,

Jyoti and Varuna.

The Perfect Marriage?

PROLOGUE

There were some things that could not be in my control and fate was one of them. Still believing in fate didn't mean a woman simply stood and let it run her down.

I was simply excited and nervous. There were butterflies in my stomach, not just butterflies it was a mild word, but all kinds of creatures creating havoc on my senses. My father Pankaj Aggarwal had just arranged a meeting with someone… for marriage. His name was Avinash.

"Avinash," I said the name aloud. I suppose it had something of a ring to it and I liked his close up, but I was not sure what to expect. He belonged to a typical well to do Pandit family. Being a part of his family business of textiles he was said to earn well.

"Asha… Asha." I heard my father talking to my mother outside my room whose door was closed but could not make out their conversation.

After a few seconds, I heard. "Smita!"

It was my mom!

"Are you ready or not?" She called from outside the door banging it.

"Coming ma." I turned away from the long mirror where I was admiring my figure and rushed to the door. Opening the bolt I pushed the door open to see my mother standing outside with one hand on her waist. Dressed in her traditional saree and wearing her favourite kohlapuri slippers she stood there trying to put on a stern expression. My mother was a simple housewife who took care of her family. But she was stricter than my father.

"We are getting late. We are supposed to meet the boy's side in half an hour and you are not even ready." Her tirade continued as she walked into the room, twirling me first left and then right to see whether I was looking thin or not. I was dieting for a year and had come down from sixty-five kgs to fifty-five kgs.

My mother's exact words were, "how will you find a good boy if you are fat?!"

Yeah, right! Fat at sixty-five kgs with a height of five-five at most I could have been called pleasantly plump!

"Smita, sit on the chair. I need to straighten your hair a bit they are all mussed," she admonished me lightly.

I had to obey her command and sat down, taking out a long huff. Taking a brush she lovingly combed my hair that was long and straight, reaching almost till my waist.

"Who will do all this for you after marriage?" She combed out the knots, leaving my hair gleaming.

"Then don't get me married. Simple," I replied instantly with a shrug.

"Nonsense! He is a good boy, well settled and educated. We know his family and you will be happy there. Oh, Krishna! I just hope the boy says yes." My mom closed her eyes briefly in prayer.

"And what about me?" I pouted, showing my displeasure at

the comment making eye contact with my mother through the mirror.

Shouldn't even I like the person? I thought. After all, I was the one marrying him and not my mother!

"What about you? There is nothing to dislike. Now don't waste time turn around, I will check your makeup." She swivelled my chair inspecting my face with an eye of a hawk. Being whitish I had a typical Indian complexion. My mother had arranged an appointment with the beautician in the morning and voila after two hours of facial I had come out fairer. She usually thought of everything, planned for contingencies and was so organised that sometimes it made me and my brother groan.

After I had protested at the appointment she had spoken crisply, "it is a fact that every boy wants a fair girl. Every girl trying to get married has to go through the same process and so will you." That had shut me up.

At seventeen, I had entered the famous Hindu college pursuing my History (Hons) course. My father was a soft-spoken man, who did not speak much, but when spoke said things that were to the point. He owned a shop of women handbags and accessories at South Extension. Being conservative and extra protective, before he left for the shop he made sure that I only travel by car from my house at Shalimar Bagh to college.

Every day I made sure to call my mother when I reached college, which would leave my father satisfied. But there were something's that couldn't be shared with one's parents like bunking classes and going to the movies, riding my friend Roshni's brand new bike and being the first one to take up any dare or challenge. The long and short of it was that though my parents were strict in matters concerning my going out with friends or alone, they gave me freedom to move around, do what I wanted and above all adored their only daughter. I remembered that when I wanted to learn Kathak, my father had instantly arranged for a guru to teach me. I was raised being pampered throughout and that's why I could twirl them, especially my father on my little finger. Of course, my younger brother Vikas was away in boarding, but he was always met with a harsher treatment because he had to earn, do something.

Even I always felt I had to do something more than being happily married and satisfied to stay at home with children and a husband. I wanted to finish my MA in history, but the idea of marriage was... humph... not repulsive I would not mind meeting him... Avinash.

PART 1

The Perfect Marriage?

CHAPTER 1

After half an hour I walked onto the white marbled hotel's lobby to meet him for the first time. The meeting was supposed to take place at the Claridges hotel where my father had arranged high tea.

My eyes moved from right to left eyeing people seated on the brown leather sofas to the singular huge china vase, complimented with peach orchids and ferns on a table topped with a rectangular mirror. A few steps ahead and I saw my face in the golden framed mirror reflecting the flowers, whose subtle colour bought a soft angelic glow to my face.

Still focussed on the mirror pumping inside me, fear, excitement was too unstable.

I glanced sideways when I caught a movement out of the corner of my eye. I saw Avinash's parents first and greeted them with a namaste while he stood with his back facing me. His mother looked round and short in a purple organza saree. As she adjusted a strangle of hair behind her right ear, her eyes were cool with suspicion. She gave me a quick up-and-down glance. I had the certain sensation I'd been studied carefully and thoroughly and the jury was still out. On the other hand, his father looked too thin I thought as if life had carved him down to the bare essentials. He wore a blue striped safari suit, had a wide smile that was more easing and comforting to the senses. I instantly liked him. It was now the son's turn.

For a second my heart stopped when Avinash made a quick turn and I caught the first sight of him. The only thought that entered my mind was that he was not as good looking as his photograph suggested nevertheless, he was impeccably dressed. He looked very sleek and cool when he stood. He was wearing grey slacks and a black shirt, and he looked as though he'd just had a haircut. He had faint lines fanning out from sharp black eyes. A narrow face, firm jaw with a long, straight nose.

I had thought he would be more muscular… Will he be able to even carry me? Carry me? Oh God! From where had that thought come? It was probably from the latest MB that I was reading. It was high time I stopped reading them. Grow up Smita! I said to myself, you are no longer a teenager, but a woman aged twenty-two and he is twenty-six.

My further ruminations came to a halt when my mom pushed me a little indicating that I move on. Avinash after giving me a small smile had by now turned around and was walking ahead. I walked beside my mother twirling my fingers with each other towards the restaurant. Inside the area was well lit and the tables inviting.

I would have laughed if I wasn't nervous as when I was about to sit beside my mother I was pushed by her.

A sweet smile plastered on her face was followed by a wise suggestion. "Beta why don't you two talk a little. You may sit there."

She pointed to another table a little ahead.

I was skeptical and hesitated. Sensing my hesitation, she scowled me and then laughed to hide her irritation for the benefit of guests. I was pushed again!

Well! There was no other choice in the matter. With as much dignity as I could muster, I walked towards the table with my light pink anarkali style suit bellowing a little. Before I could sit Avinash was beside me, pulling the chair. I beamed inside. He had scored a point! His chivalry pleased me. We sat down.

I smiled. He smiled. And then silence.

I turned my head a little and gasped aloud. Everyone was staring at us.

God, it was embarrassing! I was quick to look ahead when my gaze bumped with Avinash's. My mouth quirked into a smile as a silent message passed between us and he laughed. The ice was broken.

"Smita please don't feel uncomfortable. You can ask me anything you like," he said moving his head forward, both hands on the tables. His voice! I think that was what I fell for. It was soft and deep. A little like Amitabh Bacchan's.

"What are your hobbies?" I blurted. Shucks! What a stupid line I chided myself.

"I like watching cricket."

Oh shit! I hated it!

"Travelling…"

I always fell ill while travelling and besides, I was scared of heights while travelling by plane.

"Old songs, ghazals…

Yawn, boring! Boring!

"And long drives…"

I breathed a sigh of relief. Something matched.

"What about you?" He cocked his head.

"Me! Uh-huh… long drives…." I chewed my bottom lip as I tried to find the right words.

"Uhh.. and?" He questioned confused, studying my face.

I was saved from further embarrassment by the waiter.

"Ma'am tea or coffee?"

"Tea". Tea any day for me, I couldn't abide the smell of coffee.

"Sir?" He asked Avinash.

"Coffee."

Great! We had another point of difference.

After the waiter served and left, I gave Avinash a good study. "You don't like tea?"

He shook his head. "No, I don't have tea, just coffee."

It was just great!

"Where were we?" He asked, sipping his cup of coffee. "Oh yes! You were sharing with me your likes and dislikes."

I thought there were more dislikes than likes! I loved challenges, driving on bikes, watching movies, but he was nowhere near anyone of them.

"Yes… I love to read…"

Avinash jerked his chin. "What kind of books?"

MB's, romantic!

Before I could reply he smirked. "I hope not those romantic ones what are they called…"

"MB's," I replied with a grunt.

"Oh yes! My sixteen-year-old sister reads them!"

Now I was feeling nauseous. What was wrong with them? Shouldn't we respect all forms of literature I thought, but instead spoke aloud, remembering a book I had read. "Books like the monk who sold his Ferrari."

"Oh, so you are the philosophical types!" His lips curved a

little as he trailed a finger over the rim of cup.

Now, what did he mean by that?!

"Yeah." I evaded answering picking up my cup instead. Before he could pester me with more questions I asked him instead, "and you? Do you read?"

"If I get time generally they are business magazines, the newspaper is a must every morning and yes thrillers those I used to be fond of, but now I don't get time."

Was he a workaholic? Must be I concluded. But what about enjoying life and being free-spirited? It would be best not to share with him my hobby of riding bikes. I was feeling exasperated.

"Do you like to cook?"

Yes, Maggie! I avoided the kitchen like plague.

"If necessary," was my short reply.

"My mom makes lovely food," he went on, "you must know we are vegetarians, no eggs are allowed in the house."

Here went my chocolate cake...

I lifted an eyebrow. "That means no pastries, cakes?"

"We have but outside it doesn't come in the house. I hope you don't have a problem with that."

I shook my head.

"Good. What are your plans after marriage? I mean, do you want to work or not?"

My mouth went a little dry, but I swallowed a little tea and went on. "I want to finish my MA."

"Yes of course, if it is your wish."

It was a pleasant surprise; he was not averse to it.

At precisely that moment we were interrupted by my mom, who first looked at me and then Avinash with a wider grin.

"I hope I am not interrupting you?"

"No aunty not at all," Avinash was quick to reply, standing

up immediately as she gave him a polite pat on his shoulder. "Then come Avinash, we have arranged a buffet have something."

"Smita come." She touched my hand and blinked.

I followed my mother who was walking with Avinash at her side starting to feel a deep bout of worry in the realms of my heart. We clearly did not match, though I liked him and he was not bad to look at. Obviously, I could not expect a Hrithik Roshan, but he had fine features, a straight nose, well-shaped eyebrows and a square jaw and thank God no moustache or beard! But still, I was confused.

We partook a little bit of the snacks and at the dessert counter I could not control myself and picked the small chocolate brownie, despite the disapproving looks shot at me by my mother. The icing on the cake was when Avinash also picked up a piece. That stopped my mother's glares.

The high tea came to a quick end with both the parties eager to leave in order to discuss their respective opinions.

We were saying our goodbyes when Avinash came to me and said sweetly, "it was nice talking to you."

"Same here." I fidgeted a little, feeling shy.

As soon as we sat in the car and were a little away my mother started her tirade. "O, Krishna! I pray to you. I hope they like my girl. Avinash the boy is good looking na! Do you know he has done MBA from abroad… from some famous university, arree what was the name? Suniye Ji." She turned to my father. "What was the name? Arree the place in Australia, what were they saying?"

His hand jerked on the wheel. "Murdoch University."

At the age of fifty-two, my father was charmingly handsome and his profound looking eyes were hidden behind a pair of square big spectacles without which he could not function at all. In general, we were a close-knit family and loved each other. I was extremely attached to my father and though my mother irritated me I loved her. I could not imagine being away from them or not seeing their face for even a day.

My father looked at me through the rearview mirror. "Did you like him?"

"He is fine." My voice was meek.

My mother's mouth twisted. "Fine! Only fine? Do you know he has started his own work! Plus his father earns separately, he has a small business and properties in Delhi. Only one son in the family, the whole property will go to him."

"He has a sister," I added dryly.

"She will get married. After that, you will rule the household."

Rule the household I did not know the meaning of it at that time, but time made me learn its importance.

We reached our house in an hour due to the heavy traffic. My mother throughout the way was singing Avinash's glories, by now I was having a resounding headache. "Such a nice boy, so humble, so well-mannered and cultured… etc… etc." The list was endless.

As soon as we stepped inside my father's mobile rang.

"It is Mr. Sharma." He blocked the phone from his hand and whispered for our convenience.

My heart was in my mouth. Oh God! A part of me did not want to get married, but a very niggling part of my mind did not want a rejection.

"Hello," my father said removing his hand from the phone. "Yes, Sharmaji."

I could not hear what Sharmaji was saying, but all my doubts disappeared when my father's mouth curved radiating joy. "We have just reached home. I haven't talked to my daughter as yet. Will just call you sir."

My father pressed the off button on his cell and his look was enough for everyone to know the answer. They had said yes! My mother got angry. "You should not have talked like that. What will they think?"

My father took my hand in his, suddenly calm. "Let us go inside. It is a question of Smita's whole life. Come."

We walked through the family lounge, where the walls were panelled in brown pine, which lent a golden brownish light to the room. I loved this room with its high windows and colourful sofa and it was here that all the important decisions were taken.

He turned towards me and because he understood, he laid a hand on my shoulder rubbing it a bit before letting go.

"What is your reply Smita?"

I was quiet, unsure and confused by my feelings.

"What are you thinking just say..." my mother began, but was stopped by my father. "You will not pressurise her Asha."

My mind was whirling with thoughts. On one side, I was elated that Avinash had said yes, on the other I was scared at the prospect of marriage. Then somewhere in my mind, I had always wanted to marry in a house that was well to do, enjoying the luxuries that I enjoyed before marriage even after. My mother's words were playing in my mind. I looked up to see my father and I could sense that he wanted me to say yes. My parents would choose the best for me. And Avinash seemed like a decent guy, from a very good family. He was educated, well-mannered though some of our likes and dislikes did not match, but it was no reason to say no. The silence shattered when I whispered, "yes."

My mother literally jumped up and my father beamed. I was

getting married…

CHAPTER 2

I wore my favourite ink blue jeans tugging a white shirt
inside, and my brown leather belt around it. I still
remembered my mother saying Avinash my son looks so
good in blue. Mothers were known to exaggerate, but then
the glances of the female fraternity, whenever I wore blue,
did make me realise the value of that colour on me. I combed
my hair, spraying my favourite cologne, hurried out of the
house in a Chevrolet to egos.

I'd been eagerly waiting for Smita at the entrance of the
multi-cuisine restaurant glancing around, skimming faces
when I saw her. I had fully expected her to be dressed in a
salwar suit, but when she walked towards me, I was dazzled
by her look. She wore a long dress the kind of dress that
made a man want to offer thanks to the Gods of spring. It
was a soft, pale sea green, the colour of skimmed fluid as
water down her body. She wore sexy high- heeled sandals
hardly more than a series of bluff coloured straps and a long
thin spike.

I liked this side of her a little daring, a little shy and
innocent. I liked her hair wild and loose, an intriguing roll of
black, spilling down her back and shoulders.

"Hello, gorgeous."

She jerked when I spoke and turned away a little shyly.

I pulled a bunch of red roses from behind my back. Her eyes sparkled and her lips broadened into a wide smile. She held out her arms for the flowers.

I didn't move a muscle.

"Are they for me?" She asked.

I fumbled. "Ye..s."

Like a man in a trance, I offered them to her.

Smiling over the flowers, she inhaled their fragrance by closing her eyes and then opening them with a passion. It was true; nothing perked a woman up more than getting flowers.

I was sure to win her heart.

I then opened the door of the restaurant for her. The place was not dark, but rather cosy. The light was faintly blue and added a soft tint to the white flowers in the center of each table. The tables themselves were round, with deep chairs and small sofas circling them.

Realising her reluctance I selected a table and pulled out a chair for her. "Please sit."

She sat on the opposite side gently lowering her gaze as I walked to the other side of the table and perched myself on the chair. I saw her long eyelashes spluttering while she nervously blinked her eyes.

"How are you doing?"

She now turned her eyes upwards and I felt the breath quite simply leave my body. Checking her eyes and colour a subtle, deep brown that mirrored me in her eyes struck me with a sense of belonging for her.

"Fine, and you?"

"I'm well."

She kept the flowers that she was holding on the side of the table and again smiled.

I called for the waiter and a tall, thin man in black toddled over. "Yes, sir."

"What would you like to have?" I asked Smita picking up the brown padded menu card.

Without checking the menu placed on the table, she was quick to order for both of us.

"Stuffed mushrooms, curly fries, onion rings and veg sizzler." I liked her spontaneous reaction while the waiter scribbled the menu on his sheet.

"And sir, anything else." Smita seemed to make up for both of us and I decided to shake my head and say a simple, "lemonade and nothing else thank you."

A few minutes a young waiter again toddled over, a plump young man in a black uniform. With a practised enthusiasm, he laid her favourite dishes, appetisers and drinks.

Exposing his front teeth he nodded and left.

I could see her eyes electrify when she dug out a piece of stuffed mushroom and starting savouring the taste of it.

"Terrific." She took another bite and chewed it thoroughly.

Enjoying herself, she quenched her thirst with a glass of coke. When I continued to stare, her shyness rose she twisted her fingers when she said with a soft elegance looking a little embarrassed. "Why don't you have too?"

She quickly took her napkin, dabbed at her mouth and smiled.

My heart went out to her innocent smile and when my hand reached out for a piece, my fingers collided with hers. I liked the soft touch of her fingers and felt like taking them into mine when she moved her hand away.

She dazzled me and her nervousness made me a little

uneasy. But her behaviour attracted me. I was liking her gestures, her voice, her hesitation and her smile.

"Will you come with me for a movie someday?"

Her eyes darted up to mine. She remained silent for a while as if trying to make up her mind what to say. A brief pause and I waited for her response that I wished for. She looked up and after giving me a long look said softly," yes."

"I'll book our tickets for tomorrow." Did I sound desperate, but she again nodded, her eyes lit up at the thought of going to a movie that she probably loved to watch. She flashed her pearl white glassy teeth that made her face blossom. I was pleased that our thoughts were running along the same lines. I came to know one thing about her. She was a child at heart filled with fun and frolic. I wanted her to stay like this forever.

After the dinner, I picked up my glass and raised a toast to her.

"I will take care of you. May we live together forever happily."

Smita looked a little embarrassed but lifted her glass clinging it to mine. I drank it without feeling the taste of it.

A few couples were already on the dance floor engrossed into each other's arms with the melodious music flowing in the air.

I offered her my upturned hand and could see a glaze of shock in her eyes. She slowly placed her hand in mine. I gripped her trembling fingers and moved to the dance floor with her. She was still shy but kept her hand on my shoulder while I placed mine on her thin waist.

I could sense a ripple of shiver down her right hand that was entangled in mine while we both moved in slow steps with the soft flow of music.

Slowly, her shyness and fear collapsed into a sense of comfort and ease as her steps progressed in faster movements.

I was dancing to her tune. Wherever she moved, I moved immersed in the savouring sweetness of her first warm touch. Soon her head cushioned on my shoulder and her body moved to the inner rhythm.

"This is how love survives," I whispered as the words floated away.

Minutes passed by and though no more words were not spoken we both were lost in the world of love and compassion for each other. Her eyes were shut; her arms still around me when the ring of my Samsung that was in my pocket suddenly drew us apart.

"One second. I'm sorry."

Suddenly Smita drew away, probably flustered when she saw smiles and stares of other patrons. I reached out for it answering my mother who called me to check the time.

Oh shit! I never realised it had been two hours, time to leave her safely home.

"I think I must drop you home. It's late," as I said my gaze never left her face.

There had been the faint hint of a dimple beside her mouth when she tried to hide her disappointment. It surprised me that even she did not want to go.

I took her arm leading the way, across the dance floor towards the table. After paying the bill we started off to her home.

It was dark when we pulled up at her house. She said sweetly, "It was a lovely evening. Absolutely lovely."

The look she sent me was as warm as her voice as I walked with her to the door. "Thanks again for the beautiful flowers."

"You're welcome." She pushed open the door, the flowers clasped in her arms.

At the door, with the wind chimes singing and the lamplight glowing against the windows, I left her with a sweet goodbye and before shutting the door she turned to give me a last look.

We had, I thought as I walked to the car, just had our first official date. And it had been a doozy.

The entire night my heart flickered with her thoughts. Her face captured in the peripheral of my brain had stolen my heart. The evening continuously ran through my mind. She had a good heart and gentle manners.

I couldn't wait to meet her tomorrow for the movie.

CHAPTER 3

"Gorgeous!" My heart was fluttering. Oh God! Avinash was sooo romantic.

We went out for Friday movies often lucky to pick up the corner seat enjoying the popcorns and dinners. Along with being romantic, he was a good human being, fun loving and jovial. All my doubts vanished regarding him being boring, he worked hard and partied harder. His sweet gestures like sending me flowers, my favourite perfume, chocolates bowled me over.

I still remembered one of the dinners that was etched in my mind. We went to our favourite Thai restaurant. Both of us loved Thai food and we generally frequented this place. I was always alert of my food habits as I did not want to gain weight. We sat down and I ordered a salad without dressing. Avinash was one of those persons who could eat as much as they liked and did not gain an ounce, sadly same could not be said for me. Avinash ordered red and green curry and rice. Rice was a big no for me and I loved it.

A little later our food came. I started picking my food

disheartened to be eating the same when Avinash touched me on my hand.

"You don't need to eat that," he said lightly.

"But…"

"Shhh, you needn't explain. You can have whatever you want I will love you even if you grow fat. You will always remain beautiful for me," he emphasised.

My eyes brightened with emotion. I was ecstatic how anyone could be so charming, so lovable. I thanked God for getting Avinash in my life.

I took his hand from across the table in my hands. "Thank you for being in my life."

"You are my life," he replied. His thumb was skimming over my knuckles in a way that made my pulse unsteady.

But the greater feeling of those cherished words kept echoing in my ear, I was happy. He respected my parents treating them like his own parents. When my father gifted him an expensive watch he refused. " I don't want expensive gifts papa, you have given me Smita what else can I want".

However, my parents were insistent and he kept the same as he did not want to hurt their feelings. There was respect for him in me. I could not have asked for more.

We went for movies and had long chats generally at night about our plans for the future sharing our likes and dislikes. There was something mystical about talking to your fiancé at night when the house was quiet and everyone was asleep. It seemed a little daring and dangerous. The best part being nobody in the family minded!

And if with each passing moment I fell more deeply in love, I did so freely with absolute joy.

For the first time in my life, I began to think of a future with a man. I imagined passing through the years with him, not always content but always satisfied. I thought of a home that we would make together, with children in it. One boy and one girl. I could picture the arguments, the romance, the love and the laughter. I would finish my MA and then PhD after which have children and then teach. I would come home content and to sounds of laughter. And always, always with Avinash beside me in sickness and health, joys and sorrows. A handful of months before marriage meant so little in the vastness of a lifetime that we would spend together. But, meant so much to me. I recorded everything in my heart and branded the rest on my memory. I didn't mean to forget these moments, not even for an instant.

My yet another wonderful experience of courtship with Avinash was one of the fondest moments of my life. I was with Avinash where he navigated his car into a narrow parking space from where we headed to Mughal gardens. We both wandered on foot hand in hand entering from Gate 35 of the President's Estate located at the extreme end of the Church Road onto the pathway that was whistle clean. As we arrowed to the left, nothing could have been farther from the pleasure palaces and the glitz of the most magnificent hotel. And I realised nothing could ever call more truly to my soul than walking hand in hand with my soul mate admiring the scenic beauty.

The vast expanse of the garden was lovingly tended as if weeds were illegal. The sight of the floral designs, a riot of colours across the manicured gardens was a visual treat, putting together the magnificent Mughal Gardens of the colossal tower of the Rashtrapati Bhavan. The painting I'd seen once of the famous garden hadn't done justice to the natural beauty. Oil and canvas hadn't been able to translate the sweep of the wind, the colour of the old and sturdy building, the floral carpet and the gnarled humps of trees. As I rounded with Avinash, the painting once I had seen of course hadn't had a floral wall of white and yellow dahlias more than eight feet in height, the exotic lilies, the China oranges, which were in full bloom and the cyclamens, which added a bright colour to the Central Lawns. I was compelled to stand and watch the fantasy of blooms their colour and adore their fragrance.

Conjured by the magical scenery I blinked. "It's amazing, spectacular."

My gaze met his with a power so intense that it stole my breath.

Avinash lifted my hands, kissed the back of them. A thrill rocketed up my arm and straight into my heart. I could see the reflection of the yellow of the flower and the green in between his eyes and his eyes dazzled with the shine on my face.

"You are impossibly alluring, the shine of the golden streaks of your hair, your radiant smile. I like everything of yours," he said making me lower my lashes. Even after a period of long dating I instantly fell shy whenever he complimented me so passionately.

His smile spread, slow, easy and undoubtedly dangerous. He rubbed his cheek against my hair and kissed my forehead. My eyes fluttered open. My heart was racing so hard and fast that I could feel it vibrating between my temples.

I let out a little breath and drew one in as I gently pulled myself away.

"I'm sorry," he murmured.

The love somewhat wistful in his voice was unmistakable. Moved by it, I laid a hand on his.

He was handsome, romantic, clever and rich. Here comes my prince and I would live happily ever after. I was dazzled, flattered and in love. Avinash worked very hard to make me fall in love with him. He made me feel I'd deserved his love and he was always successful in his approach.

I knew it was about to come and he said it clear. "No other day can be better than today to say that I love you."

Another long thrill rippled through me.

I was speechless, but he knew my answer. I did not say anything but he got the message when I smiled. A few moments passed on to chat and observing the natural beauty accompanied by laughter on small jokes.

A little later, we both got up, walking hand in hand.

It was so quiet and I could hear the quiet with every step Avinash and I took over the ground.

Silence spoke more than words. Looking into each other's eyes and strolling along the curves of the garden we marvelled the Bonsai and the herbal garden.

We both had no idea when the time flew by. The sky now rested with the light yellow and orange hues of the sun. We left the magical creation of nature moving out towards the car.

Settling on the left side of Avinash, he drove in silence for a few minutes. I was still lost in my world with him in the garden.

He turned his head, slanted me a look. "Can I pick you up at ten tomorrow?" He spun the steering wheel to the left after the green signal.

The question broke my rhythm. For a moment, I could only stare at him baffled. "I don't know."

"But I want your approval for something special."

"Special." I looked at him still confused.

"I want you to see the engagement ring," he spoke so casually as if hiding the excitement behind his guileless and steady eyes.

Surprise had me, pursing my lips.

I tossed back my curling flood of black hair and gave myself a moment to think before I gave him a quick look. "Have to ask papa."

Squeezing the wheel a little harder on turning around the bridge he moved right into the lane of my colony.

"Ok, I'll take his permission, my dear."

Permission was granted and the next day Avinash took me to one of the jewellery house in Delhi.

Perched on the soft cushioned seats, both of us were greeted with a warm smile by the salesman who seemed very proficient in tapping a good client. Avinash was very particular about the kind he wanted that was supposed to be of the best quality. One by one exclusive pieces were shown to us ranging from sapphires to emeralds and diamonds.

I kept on trying one piece after the other not satisfied with any of them.

He knew I was not very happy with the types being displayed. "Show the lady something else. Something different." Avinash waved his hand over the jewellery gesturing the salesperson to keep them on the side.

"Dear choose the best," he whispered into my ear and then looked back at the salesman over the counter.

The man waited lost in some kind of thought and kept the smile on his face. "Sir, I'll show madam, something someone has never seen before. I'm sure, she will like this. It is custom made."

We waited patiently till he returned with a ring case.

He opened its lid very carefully not to mishandle the

precious piece in his hand, taking it out of the case and displaying it on his palm."Madam for you."

Oh my God! I didn't know what to do. It was out of the world. I picked up the beautified stone from his palm and fearfully wore it in my sun finger.

It was a beautiful diamond ring. The single stone was bright and clear and beautiful. It sparkled and gleamed at me. It blazed brilliantly, radiating its white light on my finger overshadowing all the other gems with its aura.

I was glued onto it till Avinash broke the reverie. "You like it."

"I love it," I murmured in a soft tone without taking my eyes off it.

"We'll take this one." Avinash had sounded firm as if he had made up his mind for it.

The temptation to wear the ring once again faded away when the salesman very dutifully and courteously informed Avinash about its price. It left my heart pounding, hard and fast as my gaze slid away from the ring to him. "Avinash leave it. It's too…."

He cut me short, kept his voice upbeat. "Pack it and send it at my residence."

Such a cool composure on purchasing the ring was yet another attractive feature of his that mesmerised me.

We both scooted out of the showroom and I flicked a look at him.

"There was really no need for you to buy that ring?"

"But I couldn't bear to disappoint my lady. She's more precious than a stone. Actually, the diamond would have lost its lustre if you had not selected it."

He was so sweet and smart, so steady without being boring or stuffy about it and I admired him. I loved listening to him, watching the way his mouth quirked just a little higher on the right corner than the left when he grinned. And the way his eyes got blurred and became focused when he looked at me. The way his hair all dark and thick was not very tidy. Then there was all that fascinating intensity balanced by the easy humour.

I simply loved him for what he was simple, straightforward and humble.

Avinash drove me back home. When the door closed behind me the only single thought shrivelled me. The problem was I wasn't quite so stable. Not quite so okay. Because I was crazy about him.

CHAPTER 4

The months from the day I said yes to my marriage passed in a blur. It seemed a tornado of preparations had struck where one task finished the other started.

I was getting married. The wedding was now just a week away and my younger brother Vikas who was staying in the hostel came down for the wedding. As usual, Vikas started irritating me; whenever Avinash called he was there picking up the phone, listening to our conversation and in general frustrating me. I felt like wringing his neck.

My usual threat to him was if you listen to our private talks I'll tell mom. But he always dismissed my threat with laughter, mimicking the way I spoke and got angry. I let him go mostly shutting the room's door before he got to the ringing phone.

I was desperately missing Roshni my best friend with whom I shared all my secrets and thoughts. She was a photographer and her pictures had been selected. She had been given a once in a life opportunity of working under the famous nature photographer Ravi in South Africa. Occasionally we got a chance to talk on the phone and that too only for a few minutes. The first time I had called to tell her that I was getting married, she had collapsed on the floor in disbelief. Her roommate had helped her in regaining consciousness after which she had hollered on the phone literally blowing off my ear. "How can you get married? How could you say yes without me checking on him?" Oh God, I missed her! The worst being she wouldn't be able to attend my wedding. But it could not be helped her whole career lay in front of her. She was a hell of a photographer. All my relatives, outstation ones were here some staying in the hotel and some at home. There was no space to even step with some relative or the other sleeping on the mattresses on the floor, on the couches and spare bedrooms. The house was chocked full. Plus everyone had free advice to give, and an endless stream of opinions.

Don't have children until three years! Have a child in the first year only! Have only two children, always please your husband, listen to whatever he says, don't answer back your in-laws, always stay humble, learn to cook for your husband, a sure way to his heart is through his stomach and many more. I was already exhausted from listening to them and I usually hissed a breath between my teeth hearing to constant advices. But it all boiled down to in the end that I was on my own after marriage.

The festivities started three days before with the haldad and mehendi ceremony. My feet and hands were painted beautifully with intricate mehendi designs. For the first time, I had applied mehendi till my elbows and on my legs. I was liking the idea of Avinash's name written on my palm, which, according to a custom he was supposed to find. When the woman applying the mehendi on my hand asked, "what is your husband's name?" It struck me husband! In two days' time, I would become Avinash's wife.

By the evening, my mehendi had taken its dark brown colour and my masi was quick to retort. "Your husband will love you a lot. It has taken a beautiful rich colour. The deeper the colour of the mehendi the stronger is the groom's love for the bride."

The other ladies laughed along with my masi teasing and then stroking my cheek and loving me.

That day I slept with the fondest of dreams that emerged one after the other with Avinash and me together in our home and I was lost in them till the next morning. Avinash's home would now be my home… no, our nest.

Today was the engagement ceremony our sagai followed by lady sangeet in the convention hall of hotel Ashoka. The entire family and relatives gathered in the huge hall half an hour earlier waiting for the groom's side to arrive. I loved the colour of the roses pure red and white carnations interspersed with golden ribbons covering the length and breadth of the hall giving it an ethereal glow.

The playfully pretty sweetheart stage and all of the floral ad décor details that had been put into place was even more mesmerising. The dramatic centrepieces carried over the ceremony look and feel rounded out the event design beautifully. My heart squeezed with admiration at the sight and I thought it was beautiful!

My eyes rolled over to see Avinash walk in with his parents and relatives. Escorted by my parents and brother, he walked towards the stage slowly. I thought he looked magnificent dressed in a black sherwani as he sat beside me on the big velvet sofa. The sofa carved to perfection was only meant for the couple and it accommodated both of us comfortably.

The ceremony started. My father smeared tilak on Avinash's forehead gifting him a watch and golden chain. I saw his smile with the corner of my eye and felt nice when he stooped down to touch my father's feet. My father blessed him and then hugged his future son- in- law with affection. Avinash and I exchanged rings in the large hall with the crowd applauding and cheering.

Then I was made to sit on a cushioned seat surrounded by the women of the groom's family and he was whisked away by the male members. We had hardly exchanged two words except a Hi.

The heavy, deep gold-bordered south silk saree that I had worn was exquisitely crafted with thread work gifted by my mother-in-law and she commented that it looked beautiful on me.

"A very beautiful bride. God bless you." One of Avinash's aunts stroked my cheeks and blessed me. One by one, the other woman passed sweet comments, giving me countless blessings. My mother-in-law, whom I had got into the habit of calling mummy made me wear the family's traditional jewellery.

A kundan necklace now adorned my neck and long green gold earrings burdened my ears with their weight. But, I was loving the feel of it that marked me as the daughter-in-law of the Sharma family. Many gifts were placed on my lap wrapped in small kits and baskets that were kept safely to be taken away later. This was followed by an exchange of gifts between the families. Once the rituals were over the DJ started to play the latest numbers marking the start of the lady sangeet.

Avinash and I were made to sit in the front row in direct view of the stage, while all the relatives settled around us themselves on the white cloth covered seats enthusiastically waiting for the program to start. I was still waiting for him to compliment me.

Our respective siblings had prepared a small skit on how we had met till our marriage. I was surprised as they enacted and danced, showing various stages of our courtship perfectly.

My cousin Rajiv disguised himself as Avinash and Avinash's sister Reema played my role. Reema started the play by saying, "this is for Avinash bhaiya and Smita bhabhi."

The first scene when Avinash presented me with flowers and a gift and the way Reema tilted her lips into a sheepish smile came as a surprise to me. The exchange of cards and gifts between us and a few of our private talks came as a shock to me.

How the hell did she know about the movie and the scenes we discussed? Oh, my God! She had not only read the cards, but overheard the conversation behind Avinash's back. I wanted to kill him for this.

At last, the mingling of love songs and hand in hand dances between the two ended with a loud I love you precisely indicating made for each other. Both Avinash and I glanced at each other literally red with embarrassment to be exposed like this in front of our relatives. After the skit was over Rajiv ran up to me. "How was it?" He winked at me. I showed him a slap and pulled his hand towards me. "I will not leave you, you silly boy that was not done."

But all was taken in a light-hearted spirit when all the guests were invited to the dance floor. Everyone hopped joyfully on the latest dance numbers, especially my mother with Avinash's mother and my father with his, skipping right and left like dancing dolls. The light of happiness that shone in everyone's eye was a wonderful feeling and I felt like capturing the moment of joy in my eyes forever.

The end of the lady sangeet was with my dance. I was a little nervous standing in front of the audience in my shimmering saree.

The beautiful diamond and red coral set changed by my mother-in-law was lying heavily in my throat in anxiety. My dance number started... As the wordings flowed I danced with my heart for my future husband and my future. I hoped...I just wished for happiness. ... My mother, father, in-laws everyone, came with money rounding the same around my head a popular custom that protected one from an evil eye.

And then Avinash came prompted by his parents to dance with me on the stage after my number ended. He was smiling... I could not meet his eyes. I suddenly felt shy when he came closer to me and lifted both my hands. His charming gaze penetrated deep into my soul and they expressed such unspoken feelings that made my heart leap with the joy of being with him. I knew him to be a gentle dancer, but today his enthusiasm was shown in the way he performed in bhangra style. I was laughing throughout the song till the number came to an end, but he was in no mood to stop. Everyone stood up, clapped and cheered us...and I prompted Avinash to stop moving.

As I walked back shyly and sat, he leant a little towards me and whispered, "You are looking beautiful sweetheart. I could not take my eyes off you the way you danced gracefully."

My heart soared and all my anxiety flew out of the window. It was as if I was waiting for this special compliment that meant the most to me... The future looked suddenly brighter. I knew that Avinash and I would be the perfect couple, truly made to love and understand each other. The function ended with loads of family snaps and a scrumptious dinner.

CHAPTER 5

It was the day of my wedding, I thought with a sudden sense of alarm as I sat up in my bed after a long night of almost no sleep. Because with thoughts of the wedding came the unwanted thoughts of my first night. The same had been giving me sleepless nights for some time. Though we had held hands and he did try to kiss me once in the park, we were interrupted by one of the caretakers of the place. Later Avinash was too embarrassed to try again.

My mother had scared me further by coming into my room last night after the engagement ceremony. I had just changed and was huddled under the covers. As was her way she had sat on my bed where I was trying to sleep and had taken my hand in hers. "Smita I want to discuss something important with you."

I had been sleeping and had replied crossly, "ma please go I am tired."

"Smita it is important getup!"

"Just go ma please we will talk in the morning." By then I was getting really irritated.

"No Smita," she had spoken sternly. "Get up!"

"Fine." Grumbling, I had jerked up throwing the bed covers. I was getting married and my mother was as insensitive as ever.

She had taken my face in her hands and had kissed me on my forehead with her eyes brimming with tears. It was getting normal for her to burst into tears for no reason.

"Please, ma don't start again!" I had panicked stopping her otherwise; even I would have started to cry.

"Ok." She had then wiped her tears with her dupatta. "I had to tell you something important."

"Can't it wait!" Protesting I had covered my face with a pillow.

"No grow up Smita, you will be a married woman tomorrow!" She was clearly upset as she pulled down the pillow shoving it on the side of the bed.

"Ma you have come to tell me this?" With my head angled, my face was set on hers.

"Smita be serious! It's just a reasonable and sensible suggestion. Now listen to me! You know what happens after the wedding."

"Yes, ma I know Grah Parvesh. I need to jerk the Kalash with my right foot and then step on the vermillion water." I had shaken my head in irritation. "You have told me this ten times!"

"Yes I have and thank God you remember it but I have to talk to you about your first night."

"Ma pleassseee." My mother was just too much! My cheeks had flushed with embarrassment and I could still feel the heat coming out of them.

"What please what I am saying is important. First and foremost don't fight your husband. He has some rights and don't stop him from exercising the same."

"Ma Avinash is not like that!"

She had smirked and replied skimming her fingers on my hand. "In this regard, all men are the same. They will not wait and you will not fight your husband otherwise, it will make a dent in your relationship."

I could not believe what my mother was saying. "What nonsense!"

"It is not nonsense Smita. It is the way of the world. You have to grow up every woman goes through it. Promise me you will not fight or say no to your husband."

"I will not promise something like this." With my jaw slacked open I could not hide my expression of disbelief and shock when my mother had slapped the hand she was tendering. I still could not digest the fact that my mother was so orthodox.

"Smita." She'd put my hand on her head. "Promise me."

"Ok, ma I promise."

Though I had promised her, but I knew Avinash would never force himself upon me.

My gloomy thoughts of last night were broken by the cell's ring shaking me out of my reverie; it seemed like my thoughts conjured him, Avinash was ringing me. I was a little surprised why was he calling me at nine in the morning on the day of our wedding?

I clicked the call button. "Hello."

"Hi."

Silence followed for a few seconds. I was getting confused by the minute.

"I just wanted to say..." he trailed off.

"Yes..." I whispered my anticipation rising, was something wrong?

"I love you."

I pressed a hand to my stomach. Emotions churned inside me. Too much to feel, too much too wonder. "I love you too."

"Just checking whether you still want to marry me or not." I could hear the smile in his voice, so warm and welcoming. I settled comfortably into the pillows, teasing. "Still haven't decided."

"I hope till eight you would have decided, the time of our pheras?" His reaction was quick and satisfying.

"Maybe." I pretended to think. "Ummm...Yes, I still want to marry you."

"Thank God!" He let out a muffled hoot of laughter. "Then see you".

"See you."

"Bye."

"Bye." I disconnected the phone. My heart sang merrily. Oh my God! I was hooked completely. All my fears subsided; Avinash was a lovely human being. Whenever I was in doubt he did something to soothe my nerves.

There was more to loving than the uncountable physical pleasures a man and woman could offer each other. There was trust and patience, generosity and joy. There was a drugging contentment of falling asleep knowing your partner would be there when you awoke each day. Partner... The word floated through my mind... My match.

CHAPTER 6

The wedding venue was a farmhouse in Chattarpur, being handled by an event manager who took care of everything the decorations, food and other small details. My father had put all his might into my wedding, ordering the best of everything that was in his capability. The money envelopes were prepared and sealed to be given to the guests on the groom's side along with one gold coin to the ones, who were important. Gifts and clothes were bought in abundance to be distributed. I mentioned to my father, why so much expense was being incurred, but he hushed me saying that it was the custom.

I had expected Avinash's family to say no to this unnecessary expense, but they did not. I did not like it, however, my mother convinced me that this was the least that they were doing and I was not to worry about it. I soon forgot about all this in the festivities enjoying the moment, after all, it was once in a lifetime experience.

In the afternoon, the beautician came to get me ready. Shina pecked and cooed as she draped the dupatta around the golden and red lehenga. The heavy zardozi work on the brocade weighed around fifteen kgs and I thought I was surely going to trip and fall on my nose in front of Avinash. I came out of my room dressed like a bride two hours later. I looked at the finished result in the mirror and it was a stranger staring back at me. My hair was immaculately tied in a bun pecked with a diamond tiara that reached till the middle of my forehead. The pink lipstick shaping my lips, a blusher that highlighted my delicate cheekbones, with a golden eyeshadow beautifying the shape of my eyes matched perfectly with my attire and jewellery.

The golden sandals on my feet added to the shimmer and shine. The huge nose ring was covering a side of my face and my neck was enclosed in a jaipuri choker, with small strings of diamonds falling from it creating a cascading effect. I was enthralled I had never looked that beautiful in my whole life. I was looking like a grown up woman. In fact, the realisation of the situation hit me hard -I would be a married woman soon.

A woman, not a girl anymore.

My mother was the first person who saw me and as expected her eyes misted. She quickly wiped a little kajal from her eyes and rubbed the same behind my ears. "Smita, bless you, my child."

My father fixed at the entrance stood to stare at me. When I looked at him with misted eyes, he moved like a snail towards me, standing to face me with pale eyes. Drained of strength first he blessed me by putting his feeble hand over my head and then he spoke in a shivery tone that sounded weak, "my little girl has grown up. My mitthi."

He kissed my forehead and I could feel the touch of his trembling lips over my forehead so soft, loving and caring. My father used to call me that when I was small. I was overwhelmed, my emotions were clogging me. The kind of emotions was inexpressible between parents and daughter all mixed with the inner turmoil of love, longing, belonging and even happiness. It seemed surreal as if I was in a dream, I felt I was attending a party where I was the chief guest and when it would get over I would come back to my house, change into my favourite pyjamas and lie in my bed. The reality had still not sunk in fully. I looked at my room for the last time, looked at the pink painted room, the fairy bed, the flowered curtains. It was funny to think that in a few hours I would be someone else, someone's wife. Who would I be then? Would it be different? Would Avinash change? Suddenly it all seemed more than a little scary.

My mother was strong and quick enough to adapt and sensing the sensitivity of my feelings she spoke quickly, "Smita come we need to reach Chattarpur farms by six. Barat will arrive at six-thirty."

I was made to sit with my mother and brother at the back, while the driver drove the car with my father occupying the side seat of the Honda. More cars filled with relatives followed ours and some thirty minutes later all the cars lined up behind each other when we reached the venue. My driver Kishore turned the car to the right taking us up on the wide well-manicured lane. I turned towards the window, an ominous silence settling towards me when my brother Vikas gasped and shouted, "look at that!"

I craned my neck upwards. We were passing beneath a wide entrance, with gateposts gilded with an arch of entwined flowers of marigold and a huge marble statue of Lord Shiva and Parvati. Shiv and Shakti the epitome of a perfect couple worshipped with reverence.

With this single thought, I calmed.

"Papa it is grand," I declared, turning to face my father.

"I am glad Smita you liked it," he answered happily.

"Papa, I love it." My father was sitting in the front seat and I could not resist myself, I scooted forward in the seat and clasped his arm.

The car came to a halt shortly and we got down. My mother caught hold of one side of my lehenga and instructed my brother to hold the other. Obviously, it was not like him to do this job and he protested, "maaa no!"

My mom glared at him and screeched, "Vikas!"

He picked one side of my lehenga dejectedly. Good! After all the trouble he had given me for all these years, it was time he was troubled also.

But who was going to fight with me now? I loved my brother with a deep, solid affection and knew that I would miss him desperately.

We walked in the house that was adjoined to the farms where I was to wait till instructed to come out. I sat down on the bed waiting alone, as everyone left fifteen minutes later to greet the boy's side.

I could hear the drums beating and the music playing. My anticipation was rising and around half an hour later I was called. We walked in a line of three with me in the middle and my two cousins beside me, two in front and two back carrying a dupatta over my head.

The garden was tastefully decorated with carved divans arranged as seats for guests, besides whom pots of huge bright flower arrangements were made. Ample lighting provided by the crystal lamp posts added shine and glamour to the area.

As I moved ahead, my eyes could not miss the smooth flow of colourful waterfall at one corner whose calm pool was lit

by the subtle glow of numerous diyas. Our procession headed to the stage where the jaimala would take place.
I hadn't looked up till now feeling queasy, but when I climbed the stage and stood in front of Avinash, he looked at me with an emotion I couldn't really decipher, but on seeing the smile on his face all by queasiness vanished like a puff of air.

Dressed in a white sherwani, with a clean-shaven face and a gold-red turban on his head, he looked like a bona fide prince. I could feel my desire returning for him, he was so handsome and pleasant. I smiled shyly and quickly garlanded Avinash. After the exchange of the garlands, we sat in the plush maroon velvet coated settee intricately carved with silver.

One by one the guests came, not even giving Avinash and me a chance to properly greet each other. In no time, it was time for the pheras.

The mandap had long rows of pink and a blue stream of soft fibre interspersed with bunches of roses and carnations hanging from the top. I was made to sit beside Avinash and the fire of the havan was ignited, after the recitation of some mantras by panditji. The entire mandap area smelled divine with the fragrance of the wood and the flowers glowing like a heavenly place of divinity.

Panditji instructed us to stand and revolve around the yajna. Both of us started moving in sync with each other. With the start of the vows, my heart started echoing them.

In the first round…. I pray to God to let us walk together so that we will get food.

In the second round… I pray to God for a healthy and prosperous life, for physical, spiritual and mental health.

In the third… I pray for wealth, for the strength for us to

share happiness and pain together.

Fourth round… I pray for the increase in love and respect for each other and our respective families.

Fifth round… I blushed on this one and everyone laughed, I pray for beautiful, heroic and noble children.

Sixth holy… around the fire, I pray for a peaceful long life with each other.

Final seventh round… I pray for companionship, togetherness, loyalty and understanding. Make us friends and give the maturity to carry out our friendship for a lifetime.

Avinash turned to me and repeated the vow, "now we have become friends after the Seven Vows and I will not break our friendship for life."

The completion of the marriage was the smearing of sindoor, the red vermillion on my head and the mangalsutra sliding around my neck by Avinash.

I was a married lady now Mrs Smita Avinash Sharma.

Oh God! What was I getting into?

I sneaked a glance at Avinash who was now joking with my cousins and brother over the joota chipaye rasam. And of course, very pleasingly he parted away with a bundle of cash in return of his jootis.

My husband, life partner, it was so overwhelming. I was not given the chance to dwell on my thoughts because we were whisked towards the dining area. A whole variety of foods were served, including Indian, Continental, Chinese and Thai. My first cousin Rakhi joked, "jijaji you need to feed didi with your own hands."

"Yes, of course, I would love to feed my lovely wife." A cheer went up as Avinash picked up the spoon filled with rice and curry to feed me.

I laughed softly, taking a bite. His expression was tender and soft making me go all weak inside.

"How romantic!" My other cousin said her expression one of enchantment.

"Again!" Rakhi shouted, jumping up and down in her pink and orange ghagra choli.

"Enough children!" My mother admonished lightly, "let them finish their food in peace; you mustn't trouble your jijaji."

"No ma let them, they have the right." His eyes were dancing with merriment.

He was so sweet! I felt my blush deepen.

After dinner, the reception started where guests came with gifts and money envelopes to wish us. I was happy, but dog-tired wanting nothing more than to go to sleep on my bed in my room. But my bed, my room! It was wishful thinking first I had to face the biggest night of my life that was giving me the jitters.

Finally, the moment I was dreading came the vidai. I was leaving my home, my family, my loved ones and everything that was known and entering the unknown. A trickle of fear went down my spine, but I inhaled deeply gripping with a sense of security with Avinash at my side.

The strong pillar in my life, my soul mate. He would be my anchor my support. I repeated to myself again.

From the corner of my eye, I saw my father giving gifts and money envelopes. The men of Avinash's side sat with their yellow turbans held high in a supercilious manner, especially not to miss was the haughtiness of my mother-in-law who laughed boisterously throughout the ceremony. Whereas my father looked tired and drawn with his silk kurta rumpled and shoulders hunched.

I felt like reaching out and hugging him.

The gift distribution ceremony was over and my mother came towards me, her eyes were red. My mother who cried at the drop of a hat was holding back her tears for my benefit.

I was ashamed of the fights I had with her, the arguments, how irritated I used to get.

"Come Smita." Her voice was low nearly inaudible.

I wanted to say something, so many words wanted to bubble out of my mouth, but nothing came out. I just walked in a daze, with my whole family walking behind me crying softly, even my brother was crying and that seemed to break the dam. The tears which were refusing to flow burst out of my eyes as I hugged my mother and brother. I looked up at my father with eyes as brown as my own and filled with tears.

"Papa," I whispered. It was harder leaving him, in some ways than my mother, who was more matter of fact.

"Everything is going to be just fine," he reassured me, just as he had the night of my first dance show… and the time when I had fallen from the stairs and broken my arm, the time of my first class twelve board exam when he drove me to the exam centre, telling me funny stories and making me laugh to ease my tension. He bent and kissed my cheek. It was a moment we both knew we would remember for a lifetime.

"It is time to go Smita." I gave a final hug to my brother whose watery eyes flashed red enough to tell me that he had been crying for quite some time.

"Take care of yourself, ma and papa. I love you, I'll miss you." Vikas nodded, trying to hold onto his emotions, assuring me with a comforting squeeze of my hand. He suddenly looked so grown up, my little brother.

I sat in the car beside Avinash, on a sob, I turned around as the car moved desperately trying not to lose my family's sight. As the car turned the last glimpse of my family collapsed behind the dark and I could not get my breath. The car's walls, my family's faces, future expectations, it was all closing in on me.

I turned back when Avinash gently clasped my shoulder. I sagged against him, all but blinded by my tears, feeling utterly alone. I felt Avinash's arms about me gently reassuring me with his presence.

I had to control my emotions and I straightened a bit, blinking back my tears. Avinash handed me his handkerchief and I murmured, "thank you".

Wiping my eyes, I looked at him and gave a weak laugh. I sensed Avinash's discomfort as he looked at me with trepidation. "Are you feeling better?"

"Yes."

He said nothing, but instead, his gaze roamed over my face and then his bow-shaped mouth stretched into a wry smile. My cheeks started burning at his scrutiny, but still, he was looking at me and then he spoke out, "I am your family now Smita."

He touched the right chord of bringing relief to my disturbed senses. I needed to be in that comfort zone desperately.

I did nod, unable to speak, yes, he was my family but so was the one I was leaving.

CHAPTER 7

I reached my new home situated in Vasant Vihar. Anticipation was singing in my nerves. I had the first view of the building from a distance. Immediately something Roshni had told me struck hard. I had heard from her that some families were a little orthodox. For them, it was considered ill luck for the bride to enter her future husband's house before marriage. And Roshni thought even mine was like that as I had never seen it before. The thought of the house intimidated me. The knowledge was a little lowering; after all, it was just a house. I saw the house stand amongst similar shaped buildings. It was a little smaller in size than I had anticipated. I forced my nerves to steady as the car turned into the cobbled driveway. I looked out of the window to see the wooden gate that was the entrance of the house dotted with people. I sat back a little against the seat nervously when the car halted. I was never a coward and would not start now.

Avinash said, "come." And exited from his side.

I plastered a smile on my face and straightened my spine when the car's side door was opened by my mother-in-law.

As I descended from the car she took my arm and directed me inside the house. Avinash stood beside me. At the entrance, a kalash filled with rice was kept. As directed by Aninash's mother, I tilted the same to send the contents falling on the floor and entered my new home.

Next, instead of my feet, my hands were immersed in red vermillion water. The same was imprinted on the wall beside a small wooden temple in the house. The temple housed a small idol of Lord Krishna and Radha Rani. I folded my hands and prayed for a happy future. I hardly had time to inspect my new home when I was whisked to my room which obviously I would be sharing with Avinash.

I gulped hard on entering inside. The bed was covered with red rose petals, the copper bowl on the side table bloated with water on which diyas and candles floated around orange marigolds. A few semicircular sized bouquets whose flowers spread like a peacock's wing adorned the corners of the room.

Oh, Lord! I was feeling weak-kneed. Thank God Avinash was not with me at that time and I was alone with my mother-in-law and sister- in- law Reema. "Bhabi!" Reema said excitedly, "I have decorated your's and Bhaiya's room. How did you find it?"

Anxiety had already crept steadily into my veins looking at the decorations, especially the bed. My heart was pounding heavily with fear. Instead of voicing my fears I spoke in a small voice, "it is lovely Reema. Thank you."

Reema, I had learnt was a complete romantic and that could be seen by the kind of taste she had. She replied in a high pitched tone, "Bhabhi you needn't thank me. It is your wedding night and…"

"Shh.." My mother-in-law stopped Reema from continuing

and turned towards me. "Smita you will be leaving for Leela Palace. We have booked the honeymoon suit over there. Avinash will take you."

Just then Avinash entered the room. He had taken off his golden pagadi and had unbuttoned the topmost button of his cream sherwani. I turned my face away.

"Bhaiya you couldn't wait na," Reema teased.

Avinash just laughed and pulled Reema's hair. "Chutki stop embarrassing your Bhabhi."

I felt my cheeks turn into a rosy pink, wishing my blush was becoming.

"I think you should leave". My mother-in-law glanced at her watch and seemed in a hurry to send us to the hotel. Guess it was the timing of the moohrat that was playing on her mind, the usual old ways followed as a tradition by some elderly ladies of the house.

Reema bobbed her head up and down. "Yes, yes, I understand. Bahiya and Bhabhi need to go". She giggled and with a parting glance filled with mirth directed at us, moved towards the door followed by my mother-in-law and then both of us.

We both sat in the silver Chevrolet. The drive to Leela Palace took around fifteen minutes, as the roads were empty, though Delhi stayed alive at night with a few joints, pubs and restaurants open.

On reaching the hotel, the car was handed over to the valet and me along with my husband entered the lobby of the extraordinary Leela Palace whose interior was more on traditional style ranging from the royal artwork displayed on walls to the silver art pieces glittering all around and cosy seating areas.

I barely had time to absorb the light, colour, before Avinash hurried to inquire about the room's booking at the reception. "Yes, sir, the honeymoon suite, has been booked in the name of Mr and Mrs Avinash Sharma." The tall, healthy looking receptionist handled the key card to Avinash with a gentle smile.

We took the elevator and as it ascended towards the second-floor panic sprawled through the pulse of my heart. The door of the lift slid open and I walked behind Avinash towards the suite. He inserted the card that opened the door. Entering in, he shut the door with a snap. I looked at the closed door as an ominous stillness settled over me. I looked around the room, so softly lit, so private, so romantic and so scary.

There were flowers and candles and the room smelled of both of them, something soft with weeping violins-drifted through the air. And more candles and flowers swiped the mantelpiece. A wide scalloped mirror reflected off it, creating a strong sense of intimacy.

I glanced back at him as nervous wings began to stir in my belly. Now, what?

"Hum." Avinash cleared his throat, coming to stand next to me covering my hand with his before I could move it out of reach. "Why don't you change? The lehenga must be heavy." He was so cool about it, but I was scared, hell scared to death swallowing the lump in my throat.

"Ya..yes," I stammered and turned towards the bathroom when Avinash clasped my arm and jerked me into his arms. I wiggled a little refusing to look up. With one arm around my waist, he raised my chin with the other hand forcing me to look up. "Did I tell you that you are looking out of the world, gorgeous," he whispered huskily.

He was so close that the breath from his mouth was fanning

my face. I was feeling weird, jittery and excited all at the same time. I really did not know how to react. I wiggled uncomfortably; all this was extremely new for me.

"I...I would like to change," I stuttered.

Avinash smiled and released me. "Yes, go ahead, I am waiting."

Waiting! Oh no! Not tonight! I was not expecting it to happen tonight...I quickly turned around to face his back. There was another door to the left of the room which I presumed was the bathroom. I walked towards my duffel bag that was kept in the corner of the suite already sent ahead most probably by my mother-in-law. I was so nervous that it was even difficult for me to admire the beauty of the room.

I quickly opened the bag and started rummaging for the new night suit I had bought. Instead of finding the night suit I came up with a pink negligee. Oh, shit! I was sure it was all my cousin's doing. I could not believe it! How could I wear this wisp of a material in front of Avinash!

"Is something wrong Smita?" Avinash asked from behind me.

"No," I replied quickly hiding the negligee behind me. "Nothing."

I sidestepped and was quick to head to the bathroom closing the door before Avinash could ask more.

I leant my head against the door and squeezed my eyes shut. The situation was entirely impossible. I walked towards the washbasin, breathing heavily completely out of my element. I slowly stripped off my clothes, taking my own sweet time to change. I looked around the bathroom. It had a shower to a side that was bisected by curtains. The yellow tiles created a pale effect around the small room. It had a western type toilet, which was right across the mirror and basin where I was standing.

I folded my lehenga, blouse and chunni in a neat pile and kept it beside the washbasin on the marble slab. I stood in front of the mirror in my underwear observing my body, I was looking fine?....Fat?...Thin?....Beautiful? Oh God! What was I doing?! I quickly turned on the tap, letting the cold water flow and scrubbed my face clean of the makeup. As the water rippled over my body I thought the situation was totally irrational, emotional and fanciful, my mind only thinking about how Avinash had pulled me.

After my bath, I turned the water off, drew the curtains of the bath tub and climbed out. Sliding the nighty over my underwear which I normally did not do, I stood inside the bathroom uncertainly. I did not want to go out and I couldn't stay in! I breathed in and out, in and out. I shook my hair free from the hundreds of pins that were holding it in a bun and combed the tangles out from them.

I rummaged through my vanity bag for a hair band and deftly combing my hair I tied them in a ponytail that reached till my midriff. I always wanted to try new hairstyles and wanted shorter hair, but my mother refused to lessen my length and anyways Avinash liked long hair so I had no problem with it.

When the knock sounded at the door, I started trembling this was the moment. "Smita," Avinash called.

"Ya coming!" Oh, how I wished I could melt away and disappear back to my house in my bed. But it was not to be. I straightened my shoulders confidently. What was going to happen was a most natural thing, every woman went through it and it had to be done. My mother's advice kept ringing in my mind like a blow horn. I walked towards the door and opened it slightly to see Avinash lying on the bed. He had changed into shorts and his chest was naked. Seeing him like this made me unaccountably ill. I averted my gaze and walked into the room clutching the wisp of material at my neck.

Once again I cursed my cousin the negligee was perpetually transparent. I looked up again and saw him staring at me. He was smiling at me and I could feel the heat glimmering in his eyes. I tensed as he stood up and started walking towards me. Damn and double damn. I thought my heart rate must be two hundred at that point of time, I could hear it thudding in my ears. I saw the desire darkening in his eyes as he took me in his arms. I closed my eyes and leant into him. The contact sent up multiple sensations floating through me and I buried my hot face into his chest. I hardly had a chance to say anything before he placed me gently in the center of the bed. He bent over me, his hand flat on the mattress and I blinked up at him, motionless as a bird that fears a cat prowling nearby. He kissed me tenderly on my lips and I stiffened. As if sensing my tension Avinash abruptly broke the contact. I didn't know if I was glad to be spared or sorry not to be taken into his arms.

This moment was inevitable from the first. Destiny had brought us together, and I had to let destiny have its way. Again, my mother's words were echoing in my mind. I had to build this relationship and it could not be built this way with me behaving like a sissy. I got on my knees and took Avinash's face in my hands. It seemed this was all the invitation he needed as he picked me up and tenderness spread through him as he cradled me in his arms his hesitation vanishing… All the conflicting emotions, the needs and doubts and wants. And as I accepted them, accepted him, I felt myself settled. I performed my duty on my first night though I was not ready for it, and then the dark faded in the unity of two souls.

CHAPTER 8

It was sunny and warm when I woke and the air smelled like roses. I snuggled in for a moment. Warm sheets carrying a faint scent, the soft drift of silence.

I rolled over lazily, blinked sat up and stretched, feeling the heavy pull of muscles. I was a little tired from last night but pleased with myself. I looked sideways and saw Avinash fast asleep.

I slid out of bed sniffed the yellow butter roses on the dresser before wearing my robe and went to the bathroom locking it. I stood in front of the mirror eyeing any change in me, but the reflection staring back at me was the same, a little tired with dark smudges under the eyes, but nevertheless the same. I used the toilet and showered making minimal noise so as not to wake up Avinash. I felt a little embarrassed at performing private tasks in the vicinity of him.

After dressing up in my new pink saree I searched my bag for my mobile. I was dying to talk to my parents missing them terribly. I dialed my father's number and instantly after a ring the phone was picked up as if they were waiting for my call.

"Mitthi." My father's throat seemed closed as if he had to swallow hard to clear it.

"Papa." My heart began to stir on hearing his voice.

"How are you, baby?" He asked me, his voice was a little wobbly.

"Fine just fine," I replied my eyes watering. "Where is ma?"

"Right beside me." There was a shuffle and my mother came on the phone. "Smita!"

"Ma?" I fought to regulate my breathing. Home, safety, security it was all there in her voice like a shiny gift.

"Hello! Why are you whispering? Is everything all right?" Her voice was bordering on panic. I laughed at my mother's typical behaviour. "Everything is all right. Avinash is sleeping and I am in the bathroom that is why I am whispering." I cradled the phone between my ear and shoulder, tugged on the pleat of my saree which I had missed.

"Ok."

"Vikas, is he all right?" I asked about my brother.

"Han han he is sleeping. How come you woke up so early? It is just seven- thirty and you never wake up before eight." My mother's questions started and I gave a watery smile.

"Ma please don't worry I am fine. Now keep the phone, I will call you later."

"You go, take care of yourself and Avinash."

"Yes ma, love you all. You also take care of yourself and everyone else." I clicked the phone shut.

After keeping the phone back in my bag, I gave myself a last look in the mirror and then opened the door of the bathroom. I paused by the window and let the sound of bird song play like a flute in my ear. A sweet little smile played on my face as I turned around to see him standing behind me.

"Hi! Good morning," I said shyly. How did you greet one's husband after your first night? I had no idea!

"Good morning," he replied, but, I had a feeling his expression was guarded. However, I realised that my worries were unfounded when he kissed me tenderly on my cheek. "I thought I'll give you a surprise."

He ran his hands over my arm as he eased me away. "Breakfast in bed with me, but before that, I need to change."

I nodded while he paced towards the bathroom to change. He came out opening the room's door at the ring of the doorbell. A waiter tooled inside with a tray easing it in the middle of the room.

With a slight bow, he smiled and exited the room.

My eyes went wide as I checked the contents of the tray. I opened the lid of the silver teapot savouring the rich chocolaty smell of the hot chocolate. The croissants, mayonnaise coated mixed vegetable sandwiches, chocolate fudge and finger chips spread across the round table with a single rose in a bud vase was the icing on the cake.

Wow! Was the one word that entered my mind as I clasped my hands together under my chin.

Avinash folded his arms around my waist and said in a low musical voice, "I hope you like it."

"I love you!" I turned to hug him.

The joy of eating together on the bed was like a drug and even as we ate, my heart jumped with glee at the wonderful sense of sharing with love. It was believed eating in happiness was the best gift one could give to one's health, but even more so the saying was correct when the food was graced with love.

"I think my beautiful wife deserves a splashing honeymoon."

He finished the last bite of the sandwich now smoothly caressing my chin with his hand.

"What...where?" I blurted with a kind of frantic glee studying the colour of his pupils that sparkled when he winked at me. "Sun-drenched days, starry nights of Australia. What do you say?"

He brushed a hand down my hair and then drew me close to his side so my head rested on his shoulder.

"Lovely...exotic...wonderful! I want to go there with you sweetheart. I have never felt so much love in my life and I don't want to lose it ever."

"And you will never ever lose it. So now what's keeping you waiting? Make a move."

"What?"

"Yes, now. Tickets have already been booked we are leaving right now."

It was perfect. Absolutely perfect and this surprise was my long lasting wish that was being fulfilled by my husband. I started to feel that he knew my instincts and what I wanted. The day was so beautiful that it was like a jewel in the palm of my hand. He made me see it, feel it and want it.

Crawling out of bed, we hurried out of the hotel and left for Avinash's house from where we picked up our luggage and headed to Australia for our honeymoon. Our flight was at twelve in the afternoon and we hardly had any time.

I wanted to meet my family before leaving, but obviously, could not. It had to wait after we came back in a week's time.

 As I sat in the plane, I was excited I was visiting Australia for the first time and was looking forward to it. Even my aversion of travelling could not diminish my excitement.

The hotel at the beach where we stayed was an added advantage of enjoying the scenic beauty of nature. I was thrilled when I saw my room. It was on the second floor and it had a huge living room and a fabulous bedroom all done in delicate flower print and pink satin. It looked like the ideal place for our honeymoon.

My week in Australia was like a dream… The sun, sand, and surf.

Avinash knew quite a lot about the local joints and tourist spots so he became my official guide. I bought presents for all my family members and I was dying to give the same to them.

On our second night, we strolled on the beach. The light was fading, going deep at the edges. A swath of light swept the horizon with a gleam of pink in the west. The tide was low, leaving out dark, damp sand that was cool underfoot. The foaming surf looked like a flowing ribbon.

Some other couples strolled on the beach hand in hand or arm in arm. I was walking beside Avinash a little uncomfortable with the openness of affection displayed on the beach. I tucked my hand in the pockets of my jeans that I had rolled up and my feet were bare.

"What about going in the water?" Avinash's face gleamed mischievously.

No way, I thought looking at the bathing suits; I couldn't be comfortable like this besides I didn't even own one. I just shook my head in denial.

"You can't swim?"

"Of course I can swim."

"Then let's go."

He scooped me up so fast that my heart was stuck in my throat. I could barely manage to breathe or scream when I was in the water. He was laughing, spinning me away from oncoming waves to take the brunt of it himself, while I was sliding and rolling trying to gain my balance when he simply nipped at my waist straightening me.

"Oh God!" Whatever I was about to say was left midway as another wave hit me knocking off my feet.

"Careful." Avinash laughed, as I surfaced the air hitting my heated face. The sea rocked us gently when he took my hand as we drifted an arm span apart.

"It's like magic," I sighed as the cool breeze drifted over me softly.

"The magic is you."

I looked at him as he planted his feet again, lifting me until I stood facing him with the water at waist level. Overhead the stars were twinkling their shadow sprinkling over the surface of the water.

He skimmed my wet hair away from my face, leaving his hands resting on my cheeks. I turned slightly, but he stopped me as I pressed my hand against his shoulder. He bent forward as I curled my fingers into his wet shirt and leant into him, parting my lips under his. My kiss under the black sky in the star-drenched surf. It was beautiful.

I think until the time I die I would remember that week where we were just lost in each other.

Though I was still a little shy with the intimacy of our relationship I had reached a stage where I had accepted it and enjoyed it. We became closer as close as any two persons could be sharing our bodies, our minds and our thoughts.

I thought this was all that marriage should be about, why people married. It was a beautiful week, the beginning of a life I had always dreamed of.

Everything had worked out perfectly in my life and I loved

living with my husband. We were both sure of each other, wanted to be together and build a family. I recorded the moments of my honeymoon period that would be cherished for life-long.

Sadly our short honeymoon came to an end very soon and it was time to get back to reality.

CHAPTER 9

We arrived in Delhi and headed straight to Avinash's house... no, our house. I wanted to go there to meet everyone and then quickly head to my place to share the gifts with my family. I was excited to meet them all again. The driver pulled off into the cobbled driveway. I noticed the little back yard for the first time; it was bisected by a trio of white marble steps and a narrow walkway.

As we trooped up the front porch my mother-in-law opened the door. I bent down and touched her feet. She blessed me and we came inside. The front door opened straight into the living area that stood twice as wide as long, with steps leading to the upper floors a few strides to the right. The house had two storeys. I learnt later that the upper storeys had been given on rent, and the family used the ground floor for residential purposes. The ground floor had four bedrooms, a small drawing room and dining room and a kitchen to one side.

I gulped down my disappointment; I was hoping for some privacy but could not be so in such congested surroundings. My father-in-law Naveen Sharma came to greet us and gave me his blessings when I touched his feet. "God bless you. How was your journey?" He asked, tossing a sweet compact smile.

Before I could answer Avinash steadied himself forward his jovial manners only adding to his charm as he said, "just great papa."

"Good."

"You both must be tired why don't you rest?" My mother-in-law ushered us to our room and left. I saw its interior minutely because the last time I had been here I had just glanced around.

The medium sized room that was painted in a light cream colour decorated a subtle painting along the left wall of what looked like a Greek goddess of love showering warmth and spreading the purpose of love through her soaring wings of passion. Brilliant in colour and shape only one word emerged in my mind. Ethereal!

My gaze travelled to the other side, the wooden cabinets for the clothes occupying the space perfectly. The bed was touching one side of the wall to the right of the wooden cabinets. Across the bed were an LCD TV, music player, DVD player and play station. To the left of the bed, there were two chairs. At the end of the cabinet, there was another wooden door that I was sure led to the bathroom. All in all, it was pleasant room.

While I was engrossed in admiring the surrounding Avinash's voice drifted me to awareness and I found him typing furiously through the keys on his phone.

Then he went to the wooden table, opened the drawer and took out a file.

He sauntered back towards me and laid his hand on my shoulder. "I have some important work, need to go." He

gave me a friendly pat. "You take rest. I'll meet you later."
 "Sure."
I saw him close the door as he moved out. I went to the
bathroom to wash up and change my clothes. After I came
out of the bathroom, I saw that Avinash had still not
returned. I checked my watch, it was eight in the morning
and I was sleepy unable to sleep on the flight. I lay on the
bed and closed my eyes slumbering into sleep.
I was startled into wakefulness on hearing some noises that
were coming from outside my room loud enough for me to
make out what was being said.
"She is sleeping?"
"Yes."
I checked my watch; it was just nine-thirty.
I hurried up part of me acknowledging the fact that I was a
married woman who could not sleep for long. At least that
was what my mother had advised me, to be on my toes all
the time and to bid laziness goodbye.
I hurried out of bed, draped my chunni across my shoulders
and opened the door to see no one outside. I came out
sliding the door shut and saw my mother-in-law and
Avinash talking in the drawing room. Their backs were to
me and they hadn't seen me yet.
As I approached them with soft steps their voices became
audible.
"You did not think of getting anything for your mother."
The side face of my mother-in-law was swollen clearly upset
and angry with her son.
"Ma, next time I will go I will get." Avinash cuddled his
mother.
"Smita also did not think of buying anything for me," she
contradicted.

Oh shit! I realised my mistake I had bought presents for my father, my brother, and mother but completely forgot to buy presents for Avinash's family.

I quickly turned and went back in my room. I opened the luggage and pulled out the two purses I had bought for my mother. The peach one that was a little better I kept for my mom and the other that was in blue I took out for my mother-in-law. I stood up but stopped looking down at the blue purse which my mom would have loved.

I couldn't help it! I had to create an atmosphere of love for my family and I knew I was wrong in this matter. I walked with determination outside and without stopping went and sat beside my mother-in-law. She looked at me in surprise, while Avinash passed a startled smile.

"Ma sorry I went off to sleep without showing you this." I gave her the purse. "I bought this for you."

She took the purse from my hand and led out a breath, putting her hand over my head. "It is lovely. At least my daughter –in- law thought about me, if not my son."

At that moment, I understood that she loved getting presents and who was I to deny her this pleasure. If I was to make a place in her heart it would be through giving her gifts. I learnt something important on my first day home; it was time to grow up!

CHAPTER 10

It had been six months of my marriage, Avinash was busy
with his work he left for work at nine and came back at
around eight at night. In the mornings I loved looking at him
getting dressed, putting on his favourite aftershave lotion,
handing him his wallet, tie and kissing him goodbye. I
remained at home taking classes from my mother-in-law on
how to cook. According to her I just didn't have the head for
it and I wholeheartedly agreed. It was easier for me to let her
do the cooking because I hated it!

My MA classes had started. This was my second year and I
was eager to finish it so that I could do my PhD in history.
Life was going exactly as I had planned it! My regular
classes, my studies and weekends that was always special
and mystical with Avinash and me going out together.

And one morning all my well-laid plans were shattered.

I woke up in the morning feeling nauseated and I was
vomiting continuously. It had been a few days since I was
not feeling well. After vomiting again, I walked out of the
bathroom to see Avinash sitting on the side chair reading the
newspaper.

"Avinash!" I called loud feeling low and breathless. Avinash hurried on, staring hard at me.

"I am vomiting since morning and it has been two or three days since I am not feeling well. I think I need to show to the doctor."

He took my hand firmly in his. "Why didn't you tell me before? You look pale."

He showed me to the bed. "I will get you something to drink that will make you feel better."

He quickly walked out of the room. In a minute he appeared with a glass of lemonade which he made me gulp down ignoring my protests.

I liked the way he caressed my forehead and said, "you rest awhile, I will tell mom, and she will take you to the doctor." He made me lie on the bed after I felt a little better and left.

Within seconds my mother-in-law was standing before me. For a fleeting moment, I detected a worried look in her eyes and then it was gone.

Then she stooped down, looking at my stomach with great interest till she became google-eyed. Only I knew how I controlled my laughter.

I could never forget the first question she asked me, "when did you have your monthlies?"

And then it hit me, I had not had my periods and was well past the due date. Oh no, it could not be! I couldn't be pregnant. I closed my eyes for a second all thoughts of laughter leaving my mind. Maybe I must have miscalculated the dates; yes, I reassured myself that is it. Anyways who remembered all this?

"I don't remember mummy," I replied meekly.

"Then it is best that I show you once to the gynaecologist".

Steadier I laid out a breath and looked at Avinash who gave

my shoulder a squeeze and agreed with the decision.

My mother-in-law and I left for the doctor, Avinash could not accompany us as he had to go to the office.

My heart was literally in my mouth, I was so nervous that my fingers had become cold.

Dr. Preeti lived nearby and it took us hardly ten minutes to reach her. I reached her clinic and after examination was declared brought pregnant! However, a pregnancy test was suggested to confirm the same.

From there we went to the chemist and I bought the kit with trembling hands. My mother-in-law's continuous excited chattering was getting on my nerves. I just wanted to get home and view the results. Here my life had turned upside down and my mother-in-law was getting exuberant, rather hyperactive over the prospect of becoming a grandmother. We soon reached the house and I literally flew to my room. My hands were sweating as I rushed to the bathroom, and locked it. I opened the kit, read the instructions carefully on the sheet of small paper, and followed the steps waiting for the inevitable. As the line turned from red to blue I went pale.

It was positive! Damn and double damn! A dozen vile and vicious words leapt into my throat. It was all Avinash's fault. But I lost them in a burst of tears. "How could I get pregnant? I was using all the precautions and damn! I was only twenty- three!" I went on and on scowling and weeping.

There was a bang on the door with my mother-in-law shouting, "Smita what is the result?"

Your head! I thought but spoke aloud, "coming mummy." I washed my face with water and then dried it with a towel. Straightening my shoulders, I unlatched the door and in my blind rush out, I literally barrelled into her.

"It is positive. I am pregnant," I declared unhappily.

Mummy clapped her hands in glee. "I need to inform everyone, they will be so happy. Smita you rest I will just come."

I simply nodded and she made me lie on the bed as if I was some worn outpatient drained of strength and energy.

"Don't move I will just come."

Trotting like a happy rabbit she scurried out of the room, leaving me restless and devastated. Everyone would be happy, but what about me? God, I was scared, scared of the thought that a life was growing inside me.

I touched my stomach, how could I take care of this life when I wasn't even capable of taking care of myself. I suddenly felt alone in this feeling of fear, only I could feel it and nobody else. I was to become a mother! A mother, the thought only gave me the shivers. I closed my eyes suddenly weary. I did not know what to do.

Like a tornado, mummy again whirled inside scooping a spoonful of curd and sugar mixture into my mouth. Gush! It tasted awful. This was the last thing I wanted. Mummy had gone berserk. She swirled something packed in a paper around my head, mumbling something in her mouth, "Krishna, please protect my grandson from the evil eye." Grandson? It could even be a granddaughter!

After satisfying her suspicious rite over me she started giving advice.

"Do not over exert for three months. The beginning months should be taken care of. Eat what you like. Keep yourself happy. I will give you almond and honey paste every day in the morning. It will be good for the child's health…" The list was endless and I gave a huge tired yawn that made her stop.

"You need to rest. I think you are feeling sleepy. Take a good nap."

She was correct this time. I needed some more sleep, some time off from the constant jabbering hammering my mind. I slowly closed my eyes, breathed in some air exhaled out and dozed off.

That evening when Avinash came home he flashed a smile and kissed my forehead. I was expecting more, something in the lines of what they show in the movies with the hero sweeping his wife in his arms with ecstasy at the thought of becoming a father. In fact, instead of rejoicing, there was an uproar in the family.

A little while earlier I had told my mother-in-law that I would be resuming my classes. She had vehemently denied. However, I was adamant; I wanted to finish my studies. After dinner, I walked into my room to see him standing in front of the long, narrow window with his back towards me. As if sensing my presence he said without turning, "why are you creating an issue Smita?"

Issue and me? This was the pot calling the kettle black. I added with a calm composure, "there is no issue Avinash I want to resume my classes."

"Classes!" He turned enough for me to see his smirk. "I think my mother has already told you the importance of the first three months."

"Yes and I am grateful for her concern, but I need some time for myself. All this is silly."

"Silly! For God sake use your head!" Now he turned towards me fully. "Listen to mummy, I know you don't want to, but for once listen to her."

"I don't want to listen to your mother!" I cried unbelievably. "Has mummy filled your ears?"

"Don't you dare take her name!" Anger danced in his eyes as he stepped forward in the middle of the room to where I was standing. "She has been so concerned for you. She only sees your benefit and you are complaining. You can always resume your classes after you deliver. I don't want any harm to come to the child due to your immaturity."

"I can take care of myself…I am not immature," I replied vehemently getting angry at my mother-in-law. I didn't know she would be a back stabber. I had only shared my desire for studies with her and she had chosen to create a mountain out of a molehill.

"I know how?" I continued to snap hard at him.

I was stopped from further argument when the servant knocked at the door."Bhaiyaji, bahuji's parents have come." "Ok." After buzzing him off, Avinash turned back at me. "Now I don't want any more discussion on this topic." He balled fists at his side and banged the door behind him when he whirled out of the room.

What little colour was left had drained out of my face leaving me hurt. How could Avinash be so cruel? I never expected him to speak to me like this.

A few minutes later, my mom came to meet me. I was still standing where Avinash had left me, thinking. She hugged me affectionately. "I am so happy Smita."

When I did not reply, she looked at my eyes as if studying the emotions that revealed themselves so clearly to her.

"Your eyes are red. Why are you crying? What is wrong Smita?"

I burst into tears and I could feel my mom panicking when I clung onto her. "Smita, my child what is wrong?" She ran her hand over my hair.

"Ma…" I hiccupped and wiped my tears pouring my heart out, "I want to finish my M A. ma, I really do, but Avinash and mummy don't want me to study right now."

"Smita!" She guided me towards the bed and placed my head over her lap gently rocking me as she used to do when I was a child. "You need to compromise a bit, baby. You are going to be a mother. It's not easy. You have to take care of yourself."

"But I worked so hard," I stammered between tears, "and anyways my exams are in six months and this is my first month."

"You will give your exam," my father said from the doorway.

"Papa!" I flew towards my father and in his arms. He held me affectionately gently patting my head. "I will talk to Avinash, don't worry."

"Suniyeji," my mom interjected from behind. "Please don't do something rash, stay calm. After all, she is this house's daughter –in- law."

"But what is the harm in talking," I argued.

"Smita please don't be childish!" she admonished me, lines of worry marking her forehead.

"Asha let me see. Now enough of all this," he took my face in his hands and spoke gruffly, "now how is my little mother feeling?"

I gave a wobbly smile. "Fine papa."

"Mitthi, now give your Papa a big smile."

I laughed and hugged him. I could always count on my father to bring back cheerfulness on my face.

"That is better. Now let us go out and sit with your family." We went out and sat in the drawing room where my in-laws and husband were already seated.

Reema was not there, as usual, busy most probably with her studies or friends.

My parents sat on a long sofa directly in front of the one on which my in-laws were sitting. I felt as if two warring parties were seated opposite each other. I went and sat beside Avinash on the right. A plate of sweets was exchanged and my parents were congratulated. After the initial pleasantries, all became quiet.

The silence was becoming oppressive and I gave my father a glance. It seemed the message was exchanged and he cleared his throat. He said softly to my father-in-law, "Bhaisahab."

"Ji," my father-in-law replied.

"Sir," my father paused briefly as if measuring his words. "Smita is a very good student and has worked really hard the whole year round. It will be a pity if she misses her exams."

"Bhaisahab she is about to become a mother!" my mother-in-laws shrill voice interrupted my father, "the hectic schedule of the exam will have an adverse effect on her and the child's health".

"You are absolutely correct Bhabhiji," my father added his voice to hers and my heart shrank. "But," he went on, "she will take care of her health and she has promised me that if she does not feel up to it she will leave the exam hall and come back. I don't see any harm in her trying. She can always leave the exam."

My mother-in-law simpered whereas to my happiness, my father-in-law gave his approval. "If that is Smita's wish then we are fine with it."

"Thank you papa." I passed a grateful smile. "I promise I will take care."

I looked at Avinash happily smiling, however; he did not return my smile. I had made him angry, though I could not understand why?

I got to know the reason soon. As soon as my parents left Avinash turned to me, sticking his hands in his pockets, his mouth curved up. "Smita how can your parents interfere in our lives?"

"Interfere? When did they interfere?" I pressed a free hand to my mouth, forced myself to stay in control.

"If this is not interference, then what is?" His tone frigid, he dragged a hand through his hair.

We were standing in the hall and on hearing our voices my mother-in-law came out.

I leaned in close so that my whisper could not be heard.

"Avinash can we talk in our room."

"If something does not happen according to your wishes will you always run to your parents so that your wish is fulfilled?" His tone was pitched up strong and high in anger.

I was shocked and stared at him in disbelief. Why was he making an issue out of such a small thing? I just couldn't reply.

"You could have talked to me," he went on.

"I did talk to you Avinash." I reminded him.

"Yes you did and you know what I said…" He was stopped by my mother-in-law. "Avinash your father wants to sleep, keep your voice down."

Without a word, he left me standing and went inside our room. For some time I was rooted to the spot.

I looked up before turning to see the look of satisfaction on Avinash's mother's face. I was confused, disturbed and though it was hard to admit scared. I was alone all alone.

I entered my room to see Avinash pretending to sleep. I changed and lay down on my side. I stayed awake a part of the night thinking...

The next day I woke up a little late to see that Avinash was already up and ready. I quickly got up and caught his arm as he was leaving. He turned towards me shrugging away his hand from mine. "I am getting late Smita."

"I am sorry," I blurted I did not want him to stay angry with me.

"Now forget it," he murmured as my eyes misted.

I locked my arms around his waist, resting my head on his shoulder. He gently patted my head and disengaged himself.

"Smita I need to attend an important meeting. I have to leave."

I nodded.

He left and I had the satisfaction of knowing that he was no longer angry with me.

CHAPTER 11

As the days passed, I spent my time preparing for my exams refusing to divulge my thoughts on anything that was unpleasant. I was now five and a half months pregnant and my body had adjusted to the changes, though I was still nauseous on occasions and tired but nevertheless I was determined to succeed. The pregnancy bought a bright glow on my face that was noticed by everyone in the house.

That morning I was again dressed in my loose yellow suit and white leggings, to hide my baby bump, everything was fine and I was rearing to go, but as I looked back, I wish I could reverse the proceedings of that day because that was the day that changed my relationship with Avinash.

I was giving my second exam, the first one had gone well and I was excited to give the second one.

Avinash, as usual, was leaving me to the college. I had hardly slept the night before and I knew I was pushing my limit but I was determined. After he left me at the college gate, I walked inside when a spell of dizziness hit me and I fainted…

When next I opened my eyes, I was in the backseat of…a car.

I got up jerkily to realise that it was Avinash who was driving.

For a moment, I was disorientated and then I remembered the spell of dizziness.

Avinash it seemed had seen me wake up in the rear view mirror because he asked anxiously, "are you all right?"

"Oh no!" I exclaimed, "what happened?"

"You fainted." I saw him through the mirror looking grim.

"My exam!"

His mouth thinned on hearing this. "Smita you fainted and the only thing you can think about is your exam!"

"No...No," I protested weakly.

"If something happens to my child I will not forgive you." He was literary vibrating with fury.

"Even I am worried about our child." Tears swam in my eyes and were blinked brutally back.

There was no time for more explanations as the car came to a halt in front of the hospital. I got down gingerly holding my stomach in fear. Avinash quickly got down from the driver's seat, throwing the key to the attendant to hold me. He took my arm.

It seemed like he had already talked to doctor Preeti because I was directly taken in her room despite the patients waiting outside.

He was told to wait outside and I was ushered inside the white sterile surroundings. A sense of forbidding engulfed me as I was made to lie down on the hospital bed. The doctor checked my blood pressure.

"It is on the lower side," she remarked. "Did you have something to eat since morning?"

I shook my head. A glass of glucose was quickly ordered and I was made to drink it. By now my knees were quaking something was not right. The urgency in the doctor's actions was making me scared. She again checked my blood pressure. She gave a relieved sigh and then did the dreaded internal check.

"Everything else is all right. You can dress up."

I quickly straightened my clothes. The doctor meanwhile, threw her gloves and called for my husband. I and my husband sat down opposite the doctor across the table.

"You need to take care of yourself Smita. You need to have food at regular intervals and Mr Sharma please make sure that she does." Dr.Preeti was insistent.

His nod was stiff and it was confirmed that I was in trouble.

"I am writing down some vitamins and iron capsules that she has to take and I advise absolute bed rest. She is weak and strained." She went on to say to my dismay, scribbling down medicines on a sheet of white paper.

"Just make sure adequate food, rest and water are taken. Today the blood pressure was so low that you could have lost the child or worse brain damage. Fluctuating blood pressure leads to brain damage in the child. You both as parents have a responsibility towards the baby. I hope it doesn't happen again. You need to come and meet me again in a week's time."

We were dismissed.

I walked beside Avinash who was completely silent as he bought the medicine from the pharmacy and then headed to the car.

We sat down in silence for some time. My stomach gave a mighty pitch as he ran over the speed breaker. "Ouch." I let out a breath.

"Shit! I'm sorry are you fine?" He stopped the car immediately.

"Yeah, I'm fine." I leaned my head over the seat.

He did not say anything else and started the car. When I could not bear the silence anymore, I spoke under the breath, "I am sorry. This will not happen again."

He drew his brows together forming a stubborn vertical line between them. "Since the beginning, you have been adamant. Even your parents did not have the sense to stop you. Now just see what your stubbornness has led to." His voice was mild but steely.

"Why are you dragging my parents into it?" I asked flabbergasted at what he was saying.

"Because they encouraged you to behave like this," he shot back.

"It is not their fault," I whispered with a wistful sigh, and a sigh that I was weakening. And twin demons of hurt and temper stabbed at my heart. Where was the Avinash who was so caring and respectful towards my family? He was not this man who was so cold and disrespectful.

"Please, now I don't want to argue, but now just listen and listen carefully no more exams or studies. You will stay at home and take rest. I hope I have made myself clear."

Was it some kind of an imperial rule where I had to obey? I knew what I did was wrong and it was totally my fault, but this was just not the way to talk to one's wife. I did not have the courage to voice my opinions, I was feeling dreadful. Despite the way Avinash had spoken it was a fact that I was wrong and because of my stupidity, I would have harmed my unborn child, I could not forgive myself for it.

And I never did after that, taking the blame entirely for everything that went wrong...

When we reached home Avinash pushed the main gate open and I waited a beat to see mummy sitting with a big face on the porch. She had half covered her mouth with her fingers. After a sharp glare darted at me she switched her attention to Avinash. "See what happens when the daughter- in- law of the family gets encouragements. Hey Bhagvan! Avinash take her inside and put some sense into her. It's the question of the future child of the family."

My hands stiffened and I could feel their cold numbness drained out of blood and life. A dreading sensation crept into every pore of my cell when I tugged my hands over my stomach.

"At least Smita obey your elders. Hasn't your mother taught you to listen to your mother-in-law?" Mummy twitched her mouth with a clicking sound that clearly depicted her anger. Her words struck me like a thunderbolt breaking my self – respect into pieces. How could my mother-in-law talk about my mother this way. It was not acceptable to me and I retaliated. "Mummy, please don't question my mother's upbringing. She has given her soul and blood for her children."

"Lo, now she answers back." Mummy snarled at me turning her face on the other side while Avinash towered on me confronting like a wounded soldier to shield his mother as if I had stabbed her. "Now you are crossing your limit. Just don't hurt mummy. If you have problems with her, she'll stay out of your affairs. Do what you like. But remember I will not tolerate anything spoken against her or you snapping at my mom."

This was what was left. A reckless taunt so ripping and mean. My illusion shattered. I think this was the first lesson of a married life. Don't question anything, don't answer, don't argue and don't put your point forward. Else you will be battered and battered so hard that you would grieve the rest of your life.

I ran into my room, locked the door, slumped on my bed, bunched the pillow under my head, curled into a ball, and begged myself to sleep.

The days passed and I became meeker. I did not discuss the matter with my mother, but my parents did come to meet me when they learnt that I had fainted.

They seemed worried and my mother cupped her hands under my chin, the warmth of her hands made me sentimental as I lay in bed. My heart knew how much I missed that touch of love and care and now her glorious scent bought me utter peace. I felt like keeping my head on her lap.

"Smita how are you feeling?"

"Ma don't worry, I am fine…" I did not want to bring her any distress.

"But your eyes, why are there dark circles around them?" She was stroking the area under my eyes moving her fingers over my cheeks.

"The doctor has said complete bed rest, no exams or studies." My mother whipped back to see Avinash remark pointedly looking at my father who was standing near the bed beside my mother.

I looked at the pain that crossed my father's face as Avinash went on, "she has said that it was because of the strain that she fainted and she should have never taken so much stress. I would have lost my child, because of some person's stubbornness and support."

Avinash was rude as he said this. He was now out of breath and his expression as hard as stone.

My father did not reply he was quiet. He knew Avinash was

pointing his finger at him.

My proud father who could not bear anyone talking to him in even a slightly raised tone was listening quietly as my husband insulted him. And there was shame on my face as I listened, feeling helpless to defend him.

My eyes watered as I turned my head, unable to bear the torment in my father's face. I had never thought in the wildest of my dreams that Avinash would speak like this to my father and I would be so helpless that I would not be able to defend him. They left without eating anything.

This cold attitude towards them left me sulking in frustration for days, though my mother made small, frequent calls cajoling me that after the birth of the child everything would become normal.

It was a part of life that one had to undergo. Some days were good and some bad and small arguments between husband and wife always strengthened the bond between them.

But I knew after that incident, my parents almost stopped coming to my house, whatever the reason my mother just gave a thousand excuses of not meeting me coated with even more advice. The major one being it's better you spend more time with your husband. You will know and understand each other better. I saw them only in some function or dinner party.

As my delivery date neared, I craved for my mother and her opinion. I realised her importance in my life and why she used to stop me from doing things, why she was adamant that I learn things.

I was lonely and the only company I had was my unborn child. I talked for hours with my child sharing my thoughts, my feelings… my being with it.

Avinash was busy with work. I just could not compare this

man with the one whom I had met before marrying. This cold, indifferent stranger could not be my husband. I realised why they said that the honeymoon period gets over in some time. My honeymoon was over.

CHAPTER 12

I woke up one night cramping badly. I shook Avinash who got up with a start. "What happened?!"

"I am having pains," I rasped between breaths.

I was rushed to the hospital that was near my house and taken to the labour room where the doctor and nurses hurriedly prepared everything, as I was laid on the delivery table.

Doctor Preeti automatically began to count. I felt the urge to push. Gritting my teeth, I bore down, grunting loudly for the first time, straining my entire body.

"The baby's in the birth canal," she said.

The nurse was about to leave my hand, but I gripped onto it, squeezing it as hard as I could. She reached for the damp cloth and wiped my flushed and heated face.

Somehow I found the strength to smile.

Within a few seconds, another pain approached. I could feel myself pushing the infant from my womb. I gritted my teeth, bearing down with all my strength.

The doctor in her strong and confident voice counted off the seconds. Again, when the pain was over I collapsed on the bed.

In the silence that followed, I could hear the sound of my own harsh breathing.

This time, when another pain came, I closed my eyes until the contraction became too strong. I surrendered to it, whimpering softly.

"The head's almost there." Doctor Preeti was completely focussed on the baby when the pain finally released me.

I did not know how much time, probably a couple of hours passed in pain.

With this final pain, I sobbed quietly. The baby was leaving my body. I could feel it now, feel the baby slipping free and then the loud, fierce cry that resounded in the room.

My relief was instantaneous.

I was drenched in sweat, my face streaked with tears. "I'm never going through this again," I gasped, thinking how my mother had gone through it two times.

Doctor Preeti held the baby in his arms and the nurse had a towel ready.

When I looked at the infant, my own tears came streaming down from my eyes with an intensity of emotion that surprised me. I really hadn't given much thought to the sex of the child, hadn't really cared.

"You have a daughter." She smiled.

Yes, a girl not a boy at six in the morning.

When I took the small infant, my heart literally burst out with love for her. She was so tiny, so fragile my baby. She had big, wide eyes and a look of astonishment as she seemed to stare at her brand new mother. The baby was carefully cleaned, examined and wrapped then placed beside me as I held on to her small hand and stared at the miracle I had birthed. She weighed seven pounds and two ounces and was twenty inches long and every inch of her was beautiful. I smiled tearfully.

A few hours later I was shifted to my room filled with pink balloons and the air smelled of flowers, exotic sprays of white orchids speared out of the crystal vase on the table. "Mom," I shouted when I saw my mother coming inside, followed by dad and Vikas. She kept looking at me with a blissful smile and wet eyes that soon started pouring out tears of joy. My family blessed the baby and then mom hugged me tightly placing a soft kiss on my forehead. After that the baby was taken away from me to be kept in the incubator for health reasons, Vikas pulled himself right across my left side and gripped my hand leaning towards me. I kissed his cheek. He was a handsome boy, and he looked a lot like our father. "How is my brother?"

"Didi super, but you know I am so thrilled to become a mama. Doesn't she look like me?"

"Yes, totally like you bro."

"Now don't make her talk much Vikas let her rest." My father was holding his hand pushing him backwards when I stopped him. I wanted to spend some more time with them. But the strain between Avinash and my family was visible because as soon as he entered the room my father became fidgety. Avinash made matters worse by being coldly civil. It was disheartening.

My family was so happy that their words, their expressions and what they were feeling could not be expressed in words. I loved to be with all of them once again and never wished this moment to pass by. I did not know if I would share the same kind of love with Avinash and his family.

My baby cried lustily the day I left the hospital and took her home. I had dressed her in a little pink knit suit and wrapped her carefully in a pink flowery blanket. I held her close as a nurse rolled me towards the waiting car. Avinash drove us home and gently put the baby in the bassinet in our room.

"Are you going to be okay? I need to go out. There is some work pending," he said the minute he helped me in the bed. I almost couldn't bear it, but I nodded, what was the point? As the days passed, I was busy and extremely tired with the small one.

I could sense the undercurrents of disappointment in the family on the birth of a girl, though nobody said so in the open, but hints were dropped. Those so called well-wishers, relatives came out with some words of wisdom. "It's okay to have a girl, but there should be a boy to complete the family."

My mother-in-law's response could not have been better. Adjusting the edge of her saree, she normally shifted in her seat coming out with her heart's grief. "Oh behenji, I had thought of distributing gold coins at the advent of a baby boy, but have to abide by God's will. Maybe next time …"

I kept quiet what was there to say? I had committed the unforgivable mistake by birthing a beautiful, healthy baby girl. How could a child be a mistake? And what did she mean by next time? Was I a child producing machine?

It was quite hard for me to believe my mother-in-law who was a Durga worshipper would speak like this, in fact, our whole nation worshipped the goddess.

In India, though a girl child was considered a goddess, but the irony of it was that here they were in fact treated as second-class citizens, thrown is dustbins, treated as trash, killed in the womb or throttled after birth. It was quite disgusting. I had never had these strong feelings of dissent within me, but what I experienced during that phase was disturbing. I had heard stories where women were forced into conceiving child after child in order to have a son, but mine was a modern family it would never differentiate between a girl and a boy, but that wasn't the case. The differentiation was there all right, it was just subtle.

After a few days, Avinash and I were sitting in our bedroom. I had one wall of my bedroom being decorated with the bright faerie-tale scenes for my gudiya. I had given my child the nick name gudiya who was sleeping peacefully in the crib. And in the crib with its glossy spindle bars, my little girl started crying impatient for attention.

"I am coming gudiya. I'm right there." I rushed to the crib, picked her up and cuddled her close. I smiled affectionately at her, as usual her arms were spread upwards, the sleeves of her top covering her palms and her fists clenched tightly in a grip. Her small pink lips were also closed tightly and her there was a red blush on her puffy cheeks. When I looked at her, she looked so perfect, so small yet so round. She was so tiny that it scared me sometimes that while sleeping, I would squeeze her.

She would have her father's hair and complexion, but my looks I thought as I cooed and swayed. It was already coming in the dark with those hints of chestnut when the light caught in. She gave another lusty cry and I knew I had to feed her. My breasts felt huge, and I had so much milk that I sprayed her face at first while she tried to eat, and she made funny faces at me.

I laughed, looking up to see Avinash furiously typing on his laptop. He wasn't even aware of the joys of fatherhood, he had become busier; he was earning more and had lesser time to spend with us. He left early in the morning and came late at night and even at home, he was busy with some work or the other.

I asked him, "I feel like going out. Gudiya is sleeping we will come in a few minutes."

Avinash looked at me with angry eyes and literally snarled at me as if like I had incurred some sin by asking him to take me out.

"Can't you see I have work? You do not have anything better to do except to snap your silly wishes at me expecting me to be some superhuman who will work and even cater to your whimsical demands."

I simply kept looking at him with an open mouth as he hastily picked up his laptop and snubbed me, "I can't stay in this room." And briskly walked out of the room, haughtily banging the door without even thinking that his daughter would wake up.

Gudiya started crying, with tears streaming from my eyes, I picked her up gently cooing to her softly, reassuring her with my presence that everything was all right in her life. There was nothing all right in my life; I had never seen Avinash behave this badly with me. It was as if some monster had entered into him and he had become someone else.

A little while later gudiya went off to sleep and I cried myself to sleep.

Avinash did not come back. I swiped at my tears working my mind through the niggling doubt that he wanted a son and now with the change in his behaviour, I became convinced that indeed he was disappointed that we had a daughter and not a son.

I did not see Avinash again until morning and even then, he

left for work. My mind was fuzzy from lack of sleep gudiya had not slept well the whole night; I had to keep some help. I talked to my mother on the phone who immediately suggested a maid whom she knew. I readily accepted telling her to send her immediately.

The maid arrived somewhere in the evening when I was sitting with my mother-in-law in the living room.

She slanted a look towards her and frowned. "Who is she?"

I glanced at her wary. "Mummy, I am unable to take care of gudiya alone. I need a maid. My mother knows Kanta really well she will help me."

"Even we have brought up children alone. Why can't you do it on your own?"

"Because I just can't," I said defensive now. "I need help."

My mother-in-law sniffed and got up. "Fine, then why ask me when you have decided." She walked out and I ignored her. I really needed Kanta. I settled her salary and took her to gudiya in my room.

Kanta slid her hand under my baby's head and picked her in her arms swaying her slightly. I saw Kanta was very careful in handling gudiya and she also did not feel uncomfortable with her.

I liked her attitude and she was ready to start work from that day itself. It was a big relief; she knew exactly what to do and how to do it. From teaching me how to hold the baby properly, to making her have milk, burping, changing diapers everything. She was a wizard; I called my mom to thank her.

After a short inquiry on gudiya my mother was quick to ask. "You asked bhabhiji na, was she fine that I sent Kanta."

"She wasn't ma, she objected…"

My mother sounded horrified, "Oh God, then don't keep her

may be she didn't like her."

"No! I will keep Kanta, she really helps me ma and no one else. Ok, forget all this tell me how is everyone at home?"

I went on speaking without realising that my mother-in-law was listening to my conversation from outside. I had no idea what was in store for me.

That night when Avinash came home my mother-in-law very conveniently started crying in front of everyone.

Avinash pressed his fingers to his eyes clearly irritated.

"What is wrong with you?"

"I have become useless; can't I take care of gudiya?"

"Who said you can't?"

"Smita has kept a maid!"

"But…" I butted when Avinash spared a glance at me and raised his hand stopping me from speaking further.

"So?" He asked his mother.

"So? Can't you understand she has kept a maid?"

"So what's the big deal ma, please stop this melodrama. I can afford a maid." He brushed aside the matter.

My relief knew no bound. I was happy maybe what I was thinking was wrong I was hasty in my opinions about him.

CHAPTER 13

Forty days later there was a small havan and the naming ceremony of my baby. She was named Naina by my father-in-law. Naina, I guess because of her large, swan-like eyes that were her most prominent feature she was named as such.

Naina was growing up well, making her way into everyone's heart, but not so much to my heart's content.

 One day some guests arrived at our place. I was called out by Avinash to meet them while I was making Naina feed. It was a hell of a day as Kanta had chosen to take the day off. Somehow I managed to make her sleep, softly closing the door behind me.

I spotted an elderly couple seated on a couch across the ornately carved wooden table in the drawing room. Avinash, mummy, dad and Reema had taken the chairs on the other side of the table.

As the bahu of the family was meant to do, I greeted them by touching their feet.

My eyes stayed on them for a moment and then turned to mummy who said, "Bhaiya is an old family friend."

I was told to get something to serve the guests.

I started for the kitchen, but sneaked for a moment into my room, satisfied to see Naina sleeping in peace.

Mentally counting the number of people, I hurried into the preparation of six cups of tea presenting it before the guests.

Before I could hand a cup of tea to the guests Rima snapped at me, "what about the biscuits? Get them."

Agitated by her remark which I found derisive, I answered back, "get it yourself!"

Sparing a glance at others, I bombarded into my room on hearing Naina's cries. I started nestling my cranky child to my chest to feed her again.

I knew I had landed in misery when Avinash barged into the room as soon as the guests left.

His tone was like an electric slice through my body. "I'm sick to death of your behaviour."

"What…what have I done?" I stared at him.

"You don't know what you have done. This is the way you talk in front of the guests to Reema. Don't you have any manners?!"

I blinked. "Excuse me. Am I a maid to be ordered by your sister to get stuff for the guests?"

"You are great! Superb! Does your high-level ego allow you to talk to a young girl that way?"

"What do you mean by high-level ego? You are so cynical that instead of telling your sister to speak to her Bhabhi with respect, you are taking her side."

"As usual, you have all the fake excuses in your bag to argue and plan. You don't care about my family's emotions or me. Many times my mother has tried to involve you in the family, but you don't seem to care. You scheme against my parents, my sister, always taking out faults in them, but they never complain about you. What else... you want me to be like you. I'm tired of your mixed signals and capricious mind and your goddamn expectations of me. You want me to run after you. Shall I work or keep on satisfying your ego because nothing seems to make you happy."

He stalked to the window, stared out while I wept wildly. He did not even give me a chance to prove myself. For him, I was labelled as wrong. Whatever I did, how much ever I tried, for him and his parents I was a fault finding punching bag.

It seemed Naina sensed my distress because she stopped feeding. She gave a loud cry. I gently put her over my shoulder, soothing her. Still crying miserably, I forced my point. "I don't have a capricious mind at least I never used to. What are your goddamn expectations from me? I never seem to satisfy you or your family. I am scared of what's happening around me and I don't know what I say crops up misunderstandings. I want you, your love for Naina and myself, but your family always has some problem with me all the time. Whether it was with my studies, with the maid or moving out freely and now over a small incident. Everything is made an issue of in this house."

Avinash came up to me and fixed me with a level gaze. "If I am that bad, and you don't like the way things are, you can leave me."

My heart tripped right up to my throat and started beating there like a big bass drum on hearing this.

"Oh! It's a good idea!" I made my voice tremble. It was embarrassing, but necessary.

He could not have been nastier when he rose and pushed the door half open without turning back to look at me.

"Selfish woman! You are ruled by selfish ego. You do not know how to love, but I was foolish to mistake your feelings for love. Leave!"

I was stupefied to hear him say such vile words. I just could not open my mouth because I realised whatever I would say would be unheard and misinterpreted. He didn't bother to even look at me and whizzed outraged out of the room. With tears rolling down my cheek and Naina weeping in my arms, he had shattered all my dreams. It felt like a nightmare hitting me over and over again. But it was all true and I was getting used to it.

I could not stand the effect of my mental disturbance on my child's behaviour whose weeps had increased in intensity with my changing mood.

I quickly swiped my tears away with the back of my hand, forced a smile on my face rocking her and singing her lullaby till her tiny eyes drooled off in silent sleep.

Then I closed my eyes, wishing to keep my baby close to my heart, I did not put her down on the bed and wondered. My whole life had been turned inside out and I could barely think, let alone make important decisions. I felt as though I were walking underwater. I wanted to understand why things had gone wrong, but I was not sure. Did I make a mistake? Was it my fault or was I not good enough? Or had I only expected too much from Avinash? How could he even think of leaving me? How could he threaten me like this? Was it like this for every woman? I remembered my mother's words always listen to your mother-in-law, don't answer back, curb your tongue Smita it is too sharp. You need to grow up. Now I realised the wisdom behind those words. I had to let go of my ego, but what about my self-respect?

Time passed. When Naina my daughter was a year old I thought about giving my remaining exams. I agreed to whatever my mother-in-law said, followed her directions and did not answer back. There was peace in the family. Avinash was forever busy, he was very ambitious, and he worked from early to late. He forever had meetings and joined various famous clubs where even I became a member. However, I became pregnant again and this time everyone hoped that it would be a boy. Once again destiny had played its role and I had to leave my studies.
After I shared the news with Avinash, he commented, "I hope it is a boy this time."
I opened my mouth, then closed it and finally spoke, "Avinash, what if it is a girl? Will you love her less?"
He did not say anything, but the look on his face made me never; ever again say anything like that.
Nine months later I delivered a healthy baby boy. The heir of the family had arrived who made everyone happy and our house got turned into a new mansion. Yes, that is what I call it a mansion, not a home.
The tenants were told to leave and the exteriors were converted into red brick. The wooden doors were now honey gold, set off by copper trim that had gone dreamy green in some parts. There was a complex arrangement of terraces, skirting or jutting from both stories. Half a dozen rooflines peaked or sloped, all with a kind of artful symmetry.
The wide lawn was now informal but the placement of every

shrub, every tree, and every flower bed had been meticulously selected and designed.

I had my hands full with two babies. Before a woman had children, she thought of what she wanted to do during the day, but afterwards, her hours were filled with what she must do. I had to feed them, check the laundry, run after Naina pulling her from switches, wash my sons bottles, change his diapers and the most difficult, try to put both my children to sleep so that I could get some rest. In all this Kanta was a big help. She was firm with Naina and gentle with the baby.

Avinsh took full supervision of the mansion from furniture to its restoration and decoration. He had to impress his clients, neighbours and relatives.

At first, there had been fights.

"You are turning the house into a museum!" I always said in exasperation. "It does not look like a home!" For a change even my mother-in-law agreed, "Avinash there cannot be antiques on the table, there are children in the house. They are going to break it!"

"Then Smita will have to keep them in check!" This had become his normal habit. Everything had to be taken care of by me. The children, home and him. I had started feeling like a robot with no charge up or rest of any kind whose body mechanism was supposed to function unreasonably every second.

And I backed down, as I always did at a confrontation. I did not know where my spirit had gone, I felt like a river that was flowing against a tide and was helpless against it.

Avinash ruled the household. There were servants, cooks, gardeners, drivers and I was congested. The house was filled with so many antiques that no one could sit on the expensive sofas or touch the tables in fear. The drawing room meant for the family to sit in was permanently closed.

I hated my bedroom that was filled with greys and blacks all sleek and modern with sharp angles. I had no idea where the man who was a romantic and dreamer had gone, replaced by this ambitious, money making machine.

I talked to my mother about it. "Smita you should be happy your husband is earning so well, he is taking care of you. You have servants, sweet little babies and such a beautiful house." She was as usual objective, cementing her views with conviction.

"But mother where has the warmth and love gone?" It was my heart that wanted nourishment, not the mind.

"You have always been a romantic. What about your two children, they are your love. Now don't be silly Smita. Avinash cares for you."

Yes, he did. Avinash was a great believer in men taking care of woman, or controlling them whether it was at home or outside. Even my social life revolved around my husband and his friends and clients.

So I became the perfect wife, we became the perfect couple. Our friends were envious of us. We entertained, we travelled and we were the picture of the perfect affluent couple. We had a perfect Marriage. But did we?

PART 2

The Perfect Marriage?

CHAPTER 14

I feigned sleep in the early morning light. There had been a time when I had loved to watch my husband get dressed for the day, choosing his clothes, giving him his wallet and watch and just in general being near him. That was so long ago the romantic mind of a young girl. Now I dreaded watching him fuss and fiddle. Oh, he had the looks, but I Smita Sharma had deteriorated considerably in that department. I looked from beneath my lashes when Avinash left the room most probably to meet his mother, as he had a habit of taking her blessings every morning and I sat up hugging my knees close to my chest. No mean feat with the extra kilos I had gained over the years. It had been thirteen years and six months of marriage and my life had completely changed. Avinash hardly looked at me. Once I had cared about every little thing he did, but now it was just routine. I could not explain that though everything was good, everything fine, but now the question was what more that was needed. I would never be able to fill the empty spaces between us to feel the same again. Would it be never? The thought was terrifying.

I got out of bed, dressed, then, tiptoed downstairs to put together the ingredients of the mango pudding. Today was Sunday and I wanted to make something special. Not that anyone would eat any of it, I thought with a sigh. Naina, my daughter would be horrified at the calories, Samarth my son would come down with only seconds to spare before he made his way to his friend's house, and Avinash would only eat his cornflakes, something high fibre, and low cholesterol. Attempts at gourmet cooking were wasted on my family. Overhead I could hear my thirteen-year-old daughter Naina's quick step. She would be the first one down, the first to ask her mother why she had made something that was guaranteed to clog all their arteries with one bite. She was so much like her father that it was scary.

Samarth had gone more on me and when he was away from his friends, he would sit with me and talk. He liked the colour of his room when all disapproved, but he agreed with me. I remembered he was always an easy going child, sleeping through the night when he was just weeks old, so unlike Naina who seemed to cry and cause chaos the entire night. Even though my daughter had gained a suitable height for her age her fair complexion would instantly become pale and her sharp nose would start twitching whenever I got angry with her. Though I tried to remain stricter with Samarth, he was more understanding than Naina who was pampered by her father. I remembered that this was the girl child whom her grandmother never wanted and now she was the most spoilt.

Soon Samarth came bustling down. At the age of eleven, he was chubby. His eyes dominated his round face and were said to resemble mine, while the lower half of his face had gone on his father. Samarth gulped down the milk and pudding happily. He was a growing boy and just loved to eat. Naina looked at the pudding disdainfully, picking up a piece of sandwich munching it in small bites. The way she chewed and moved her mouth resembled the way Avinash ate food, even going on to acquire his complexion. She had sharp features that reminded me of my youth, but unlike my nature, she was as stubborn as her father.

The hurry to go out was more than wasting time at the table. So, both of them presently left Samarth with his cricket bat and Naina with her brand new mobile phone.

I was alone with Avinash who as usual, ate his cereal reading the newspaper. I put the pudding in front of him. "Would you like to have some?" I asked, knowing I sounded whiny.

He looked at it in distaste. "Smita I will not have that. You need to become more health conscious. If I eat that I will become fat like you."

Tears burned my eyes. But he did not bother even to spare me a look busy reading the economic section. He had made investments in the stock market and he was forever looking for favourable investment opportunities.

Where was the young Avinash who had said that he would love me even if I became fat? I looked at him closely; in the thirteen years of our marriage, he hadn't changed much physically. His hair was a little grey at the temples, making him look distinguished. He was physically fit by going for regular jogs in the mornings.

"I need to meet some clients," he said without looking at me and picked up his suitcase, making his way out of the main gate. I picked up the pudding and threw it in the basin and felt my insides shrivel. I was sick of his attitude, sick of his taunts and sick of his indifference.

I realised that what had changed about him was that he no longer seemed to actually see me, or in fact, his children and it had become worse over the years. I was just a convenience, someone who was dumped at home to take care of the family.

I couldn't remember the last time we had dinner together, not the social functions, but just the two of us. I couldn't remember the last time we had done anything together. We hadn't even made love since a year. Avinash did not even have time for making love. It seemed that my life was just moving away from me. Over the years he had said so many things to me, but I didn't know why what he said to me today hurt me. I thought I had become immune to his tantrums, but no it still hurt. I sniffed, remembering our dinner during the courtship period where he had held my hand and said: "I will love you even if you grow fat." Where was that love? And what he said today pierced my heart. I ran into my bedroom and then locked the bathroom door. I sat down on the edge of the Jacuzzi and cried for what had gone wrong.

An hour later, after composing myself, I was barely out of the shower, when I remembered I had to meet Roshni in half an hour. I belted my robe, snagged a towel, and wound it around my hair as I hurried out. Avoiding the mirror, I dressed hurriedly in a simple cotton suit.

On my way in my Ford after fighting the horrendous Delhi traffic, I reached the club strictly forcing my thoughts on Roshni and not on what Avinash had said earlier so carelessly. Roshni my best friend, she was my only support left. My parents had moved to Mumbai as my brother was posted there. He was married to a wonderful girl and had two beautiful daughters. They were happy together and I didn't want to burden them with my problems.

I pulled up beside a white alto, stepping out to move towards the red brick building that was not ostentatious although the construction of old brick due to years of sun and the elements had polished it to a red rosy colour. The walkway was made of red flagstones bordered by multi-coloured flowers that bloomed profusely. The building had a cosy, welcoming look. I noticed the posters and banners being posted around the club.

I stopped in front of the pink banner on which a curvaceous woman was drawn.

Size 36-24-36.

I read the caption. Mrs. Perfect.

Oh well, it certainly wasn't for me; the competition was for married woman something like Mrs India but on a smaller scale. The club organised such competitions once in four years and the preparations for the same would start six months earlier so that the married participants were given time to prepare. They got contestants from all over Delhi. It was considered quite a lavish affair.

My eyes were still on the banner when I heard a voice from behind. "Smita why don't you participate in the Mrs Perfect contest of our club?" The familiar tone was none other than my friend Roshni's. I snorted thinking, Ya right! My husband thinks I am fat and I will participate in Mrs Perfect.

My expression was one of astonishment as I mocked at my own self. I swung around. "Roshni are you joking? It is easy for you to say, but an eighty-five kilo body walking down the ramp. Forget it!" Roshni had a small, trim and tidy little body. She had lively glass green cat eyes under elegant brows. Her mouth was mobile and quick to smile or sneer and when she smiled it curved up and teased out the hint of dimples in her cheeks. Her hair was a rich dark brown, short up to her shoulders. She was Mrs Opinionated, loud and Avinash disliked her. But surprisingly, she had been my best friend since eighteen years from right before my marriage. During my marriage, she had gone for two year internship in photography and now was a renowned photographer of nature.

"This is not entirely a beauty pageant. It's about searching for a right talented woman and besides that just look at your features and complexion. You are beautiful dear. You just need to discard this extra fat around your waist. All will be well handled by a professional yoga teacher. Trust me, I know all the angles." She pretended to snap my pictures.

I laughed trying to hide the hurt. "Avinash thinks I am fat. Even a yoga teacher can't help me."

Shielding my face with my hand, I walked over to the window that overlooked a patio of sorts in the back of the building. I looked down at a fishpond to see huge goldfish swimming lazily from one end of the pond to the other. Colourful lawn chairs and small tables with umbrellas sat under a line of huge trees surrounded by lush grass. The oval swimming pool occupied by two or three people diving in and out of it.

Roshni stood beside me. "You need to kick some ass Smita! Where is that young Smita I knew in college who was the first one to take up a challenge?"

I answered, still looking straight ahead. "That Smita is long gone."

"Bullshit! Smita look at me."

I took a right turn giving her an uninterested look as she continued, "I have been your friend for eighteen years. I have seen the change in you. You have got to do this for yourself."

"And what about that question answer round. No, no I just can't answer those questions."

"There is nothing in them that shall disturb you. We will go to the best professional trainers to build up your confidence and train you in speech. They have this art of bringing out one's personality."

"But…but it's difficult. I mean I am not up to it."

"Look Smita I know you can do it. With the kind of education, family background and looks you are one of the most eligible women in the Mrs Perfect contest. And you know what that husband of yours should also get to know the real you. Don't you want to show him this side of yours? He should be taught a lesson. Given a tight slap…"

"Roshni!"I slapped my thigh to stop her, unable to think and answer logically. I forgot to mention she was also a hard-core feminist. I knew personally that there were always heated arguments between her husband and her, but what was surprising was despite the fights they were happy together. It seemed they enjoyed bickering at each other. Roshni definitely loved her husband Kunal, who equally loved her.

"Ok…Ok, fine, but just think about it."

"Hmm." That was the end of the conversation and we had lunch together talking mainly about Roshni's family and professional life. She loved photography and her face always sparkled when she spoke of the latest pictures she took. She talked about flowers, birds, dogs, trees all nature captured in her memory flowing out of her mouth like a fresh beautiful poetry.

Roshni zipped open her handbag shoving her fingers inside

to take out a square shaped photograph. "My latest piece of art." She winked showing the same to me.

My eyes were viewing a silver waterfall slinking down smoothly into a frothing river surrounded by huge boulders and emerald colour trees. The left side of the picture was bright because of the angling of the rays of the sun falling directly over the water and trees while the uppermost of it experienced a shadowy effect. Perfection with style was Roshni's forte, yet she managed to portray nature in its simplest of forms.

"It's lovely. How do you manage it?" I asked, still in awe.

"I think I kind of know the trick of the trade. Guess support of beautiful people like you keeps me going the right way."

"Ya..ya modesty goes along with praises."

"Indeed…well-wishers like you always keep me on the high praising me all the time. But you know when you get into something and work hard at it, you get results."

I knew what she was hinting at. With the usual round of jokes and fun-loving conversation, we enjoyed our lunch, and I bid Roshni goodbye without giving my confirmation to her.

I slowly walked out of the club towards the parking lot. I was lost in my own thoughts, thinking nothing else, but her words. *And you know what your husband should also get to know the real you. Don't you want to show him this side of yours?* Oh boy! She knew how to shake me up.

CHAPTER 15

I reached my Ford. Unlocked the front door, perched myself on the driver's seat shoving the leather purse onto the left. I sat still, staring blankly at the window shield of the car with my hands placed on the car's wheel.

Once again, nothing but Roshni's words echoed in my head. I closed my eyes and then did not know what happened. Something struck the peripheral of my brain and I swung my eyes open, glancing a look at the rear view mirror at my features.

I rotated the key in the ignition that started the engine of my car with a roar and laughed. Should I go for it?

Tooling along in my car over the busy, windy road, I left the parking lot behind. My heart raced with the speeding movement of its wheel. I turned to look out of the window at the gorgeous Gulmohar tree. The tree emblazoned with red colour flowers and the leaves were flamed with pure shades of green. It was my favourite spring month when the breeze was pleasantly cool and the surroundings brightened with the brilliant colours of a huge variety of flowers. After the lethargy of the winter, the spring seemed to enlighten people up. My spirits had suddenly risen to a new height.

The season of flowers seemed to wake me up, bringing hope

into my life.

I took another right turn with a smile that came from within and after entering the main gate of the house, I quickly got out of my car and hurried inside my room.

I stood before the elongated mirror over the dressing table and started looking at myself. The mirror was something I avoided, especially when I was naked. I turned sideways, making a long face at the bulge of my stomach that was prominent. Then I again turned, pushing away a few tendrils of my black hair with a few streaks of grey in them that I refused to colour or was just too lazy to bother, scanning my face at the mirror. Dark circles surrounding two big puffy eyes were staring back at me.

"O God, why hadn't I checked them out."

I quickly pulled out the dressing tables draw taking out the concealer from it and wearing it around my dark circles to cover them. Then I wore a compact over my face, smoothing my rough dry skin. I moved forward roving my fingers on my cheeks. "Not bad."

Then I applied a blue eye shadow over my eyes and kholed my eyes till the edge giving them a swan-like smoky look. Finally, I wore a pink blush on and applied a rosy pink shade Avon lipstick on my lips.

I pouted and remarked, "looks luscious!"

After wearing all the proper makeup I was taken aback wondering at my looks. "I still do not look that old. I look hmm… I look nice. In fact, I am looking beautiful. After all, age is just a number you have to feel young to look young."

I was on a move. "She was right. I should try for the contest. I will talk to Roshni and ask her about the entire procedure. Let me check Avinash's reaction after he notices me wearing makeup."

I waited for Avinash to come. It was seven pm. The bell rang and the door of the gate was opened by the servant. As usual, my gaze went down to his grumbling and tired face. He threw his suitcase on the table, loosened his tie and sat on the sofa in the lobby. I saw him gulping down a glass of water offered by the servant and walked towards him. I moved closer to him, but he deliberately seemed to ignore me busy taking out his socks and shoes. He still wasn't looking at me.

I bit my lower lip as I called out, "Avinash."

For a second his eyes moved up to my face, but he simply said, "put the dinner. I want to sleep. I am tired."

I felt humiliated again. How could he ignore me? He hadn't bothered to notice me at all, even after I had taken all the pains to look so well.

I was angry and maintained a cold silence, though I was restless from inside as I moved towards the dining room.

A piercing yell jerked me away from the dining table. I rushed to the source of the noise that came from the room.

I banged the room's door open, to see Samarth and Naina shouting at each other.

"Give it to me!" Samarth demanded, rounding Naina, his face red and furious.

"It's mine!" Naina shouted, pulling the book from his hand.

If they didn't let go of the book, it would be torn to pieces. I thought.

"Give it back," Samarth said menacingly edging his way toward the bed which was big enough for half a dozen people, scattered with Mickey Mouse and Barbie pillows.

It was a beautiful room: high ceilings, tall windows, One wall had an enormous bookshelf with two carved marble sculptures.

"Stop fighting. I will not tolerate all this!" I said in my most authoritative voice. Intent on each other, both the children ignored me now climbing on the bed.

They were now turning one way and then another on the bed as if playing a game of ringa-roses. Arms and legs were kicked in every direction, making it impossible to stop them. The condition of the new bed sheet was nothing more than a crumpled piece of rag suffered from many washes.

"I said stop fighting." This time I was more forceful, but still unheard I headed over the top of the bed myself.

I grasped hold of Samarth's arm and at least, having as much success with that I grabbed him down the bed.

"What was that for? You are fighting with your sister." Samarth simply glared at me in silence. His face swollen like a hot potato.

"Answer me," I scowled shoving the fallen pillow on the bed that was coming in my way.

With defiance in his tone, he answered back, "she has taken my book. I was reading it and she snatched it from my hand. Why don't you scold her?"

"Well, I see so that is the way you should behave to get your book back."

I now glared at Naina and demanded, "come down. Why are you still on the bed?"

Naina struggled to come down and stand with her head low.

"Why did you take the book from your brother? You could have asked for it in a decent manner."

"Because it's not his its mine! I wanted it first. He could have waited to read it later." She confronted me with a stronger tone of defiance.

"So you both acted in an uncivilised manner for a book. Is

this what I have taught you? To hit and act like hooligans and then even snap at your mother for your unruly misdeeds and behaviour. Instead of sharing you chose to be selfish like your…" I was furious but stopped gulping down the word father. I pointed with a shivery finger at the bed. As it is I was in a bad mood and the anger rose inside me when both of them answered me back.

Still shaking with anger, I dictated, "you both have spoiled the new bed sheet. I feel like slapping you. Now both of you are going to wash it properly and together in harmony. This is your punishment. Now if you both quarrel like cats and dogs I am going to give you a harsher punishment. When I say harmony I mean it."

I walked over to the bed where the book was thrown, picked it up and stiffened my back. Crossing my hands, I drifted a furious gaze at both of them.

"I am taking this book with me and will only give it to you one at a time. Now both of you wash the sheet and after you finish the task come out for dinner."

 Both children nodded their heads with a stunned expression. More of it was a mixture of surprise, as they had never seen their mother so violent before. For the first time I had raised my voice at them, usually, I just ignored their fights preferring to stay away. But I was on fire and stomping my foot hard, I whirled around storming out of their room and then I felt bad. I knew I had gone overboard. Maybe I took out my frustration on the children. Anyways, I thought I needed to stop acting patiently with them.

Dinner was ready. I slowly crept in the children's room to see them drying the bedsheet and putting it over a small rack at the corner of the room.

"Good." Samarth and Naina instantly tilted their head to the right to see my smiling face.

I came closer to them.

"Sorry mom," Samarth said followed by Naina who added, "We would have listened to you, there was no need to shout at us like this!"

I knew I should curb Naina's wayward tongue but emotions overcame me for shouting at them, maybe I was wrong on being so soft but I couldn't help it, it was my nature. I simply didn't want to be angry, I snuggled both of them into my arms and caressed them with affection.

"Come for dinner. Love you." I took their hands into mine and moved out of the room reaching the dining table with them.

The family ate dinner in silence. My thoughts again transferred back to Avinash now. I was looking at him. Mentally, I knew I was upset because of him. Did I expect a lot from him? Wasn't he expected to know all the things a husband did, things like caring for the children and things like romance and compliments? Even if I produced a series of unsettling questions, he would not come up with answers. He had no time for me. After dinner, the children quickly left the table and headed to their room.

Avinash had a few gulps of water, pulled back the seat and steepled his way upstairs towards the bedroom.

After settling the dining table, I went to my room where he was already drowned into a deep sleep. I led out a sigh, with a twitch of my lip a boring gesture that had become an everyday affair. I slumbered towards my cupboard, opened its left side softly, careful not to make a noise and took out my nightclothes. I changed into my nightgown and lay beside him on the bed with open eyes staring at the ceiling fan. I made sure to stick to the edge of the bed the farthest

side away from the insensitive person I had married.
I had to change for myself. I had to think for myself and
now I would live for myself. Where was my self-respect?
Unable to sleep, I got up and walked into the bathroom,
closing the door shut. I took off my nightgown and stared at
my unflattering figure with wide open eyes. I looked like a
pumpkin with rolls of fat. I stared and stared, I couldn't be
called pudgy or chubby I was plain and simple fat and fat,
from my swollen cheeks to my swollen toes. I whirled
around to notice more ounces of fat; I stared over my
shoulders at my buttocks, my thighs and finally looked at
my face. I could instantly note the expression of misery in
my eyes, but there was also determination. I would change!
Not for anyone else, but for myself, only for myself!
These thoughts somehow made me calmer. I was ready.

.

CHAPTER 16

The next day I again met Roshni at Starbucks. The determination I was feeling yesterday seemed to be slipping again. I was concerned about Avinash's reaction when I would tell him that I would be participating in the show. He would probably laugh at my face and say, "you must be mad, just look at yourself!" And I was not prepared for the humiliation.

Roshni was my regular distress absorber.

She was naturally very upset getting, even more, every time I told her about Avinash's behaviour. Outspoken as usual she punched a finger in the air. Her lips folded into a thin derisive smile. "You need to leave him."

"What nonsense!" I remarked.

"Yes! If you left him, he would realise your worth. He'll get to know how much he needs you. You need to shake up his perfect world. The world where his slave takes care of his tidbits and still serves as a punching bag for him, being beaten up mentally at his wish. He cannot take you for granted like this! He will learn how to respect you once you leave him alone to take care of himself!"

I didn't have the heart to do that. I very well knew what happened to woman of my age who left their husbands. How the world looked upon them. I had no desire to leave my husband and live a dreary life. Besides, I still loved him, despite his flaws he was the man I had married and bore children with. "Roshni, I am not a famous photographer like you. I cannot earn and live on my own."

The incident of my first pregnancy when I had tried to do something on my own still haunted me. My failure as a competent mother in my stubbornness and attempt of doing something on my own still left me shamefaced.

It seemed that Roshni interpreted my sad expression correctly because she reached across the table to hold my hand. "Smita you need to let go of that incident. Naina is fine now; she is twelve years old and healthy."

Unconsciously, I pressed a hand to my belly, as if to protect what had lived there.

"Please let go of the guilt, you did nothing wrong. Ok, forget all this!" Roshni started making kissy noises. "At least do it for me. Eighteen years of friendship ka vasta… Pleeease."

I rolled my eyes. "Oh God you have started your melodrama, but what about Avinash?"

"Again, that husband of yours. We won't tell him! So even if you don't win or want to leave it in the middle, no one will be wiser. It would just be our secret and if he asks you just say you have joined some committee consisting of wives of rich and important men and he will become happy."

I gave an ear splitting laugh. How well Roshni knew my husband.

Roshni went on conspiringly, "and besides, it won't even be a lie because last I heard even Mrs Kapoor, wife of that famous writer who writes love stories that are being adapted into some movies is participating."

"Fine, I will participate. Nobody can win an argument with you." My apologetic smile turned into a huge laugh.

"That's right, even my poor husband says the same thing." She mimed acknowledgement, delight, then did a bootie shake sitting on the chair.

I joined the party grinning at her.

"Finally, you have taken the correct decision. But first, you have to reduce your weight. The contest will take place in around six months. I will take you to a real good yoga teacher who will help you out with your body and then side by side the overall grooming session will be handled by Mrs Karen Verghese. She has the best grooming classes in Delhi." Roshni promised me that she would fix the appointment as soon as possible before she left. An adamant Roshni actually managed to fix up an appointment with yoga guru Bhattacharya, who happened to stay in South Delhi at three in the afternoon the next day itself.

The next day I quickly catered to the needs of both my children who came at two pm from school.

Naina had to go for her piano classes and Samarth for his tuitions and I had to leave Naina though Samarth had already tied up with his friend. I checked my watch it was already two-thirty. Oh, God! Hurry! I said to myself.

I quickly freshened up and shouted, "Naina come fast. I have to go somewhere. Hurry up getting late."

"Mom coming." Naina came rushing, huffing in front of me. "What work do you have now mom!?" She was clearly irritated.

"Nothing, just hurry up!" I kissed my son on his forehead and bid him goodbye.

After leaving a puzzled Naina to her class I took a u- turn following the directions given by Roshni to the yoga institute.

Managing to reach five minutes past three I rushed inside a white polished house that had a small potted garden with a bed of green grass in a semicircular shape. As I took quick steps to the gate and rung the door bell, the gate was opened by a young servant.

"Mr. Bhattacharya, please."

He nodded and let me in a hall where I was greeted by the lovely fragrance of potted jasmine flowers that purified my senses perfectly placed in front of Ganesha's statue. Leather sofas were kept all around the four sides of the hall most probably for students. About six people were seated around, where three were busy reading yoga magazines and two were engrossed with their mobile phones. I was instructed to sit and wait till my name was called.

Soon I came to know that the teacher liked to take personal interviews of his students.

After half an hour my name was called. "Smita Sharma."
I let out a shaky breath. "Yes."

"Ma'am, please go inside." I removed my slippers in line with the others outside a wooden door and moved inside a room that was spacious enough to accommodate around eight students at a time. Stepping on a neat red carpet I understood why my slippers were removed, I walked towards a middle aged man around forty-five years of age with a glowing complexion and a radiant smile who pleasantly asked me my name.

"Sir, my name is Smita," I answered.

He smiled. "You can call me Guruji."

"Oh yes of course."

Before I could say anything else he instructed me to sit on the carpet before him. After sitting down I noticed an emblem of Om carved in brass seated on a velvet cloth that was covered with marigold flowers over a rectangular table. "So Smita. You have come for yoga classes. If I am not wrong, you want to have a healthy body."

"Sir, I mean Guruji, I want to reduce weight."

"Ok, I would like to ask you a few questions."

I nodded, as he continued, "any surgery?"

"Yes, only one a caesarian but that was ten years ago."

"Ok any BP problem or diabetes?"

"No."

"Any bone problem or disease?"

"Not as such, but I do get lower back pains at times."

"Ok, that will be taken care of."

"Any other disease or any precaution prescribed by your doctor?"

"No. I am fine."

Mr Bhattacharya took some time to write down all my details and family history. "What is your diet?" He was following a very methodical procedure where minute details were asked.

I knew I didn't have good nutritious food, but I had to tell him.

I shifted with unease and coughed a bit thinking that he would probably snap at me for my irregular food habits.

"Guruji mornings are in a bit of a hurry, looking after children and home so I usually skip my breakfast. At lunch, I have two rotis and vegetables. Tea in the evening and at night normal food, whatever is cooked, but I do have a sweet tooth."

Spilling out a brief outlay of my daily diet was the best way I thought I could handle this serious man. Nevertheless, I could make out from the twist of his lips that he was not happy. Thankfully, he did not retort back at all, but instead got up and went to the table where the Om emblem was kept. He opened the side drawer and pulled out a sheet of paper. I saw him going through it before he walked back towards me and sat before me. He handed me the printed sheet.

"This is the diet plan you have to follow. See, you have to take a correct dose of nutritious food daily. Correct food and the right kind of yoga will make your body toned and healthy. This is necessary."

For a moment, I thought whether I had come to a yoga teacher or a dietician. Well, I guess he was both.

I quickly scanned the printed sheet that had a real diet plan that seemed healthy and strict.

"I take classes in a group of four to six and you shall come from Monday every day until Friday."

My spontaneous reaction was to ask for the time as I knew early mornings would not be possible.

"Eleven am."

Perfect. I thought that was the ideal time when my children would be at school and my husband at office. I was free at that time.

I tossed a grin delighted at the timing. "I will join from the day after tomorrow."

I could not resist myself from asking the most pertinent question. "But in how much time will I get rid of this fat."

Mr Bhattacharya gave a slight laugh. "Patience. Yoga takes time, but the results are excellent. Around three months and you will see a lot of difference in yourself and by six months you will get into shape."

Three months was a long way I thought, but I was happy at his positive reaction.

I joined my hands in a namaste and walked out of his house.

CHAPTER 17

I lay on my bed that night while Avinash was sleeping soundly. I was so restless that I was unable to sleep. I was excited, for the first time in thirteen years I was doing something for myself. Suddenly I wasn't anyone's wife or anyone's mother. I was Smita who was finally ready to do something for herself. With this thought I hugged myself, tomorrow I was joining the grooming classes along with Roshni.

I smiled, thinking about Roshni, when I had asked why she was joining me in the grooming class.

She had replied in her usual dry tone, "firstly, I have no one to irritate and annoy, my husband is out of station and secondly its time I behave like a lady."

But I knew why she was joining, to help me and give me moral support. She was a true friend in every sense of the word. I felt warm all over; happy for the moment and with this thought in mind I slept.

At five am in the morning, I tiptoed into the kitchen to make breakfast. I quickly followed the routine, first packing lunch boxes. I made roti and paneer for Samarth. He loved paneer and always wanted that in his tiffin. Next, I made small, dainty sandwiches for Naina. If anything was not proper in her tiffin she had a habit of throwing a fit that I had embarrassed her in front of her friends.

Samarth, on the other hand, was easy going he did not complain and would eat anything that was put in his tiffin. It was sometimes a surprise for me how the temperaments of both my children were completely opposite. It was six am by the time I finished and I rushed to the children's room to wake them up. It always took me around fifteen minutes to wake up Naina, I would push, shove, throw the covers and finally scream, "Naina wake up now!" In order to make her move. Samarth was a good boy; he loved to wake up early. After waking my children up I dashed into the kitchen to make toasted bread and milk for Naina, a big sandwich with cheese, cucumber, tomatoes and mayonnaise for Samarth and kept a box of cereals for Avinash on the dining table adjoining the kitchen.

In half an hour I heard quick steps and saw both my children. I sighed as I always did on noticing that the hem of Naina's skirt was higher than usual showing a little of her thighs. I could make out the crisscrossed uneven stitch across the skirt which I knew I would have to open again.

Nowadays children grew up so fast it was hard to believe, in her age these things did not even cross my mind. As usual, she was trying hard to hide behind her school bag. She quickly rushed across the room to sit on the chair and gulped her breakfast.

Samarth came and gave me a tight hug kissing me on the cheek; he then turned and sat down on the table. By now, it was seven am. They finished, kept their tiffin's and rushed outside running towards the waiting car that would take them to school. I let out a pent up breath. Every day was like this except the weekends and holidays.

By eight Avinash was down ready to start his day, as was his habit, he ate his breakfast while reading the newspaper and then left in his prized chauffeur driven Mercedes. I gave a sigh of relief finally free I made a cup of green tea no sweetened milk tea for me now. I had to avoid sugar and carbs.

Next, I hurried into my bedroom and stood uncertainly in front of my closet. What to wear? A row of saree's all beautiful and expensive were hung on one side. On the lower shelves, stacks of suits were folded. Besides which, my two pairs of jeans, black slacks, a few shirts and pyjamas were kept. I took out the jeans, but then as an afterthought shoved them back. Maybe they won't fit any longer.

It was better if I dressed in my usual salwar suit. With every kilo I had gained, my clothes had become bigger until now I could hardly keep them on my body. I knew it was an illusion, but I hoped that if I covered myself completely no one would look at how big I had become. I took out a blue coloured suit that was simply cut with pink flowers embroidered on it. After having a bath, I got ready, waiting for Roshni.

I was sitting in my bedroom when I heard steps and saw my mother-in-law coming inside. Time had not been kind to her, she had lost her husband, my father-in-law just last year plus had developed osteoporosis because of which she was mostly bedridden.

I saw her limp inside dressed in an off-white salwar suit. She had lost weight as if life had carved her down to bare essentials. I instantly shot to my feet. "Ma you should have called me in your room. Why did you walk all the way from there?"

My mother-in-law's room was in the left wing of the house.
Originally when the house was renovated it was divided
into two wings the right mine and left my in-laws. It was a
huge house with six bedrooms a huge dining and drawing
area that connected the two wings. My sister- in- law Reema
was settled, happily married to a doctor in America.

"Smita, the doctor has advised me to walk a little. Anyways,
I was just getting bored." I made her sit on a chair. She saw
me dressed and asked, "are you going somewhere?"

"Yes. With Roshni."

"Roshni," she snorted. Even she did not like Roshni, not
because of any other reason, but because Avinash did not
like her. Whom her son did not like even she did not like,
period.

"That woman is not good, she wears such clothes."

To vent some of that old anger I sent her one sharp look.

"What have clothes got to do with a person?"

In a gesture that mirrored both disgust and bitterness, Sheila
flung out her arms. "How will you understand if you
haven't understood for thirteen years?"

I sucked air through my nose trying to control my anger.

"Anyway, I didn't come here to talk about your friend, but
about my son. You are not taking care of him properly. You
have kept so many servants who just cook rubbish and you
laze around on the bed."

I was sick and tired of the same barbs, the same insults…I
was no good, I kept so many servants, I didn't take care of
my husband properly, I was lazy, in short, my husband her
son had done a great favour by marrying me. Once in anger,
I had answered her and she had pretended to fall sick, and
the whole blame had come on me. It was disgusting since

then I preferred to just listen and avoided getting into any arguments with her. It just wasn't worth it.

At that moment, Roshni came in the room and had seemed to hear her. "Yes aunty, you are absolutely correct Smita is sooo lazy. She doesn't take care of poor Avinash."

The dislike was mutual. Roshni knew the hard time my mother-in-law had given me during the initial years of my marriage. She was a person who never forgot and never forgave, but if she befriended someone she would always stay by their side.

I intervened on noticing the flags of angry colour riding high across Roshni's cheekbones. "I think we are getting late. Ma should I get anything for you?"

My mother-in-law waved, her face screwed up showing her displeasure.

Oh great! I knew what was to come now; despite her problems she still had a habit of filing Avinash's ears. Now there would be questions to answer.

"Bye aunty, namaste." With a roll of her eyes, Roshni brushed her palms together as if her task was over, grabbed my hand and led me outside.

She did not stop till we reached her car. We sat inside, with the vroom, she started the car and with practised ease reversed it outside the driveway, the gatekeeper was quick to step aside to open and then close the gates.

"How do you take her?" Roshni squeezed the wheel, as if trying to control her temper.

I remembered all the times when there were disputes between me and my husband due to her and how she had manipulated him against me. "Sometimes when you are in an intolerable situation, you can never make anyone understand why you remained as such. Sometimes even I don't understand it myself. It's just the way it is and not just with me, but hundreds of women just like me."

I rested my head on the car seat and fumbled with the clasps of my handbag. "Anyways, now it is better, she has mellowed down and besides she is old and in pain."

"But that hasn't changed her nature. I know she will fill your husband's ears and then all our plans will go down the drain."

I looked at Roshni, her brows were furrowed in a frown while she concentrated on the road manoeuvring the car expertly in the traffic. "Feel how your husband feels when you torment him," I said lightening the situation. Of course she didn't torment him; in fact, she loved him a lot. It was just that she was outspoken and basically loved to argue.

"I don't torment him!" Roshni's jaw dropped as though horrified at what I was saying. "I just find new kinds of tortures to inflict on him."

We laughed. I loved this back and forth teasing dialogue between Roshni and me. We didn't have to pretend to be something we weren't, I felt younger with her as if the years had vanished and I was again that college going young girl with dreams and aspirations.

In another ten minutes, we reached the grooming school and I sat up straighter on seeing the house. It was a cheery house; I didn't expect something so homely. The driveway was dotted with various flowers as if tended lovingly. The creepers on the upper wall seemed to celebrate the music of soft wind by swaying with it and the subtle light of the sun provided a glow to the green of new baby leaves. The leaves settled comfortably without feeling the burn of the heat that was not harsh to them.

We got down and walked inside the white gate that was

guarded by a gatekeeper. I stood uncertainly in front of the open wooden door. It looked like a normal house, not a grooming centre.

I stopped looking at Roshni. "Are you sure this is where we should be!"

"Oh yes, this is Mrs Karen Verghese house and her centre is in South Extention. The first meeting is a counselling session, where she decides according to the person's nature, characteristics and level of confidence which kind of classes have to be taken."

"Oh God, no way!" There was a tickle at the back of my throat, a kind of sick nervousness. "I don't want to get into all this. Not some psychiatric session dissecting my brain."

Obviously puzzled, Roshni lifted her shoulder. "What is wrong with you?"

I was now cursing myself for agreeing to get into this.

Roshni stepped forward as I backed up. "Oh C'mon Smita. You can't back out now!"

"I can't discuss my personal life with a stranger!" I continued daunted refusing to budge from where I was standing.

"Nobody is interested in your personal life Smita." Impatience pumped through Roshni's voice.

I shook my head.

"Very well." Her face became stony. "You probably no longer have the spine to do this anymore. You mother-in-law is correct, you are so lazy."

Because of the years since I knew Roshni, I had come to understand her very well and knew what she was up to, but I could not control my emotions.

"Don't tell me what I can't do and that my mother-in-law is correct." I piped angry at what she was implying.

Roshni let out a satisfied cackle, baiting me further. "Of course that is for your husband to tell you."

"Stop talking like that!" I was getting really agitated now.

Roshni made a dismissive sound and waved my words away. "Why are you here Smita in the first place? I knew you would chicken out at the last moment."

I gritted my teeth at the word chicken. "I never chicken out."

She gave an irritated shrug. "Prove it."

"Fine." I snapped moving inside the door with Roshni besides me.

From the corner of my eye, I saw Roshni's lips twitching. I hissed like a snake. "You did that on purpose."

"Perhaps." Her eyes were twinkling as I smirked.

"Yeah right!"

"Ok, I did!" She punched me lightly on my shoulder.

"Isn't there someone else you can go and annoy?" I muttered.

She slid an arm around my waist. "No only you, because I love you like my sister."

I opened my mouth, closed it again and then just gave Roshni a squeeze...yes she did and so did I.

CHAPTER 18

I entered a small, charming reception area comprising of pink and off white comfortable sofas, arranged in a semi-circle, a round wooden table and a desk. Two women of around my age were seated on the comfortable sofas.

We went to the young girl who was seated behind the desk. She was dressed immaculately in black slacks a floral shirt with a scarf around her neck. I really liked the way she had tied the scarf in a knot in front.

She smiled showing perfect white teeth. "Good morning Ma'am. How may I help you?"

Roshni answered, "we have an appointment with Mrs. Verghese at ten for Mrs. Smita Sharma and Mrs. Roshni Sachdeva."

She looked down her diary. "Yes ma'am please take a seat, I will just inform ma'am."

We sat down on the sofas waiting while the young girl disappeared behind the wooden door. I looked around when my eye caught a photograph. A beautiful woman wearing a shimmering white gown, her hair bound in a huge bun that was surrounded by a beautiful crown had her hand held high in a wave. She was wearing a sash on which it was written in blue Mrs. India 1988. There were two more photographs, where there were two more women in the frame. Then there were more photographs of a group of women with certificates, they were surrounding a woman who was seated on a chair. On looking closely I noticed that it was the older version of the woman who was crowned Mrs. India.

My thoughts got distracted when the young receptionist said, "Ma'am you may go inside."

I nodded, now I was nervous. It did not seem like a small institution, it was a proper grooming centre.

"Smita lets go." What had Roshni got me into? I felt like strangling her, but now I was in a fix.

Like a soldier going to war, I straightened my spine and walked behind Roshni into the room. My first impression of the room was of light. It was a cheerful, light yellow coloured small room with huge windows on the side through which sunlight was penetrating. I looked at the woman sitting behind the mahogany desk. I was about to meet a Mrs. India...oh God! The same woman as in the photograph!

But there was nothing formidable about her. She was dressed in a red skirt with a sleeveless shirt. She managed to look both casual as well as glamorous in the simple outfit. The woman was not by any standards thin, but she looked healthy and fit. The transition from a girl to a woman it seemed had only added polished layers to her beauty. Her eyes were light brown, mouth wide and dominated a flawless face that was as soft as dew. There was a certain attractiveness in her, not necessarily due to her good Anglo-Indian looks, but the air of confidence that oozed out of her.

As if she could take on the world, even alone on her own. I crossed the room and she stood up to shake hands with us. "Please be seated," Karen said.

We sat on the chairs across from the desk facing Karen. The receptionist discreetly left.

"How can I help you?" Karen's voice was deep… Sultry, smoky, silky.

Roshni instantly replied, "if you remember I had called you earlier, regarding the Mrs. Perfect competition and if you could groom us."

"Ah! Yes, of course, I remember having a talk with you day before yesterday. Mrs Sachdeva and Mrs Sharma."

"Yes, Mrs Verghese."

Karen shuffled a few papers that were kept on the desk and then took out a notebook. She handed both of us sheets.

"These are the numerous classes that are offered. The basic is essential and is mandatory. The level one and two I decide after talking to the individual concerned."

I looked at the list of classes.

BASIC

Public speaking

Hair and makeup

Mind and Body

Skin

Health and fitness.

Body postures

The list went on…

"Now if one of you would please step out. I would like to talk to each of you separately." Karen tossed back her hair and I could make out the rubies at her ears.

Before I could stand up Roshni got to her feet. "I will wait outside. Smita you first."

I looked at her and grimaced, but she just winked and left.
Karen merely angled her head. "Smita what is your age?"

"I am thirty-five years old."

"Then I suppose you must be married."

"It's been thirteen years of marriage…to be precise thirteen
years and six months with Avinash and me being blessed
with two children."

The emphasis on six months deepened the look in Karen's
eyes, as if she knew I was about to say something more to
her, but I chose to refrain myself from speaking further,
waiting for her next question.

"Would you like to tell me what precisely are you here for?"
Karen looked at me expectantly, as if I was about to pour out
all my secrets to her, telling her everything. Telling her how
unromantic and insensitive my husband was, how I was
reduced to nothing else but a caretaker of my husband and
two children who liked to live in their own world. How my
world only revolved around my own nest and nothing else.
And now I was here to be the change I always wanted to be,
to be myself.

After waiting for a moment I kept my voice low, spoke
slowly while directly looking into her eyes. "I want to look
attractive. I mean a little up to date."

"Oh yes, of course, I can understand." Karen leaned back
against the leg of the big chair as if trying to read my eyes.
As if she knew what I was coming at, but preferred to go
about it very slowly and patiently.

"Can I become that?" I asked desperately.

"Why not? That is what we are here for. All women have
underlying talents that they tend to bury overtime under the
duties of their family life, but these talents cannot ever die.
Once you reach out to your hidden potential then it will flow

out of you like a smooth wave."

Karen was now speaking like a therapist. "You do not seem really happy and I can make it out of the way you have taken shape and kept yourself. It's time you generate faith in yourself and come out of your little cocoon into a new world of life. If you do not mind my asking would you like to tell me about your husband?"

I was opening up with this woman who seemed to be a center of hope for me. "Well, my husband Avinash you know is a good father and caters to the financial needs of the house…"

Karen cut me short, "that's fine but how does he look at you."

My eyes moistened and I started in a low voice, "actually he does not look at me. Over the years he has not been very kind to me in words. He does not give me attention or love and I don't understand whether he really respects me also. The years have really changed him from a lover to a harsh householder who only thinks of earning. Moreover, my kids, I feel do not really need me or want to spend enough time with me. Maybe generation gap I guess. I want a little freedom and if I have a choice, I would really want to earn the respect I have lost. But I don't want to leave my family." I simply burst out everything from my heart and then felt a little jittery at what I had just said. But Karen's expression did not change. It seemed she was used to a helpless woman's outburst.

Karen reached out to take my hand, placing hers softly over mine. "I knew your case after seeing your condition. After all, the man has spent all his energy on making, you feel incompetent and inadequate. And you don't want to leave him. Then why don't you give him a shock of his life."

I looked up at Karen's twinkling eyes that actually electrified me. "I will give you a makeover. Look at this, twenty kilos of unwanted mass who would look at you or even bother to care for you. You have to shape up girl. Shake yourself up and let the sleeping beauty come out. First of all, you need a good yoga teacher and then the rest I shall take care of."

"I have already joined Mr Bhattacharya's yoga classes."

"He is good and will get you in shape in no time. See already you are on a roll. I believe the competition is in six months time."

All my tension that had gathered in my shoulders eased at the realisation that I had taken the correct step.

"Fine now it's time for you to show the world what you are made of. Do not bother about what the others would think of you; think of what you feel about yourself."

I was listening to every word she was saying. To my ears, they were the words of an angel.

"Now you head outside. My assistant will tell you the procedure."

I got up and shook hands with Karen. Walking out with enthusiasm, I looked at the smiling face of Roshni who clicked her finger on seeing my beaming face. "You seem to be rocking lady."

I laughed. "Your turn."

Roshni gave me a hug and went inside.

I waited for Roshni. I felt nice, actually energised. This new hope of life felt wonderful. Everything would turn out right for me, just me. I knew a new Smita would come out soon. I was at the right place to discover myself.

After a fifteen-minute session, Roshni came out and let out aloud, a whoop of sheer joy. "I think it will be fun real fun."

"Ditto…I think the same."

Both of us went to the reception greeted by the same young lady.

I was the first one to speak, "we were told to fill in the forms."

"Yes, ma'am." She smiled, handing two forms, one to Roshni and one to me.

We again sat on the chairs studying the forms and filling them without missing any vital information.

We then handed the filled forms back to the receptionist. She told us the amount. Roshni quickly unzipped her handbag and took out the credit card, handing it to the lady.

Obviously, it was decided between us that I would pay my amount to Roshni later. That was what a true friend was for. Money was immaterial before her kindness. God, she was just great.

Roshni looked at me and frowned when she saw me staring at her. "What happened?"

The momentary silence was like a unified holding of breath. After a beat, I shook my head. "Let's go."

CHAPTER 19

The next day I was standing at the entrance of the yoga class dressed in black flannel pants and a black shirt. Six mats were placed on the floor on which woman of all shapes, ages and sizes were sitting. The room was bare of all furnishings, except on the side where a table on which a music player was kept. The sound of Gayatri mantra was coming out of it. I could see Guruji sitting in the middle facing his students. As soon as he saw me he motioned me to come in. He pointed towards the right where various mats were kept, indicating me to pick up one. The room was quite large and could easily house ten students maybe more. I placed the mat a little away from the other ladies.

The class started with Pranayam. Guruji sat crossed legged, his upper body straight and erect. His head, neck and back in alignment and the hands rested on knees. "Now slowly take a breath in from one nostril, close your other nostril with your thumb. Now hold your breath till the count of eight and then exhale."

We followed his directions and the session of Pranayam was for fifteen minutes.

After which he tried to relax the mind. "Now we will meditate for ten minutes. Close your eyes and concentrate on the middle of your forehead. Keep repeating Om in your mind while concentrating on the light in the middle of your forehead. Stop the riot of thoughts centering them in the middle. Feel the light…"

No matter how I tried my thoughts were in all directions from my children, to my husband, whether the cleaning lady had cleaned my room properly, whether I had locked my almirah before leaving for class, the expression of my mother-in-law when I told her that I was going somewhere and what she would do. She had not said anything to Avinash yesterday, but I knew that today there would be an argument. I was thinking of ways to reply… I have joined this committee where rich and famous people come because of which I had to join this yoga class… No scrap it…I have joined this yoga class because I have gone fat?

"Om!" Guruji's voice jolted me from my thoughts. "Remove negative thoughts from your mind. Cleanse your system…"

Yeah, right! As if anybody could?

"Now let's start with the Asanas."

In his white shirt and blue track pants, Guruji showed us the various poses with all the students trying them out. Our limbs and arms stretched awkwardly in various angles making us look like a bunch of lunatics on a rampage. In no time I was perspiring and breathing hard. My body was completely out of shape. Guruji from time to time stepped in front of the students admonishing them, "this is not the way to do it. Stretch harder, yes…"

He came to me. "Smita while bending exhale out. Breathing is very important part of Yoga." I exhaled crouched down on all my fours like a dog. "Yes…yes good."

Finally, after an hour and fifteen minutes, the class was over!
I did not walk, but limp my way towards the door when he
stopped us. "Wait a minute."
All of us stopped grumbling, was something else left?
"Please stick to your diet if you want results and go home,
rub some mustard oil on your body then have a hot bath. It
will relieve some of the tensions in your muscles. They are
not worked out; after a time your body will get used to it and
become flexible. Now I will see all of you tomorrow."
All the women walked too exhausted to chat, most probably
just thinking about a cup of tea and a warm bath.
My phone rang as I was sitting in my car. It was Roshni.
"How did it go?"
"I think I am dead. I cannot even walk straight, how I will be
able to drive home." I sulked. "Muscles I did not even know
existed are hurting."
"Stop whining, Smita," Roshni said cheerfully. "No pain no
gain."
"Oh Shut up Roshni!"
Roshni cackled. "Drive safe," she clicked the phone shut.
I banged my head on the steering wheel. What had I got
myself into?

On reaching my house I rubbed oil and then showered,
feeling instantly better. It was one -thirty and the children
would be back in another half an hour. My mother-in-law
was as usual in her room. She had her own set of servants,
she preferred it that way and even I was happy with the
arrangement because it took her off my back. My cook had
already made lunch and kept them in casseroles. Normally I
had my lunch alone before my kids came home. My mother-
in-law had lunch in her room that was taken from the

kitchen by her servant. I took a plate, just one chapatti, one bowl of cooked pulses and vegetable. I chewed my food slowly as directed by Guruji because it made digestion better. A few minutes later, there were shouts and scrambling feets and I knew my children were home. I went to their room to see their school bags thrown on the bed, Naina was in the bathroom and Samarth was sprawled on the bed wearing his shoes.

"Samarth take out your shoes before you climb the bed". He gave a grin and scrambled out of the bed, giving me a sloppy kiss on the cheek. I laughed, hugging him. "You are one smart kid. C'mon downstairs lunch is ready."

The next hour was spent with the children, then they went off to their study rooms. They had separate study rooms joined by a common bathroom. They would rest till the time of their tuitions and classes. Naina was learning Jazz on the weekends whereas Samarth had joined the cricket academy with his friends. Though now my children did not need my attention, having a life of their own with friends and other classes I still liked to stay close to them. I had requested that the grooming class would take place from four -thirty to six so that I could be home before six-thirty. Karen had obliged, adjusting the schedules from four- fifteen to six in the evening at alternate days and twelve -thirty to one -thirty on other days. It was perfect.

The day went as it usually did with me directing the cook on what to make and just puttering about the house till it was eight and time for Avinash to come home. He came as usual and asked for dinner. We were sitting in the formal dining room as Avinash liked to have food there. He liked to see the table set with cutlery and napkins with the helpers and that included me also serving dishes. As if he was royalty to be waited upon. My mother-in-law was sitting to his right, with the children properly behaved sitting in their respective seats. I served everyone the dishes. Avinash preferred having soups, salads in the evening, my mother-in-law wanted phulkas and vegetables.

The servant was running back and forth serving hot phulkas to everyone when my mother-in-law remarked, "Smita you were gone for over an hour today and yesterday also you had gone out with Roshni. Where did you go?"

Avinash looked at me. I knew my mother-in-law would bring the subject up and I was prepared. Thirteen years of marriage had taught me what to expect from her and my husband. "Avinash, Roshni has made me a part of a committee. It is a woman's club."

"I am not aware of any such club," he said.

"She has just started it." I threw my trump card. "Even Mrs Kapoor is a part of it."

"Mrs Kapoor? The writer's wife?" Curiosity seemed to creep inside him like a lizard and it gave me the satisfaction of winning over his weakness.

"Yes! I just have to be a part of it two hours every day."

"Fine. At least you are doing something good." This answer was expected out of him, he was sarcastic as usual.

I gulped the retort as I always did. I had to tell him even about the yoga class, chances were high that he would know about it as they were in the neighbourhood. Though he did not bother to look at me, but over time he would notice my weight loss and comment on it.

"I have even joined Mr. Bhattacharya's yoga classes."

For a moment there was silence and then Avinash laughed out aloud. His expression was such that as if what I had said warranted hysteria.

"You and yoga classes?"

My brows beetled and my eyes flashed pure annoyance.

"Yes Avinash I and yoga class. I want to lose weight."

"Yes, you will if you stuff yourself with food." At that precise moment, I had finished my first chappati and was contemplating having another. After all, I was hungry! His remark stopped me from reaching for the second chappati. My anger was boiling what was it with men, they did not have to bear children, raise them and fight raging hormones.

Naina struggled to hide her giggles. "Mom, I cannot imagine you thin! I have always seen you round."

Naina who had enveloped Avinash's neck seemed to be taking out chuckling sounds from her chest. Jokes about my weight seemed to be amusing to them. Needless to say, I didn't see the humour.

As always, Samarth was sensitive to my feelings. He rounded his arms around my waist in a tight protective manner. "I bet mummy will become even prettier."

I kissed his forehead, silently thanking God for giving me such a good boy for a child. His remark stopped the laughter and everyone concentrated on their dinner.

CHAPTER 20

The next day I skirted my way through the traffic to the grooming centre, after finishing the yoga class. Avinash's remark had renewed my determination. I had to again gain my self- respect. I parked the car in the parking and leant my head against the seat, for a moment closing my eyes. I was actually taking the first step; I still could not believe myself. I bet the other woman would be all high fie, fully confident, thin and full of themselves. Would they laugh at me?

I must stop, stop I chanted to myself. I must force myself to look at the positive and not the negative. If nothing else, at the least I would learn new things. With this positive thought, I opened the seat belt, got outside and locked the car. I was feeling like I felt on the first day of college, excited as well as nervous.

I entered the building in South Extension and was greeted by a photograph of Sophia Loren on which it was written. "Beauty is how you feel inside, and it reflects in your eyes. It is not something physical."

I gulped would there be models? I looked to the right to see a wooden door with a stained glass window. Maybe it was cowardly of me, but I had requested Roshni to wait for me in the reception area. I took a deep breath and opened the door expecting the worst.

My first impression of the room was of warmth, lovely deep burgundy sofas, a few tables and similar coloured chairs on one of which Roshni was sitting. The area was empty.

On seeing me, she jumped to her feet. "Smita you are late! The class has started everyone is inside."

She hurried forward towards the corridor in front with me following her.

I saw the other ladies before they saw me. And when I saw them, it was as though a thousand pounds of worry was taken off my chest. I gave a great sigh of relief and took a step forward.

There were four more women in the class, two looked in their thirties while the other two in their twenties. I was already told that the class size would be small with just five to six people in it. I went and sat on a seat to the right, I was a little on the corner. On the mirror in the front, I could see the whole class. The instructor was a young girl, very pretty and dignified dressed in black trousers and cream shirt.

She gave me a slight smile before immersing her head in the forms in front. She was writing something on plastic sheets, which would go into the projector. I took the time to study the other women in the mirror. As I was sitting in a corner, I had the advantage of not being reflected in the mirror. I could see and not be seen, I couldn't resist the temptation to look and observe.

I looked at the woman at the extreme left. Her eyes looked sad. She looked like a middle-aged housewife. She was slim, but did not have a definition. Her hair was dull lying limply around her head with many grey strands running through it. Her skin was good, but showed the lines around her eyes. She seemed unhappy about something. Besides her there were two girls in their early twenties, they seemed to be friends and were busy chatting with each other oblivious to their surroundings. It was clear to me that their respective mothers had sent them here so that they could learn etiquettes and get married in good households. I sighed, suddenly feeling old on hearing their giggles. I was too old for this. I was past this stage and it seemed so long ago. I continued my survey and just stared at her...

She must be in her early forties, her hair coloured a fiery brown and had unbelievably beautiful and large eyes like a swan. Untamed and entangled, her hair circled her head like a halo. I could not make out her skin because it was covered with foundation and topped with white powder. Her nose was sharp and pierced, on which a diamond stud glinted. Her lips were also painted a deep red. If I looked hard I could see her beauty under the layer of makeup. For a moment, I closed my eyes giving a little prayer before I saw her clothes. She was slender, almost being gaunt, but there was a hint of muscles beneath the shocking pink kurti that was in animal print and blue tights. Pink and blue? The combination would look funny on any other woman but this woman carried it with panache.

I felt a twinge of jealousy, despite being overdressed, despite wearing loud clothes, despite her painted face; she oozed confidence, strength and happiness. She squirmed slightly and I noticed round gold earrings dangling from her ears. I stiffened realising that she was studying me just as I was studying her. I turned my head slightly in her direction and our eyes clashed. I could see a slight smile on her face as if she knew I was studying her. I blushed, embarrassed and averted my gaze. I concentrated on the instructor who was now standing in the middle.

"My name is Linda and I am your instructor for today's session, before going into the details of the class I would like to know all of you." Her voice was soft and melodious. "Please if each of you would stand up and introduce yourselves one by one."

She started from the left; I was correct in assuming that the two girls were aged twenty-two and were friends. They had joined the class in order to learn how to be a proper lady. One of them was even getting married. The girls were named Shikha and Richa.

The middle-aged woman as correctly interpreted my me was a housewife, had one girl. She did not say anything else. Her name was Chandini Gupta.

I sat up straighter as the woman in pink kurti stood up. "My name Durga Mooken. Karate specialist, I also teach karate." The girls giggled and Durga stopped. Her English was not good.

The instructor said calmly, "Mrs Mooken that is admirable. Despite being a woman you learnt something like Karate and are even teaching it."

She turned towards the class clasping her hands. "A person's worth is not measured only by the way they can speak English. Ma'am." She indicated towards Durga. "Is truly exceptional, she is in a field that is normally predominated by men. I am proud of you." She clapped her hands and everyone followed even the two girls.

Her praise seemed to boost Durga's spirits and she straightened her spine. "I have two boys aged twelve and fifteen. And I love them…"she trailed off.

"And your husband?" The instructor prompted.

"I control him," Durga said simply, as if an owner controlled a pet.

Everyone laughed.

"Fine ma'am, thank you," the instructor said smiling and Durga sat.

Her words had hit me with a bang, but I did not have time to ponder over it because Roshni pushed herself to her feat. Oh no! After her, it was my turn.

Roshni slid her hands in the pockets of her grey and black dress. "My name is Roshni Sachdeva and I am a photographer…"

Linda stopped her. "Ma'am are you the famous photographer who clicked the picture of the beautiful falls in Chattisgarh."

Roshni nodded a yes.

That was one of her best pictures.

"Ma'am, let me say I am a big fan of your work. You capture nature in its wildest and untamed form beautifully."

"Thank you so much." Roshni looked a little uncomfortable with the liberal praise.

It was a surprise to me how such a woman despite her success could stay so grounded. Even now instead of going to Manali as was originally planned by her, she was here with me supporting me. I again thanked God for the gift of such a friend.

Roshni rattled off about her children, husband and then sat down. It was obvious by her confident tone that she was not in need of such classes.

My turn next! I got up gingerly on my feet and straightened my chunni. "My name is Smita…Smita Sharma. I am a homemaker and have two children, one girl and one boy. My husband's name is Avinash and he has his own business. I have joined these classes to gain confidence and also as I am participating in Mrs Perfect competition I have to groom myself for it."

"That is just amazing Mrs Sharma. And let me assure you that you don't need grooming, but just a certain finesse and surely then you will come out sparkling."

The class went on with instructions on how to gain self-confidence

"Self-confident people have qualities that everyone admires. It is extremely important, yet a lot of people struggle to find it." She paused putting a plastic sheet in the projector.

I could see two people, one looked harassed and the other confident. "As you can see that a person who is nervous, fumbling is unattractive, on the other hand someone who holds his or her head high, answers questions assuredly is attractive."

She changed the slides. "The good news is that self-confidence can be learned and built but the bad news is that there is no quick fix." The slide had a lot of points...

Look at all that you have achieved.

Count your strengths and not your faults.

Think about all that you have got and the others don't have.

Learn to defeat the negative thoughts. As the mind is a powerful instrument and thoughts tangible one should imagine that what you want has been achieved by you.

Step out of your comfort zone.

Make an unequivocal promise to yourself that you are committed to the change in you.

The power is inside you; finally, it is you who was important!

Linda explained all these points properly that were inspiring and made me feel energetic and surer of myself.

I was sad when the class ended, I could have gone on listening. Roshni and I walked out together after thanking Linda.

In the parking lot, we went to our respective cars when suddenly I received a rude jerk and a young boy of around eighteen snatched my purse. Robbery in bright daylight! "Hey, you! My purse!!" I screamed.

I saw him skirting between the cars and though there goes my purse when out of nowhere I saw a flash of pink and my eyes literally popped out.

Durga in all her magnificence jumped the white railing directly and ran after him as though the gods were chasing her. It looked like as if I was watching an action movie, something like Charlie's angels except in this one the female protagonist was dressed in a pink kurti and blue tights! The robber swivelled directions heading in the opposite direction when Durga leant forward and grabbed his hair, but it came off in her hands. The young boy was in a disguise! I tried not to laugh as the boy tried to reach for it, but Durga clipped him on the side of the head before she grabbed both his ears and held them tight. By this time, a group of men had gathered and I also reached them with Roshni beside me. Durga had by now grabbed the boy's collar and was shaking him. "How dare you steal? This is what your parents have taught you."

The boy whimpered his hands joined. "Aree aunty please leave me. I promise I won't do it again. I realise my mistake." Durga shook him some more, "aunty… do I look aunty to you? You stupid boy. Come, I will take you to the police." I could not help, but laugh Durga looked more flustered at being called an Aunty than on the robbery.

A few seconds later, two policemen approached us. It seemed like someone had called them. They caught hold of the boy and instructed us to come to the station to lodge a FIR. The crowd dispersed, leaving only Roshni, Durga and me.

Roshni backslapped Durga. "Girl, you are just amazing! Charging towards that thief."

Durga blushed rosily at the compliment. "Thanks."

I stepped forward clasping Durga's hands warmly. "I am in your debt; I am so grateful thank you so much."

Durga shifted her attention towards me, seeming uneasy with the praise. "It's ok. No big deal."

"No, it's a big deal. I just wish I could be just like you. Tough and strong!"

Durga gave a quick, baffled laugh. "Thanks."

"You have to come with me home and have lunch with me," I really wanted to know this woman, a woman who was shy in receiving compliments, but fought like a warrior.

"No...No...no need," she said haltingly in her English. "And anyways we have to go police station, FIR remember."

I laid a hand on Durga's shoulder. "Yes, but after that, you have to have lunch with me."

"No..."

Roshni cut her short. "Aree C'mon na...come." She grabbed Durga's hand and tugged as I took her other hand... linked.

At that moment I could feel it my bones that we three would become close and this was the start of a friendship that would last a lifetime.

CHAPTER 21

It was a Thursday morning and two weeks had passed, the children had already left for school. Avinash was, as usual, sitting at the table, reading the paper and drinking his tea. With his eyes glued to the paper, he said, "today we have to go for dinner to meet Mr Vipin and Mrs Shalini Sehgal. Be ready by seven thirty. I'll pick you up."

Oh no, my heart stopped, or at least I thought it did at meeting that snobbish woman. I had met Shalini twice and had developed an instant dislike for her. She was arrogant of her looks and figure and too big for her boots thinking everyone else to be less smart and intelligent than her.

I disliked the idea of meeting her once again, though her husband was decent and intelligent. He was someone worth talking to, someone, to spend a few minutes of intelligent talk.

"Smita?" Avinash face turned to look at me when I didn't answer. My face had taken a dreamy look when he sharpened his tone, "are you daydreaming. Have you heard what I said?"

Irritated I snapped back, "yes, I have heard. I'm not deaf I'll get ready."

Avinash simply gulped down the tea and picking up his bag, raced out of the house. He did not even retort back, my opinion hardly mattered to him. The order was made and had to be followed.

I poured myself a cup of coffee instead of tea, making sure to keep it sugar-free strictly following the diet menu that I hated, and carried it upstairs.

What to wear? I opened my cupboard moving my fingers over the outfits that comprised mainly of sarees, suits, a few pants and tops.

Not that I had much to choose from the collection of my western outfits. I yanked a pair of single black parallels off the shelf and a crème shirt. I dressed myself up noticing that both had loosened on my frame. I felt ecstatic. The yoga classes were working well on me. But even with a minuscule of difference, I was on the top of the world. Even a centimetre mattered to me.

The entire day passed as usual with my yoga classes and grooming classes.

I told Roshni and Durga about my lost weight and they were happy for me. Good friends were a blessing and I was blessed in this department.

In the evening again wearing my outfit, I stuck the pant with a safety pin feeling a small sense of satisfaction that it had become a little loose though obviously, even without the safety pin it would not slide down my ample hips, but nevertheless, this small action boosted my ego giving me pleasure. This, plus the self-confidence classes were helping me to relax and lessen my nervousness.

Oh, how I hated that woman who made me feel dowdy and

ugly. I wore light makeup finally adorning my ears with the long diamond earrings which Avinash had presented me on our first anniversary.

Waiting for Avinash without a hint of desperation, I sat crossed- legged on the sofa in my bedroom. I turned around to hear the door knob click open when Avinash entered and rushed to the closet taking out his suit. Locking the bathroom, he came out in five minutes fitting his tie and dabbing his favourite aftershave lotion on his face. It smelled good.

"Let's go, it's getting late."

I obliged dutifully trotting down the hall, down the steps opening the main door for him. Following him, we both sat in his prized Mercedes that he loved more than anything else in the world.

In fifteen minutes, we reached The Hyatt Regency. We walked through the lobby into the Mughlai Khanna restaurant. It was known for its ambience, good food and colourful drinks.

From a distance, I could see Shalini. Her nose and chin upright, unmoved she sat beside her husband like a black skinny crow, waiting to prance at any moment. Vipin was well-known to the establishment, probably one of their best customers.

With the final step we approached the couple Avinash was quick to shake hands with Vipin whereas Shalini chose to hug him. I twitched my lips.

"Oh! How very nice to see you Avinash!" That sounded so very sugar coated to my ears, must be in want of some attention that her husband did not give her I decided.

"You are looking really nice Shalini." Avinash was quick to give her a false compliment. As if she was, she was looking scrawny. The black dress that she was wearing till her knees was shining like a light bulb, sticking to her zero -sized waist that was not at all appealing. Nevertheless, she had sharp features, but her eyes were not so Indian like, they were small. She used extra kajal to give them shape, painting her powdered hollow cheeks with coats of pink. Above all the baby pink flashy lipstick made her look like a perfect witch. In order to maintain her ideal figure that no longer was perfect, she had lost the glow from her face.

"Oh, dear Smita! Looking the same." She paused as if forcing the words out of her mouth looking at me up and down.

"Good to see you too."

Looking the same was meant to be a punch line to make me aware of my weight.

I worked my facial muscles into a smile. "Same here."

Vipin greeted casually in his normal dignified manner. He wore an elegant crème suit. He was not the typical show off Richie rich. With his appearance and humility, one would take him to be a simple professor instead of a successful businessman.

"Come, please have a seat," Vipin waved his hand.

All four of us sat around the table. Avinash and Vipin were discussing the new economic policies in business with Shalini butting in a few times with her misfit comments.

"The real estate market is picking up after the new government has come into power," Vipin commented.

"There have been positive changes in favour of building the markets." Avinash replied, "I am thinking of buying a few plots in…"

"Darling," Shalini bounced in between like a cannon ball that I felt like smashing hard. "Why don't you tell Avinash about the new plot that we had bought for…?"

She rattled off a figure in her usual show off self.

Vipin dismissed her remark with a smile looking for the waiter.

The waiter was motioned and we ordered drinks.

"Fresh lime juice, without sugar," I was first to speak.

Shalini raised her eyebrow. "Likewise please."

The drinks were served and as I did not want to look at Shalini, I concentrated on the drink instead.

Soon vegetable clear soup was ordered for the four of us. I took a few spoons of it, leaving the rest as I had to stay on the diet. Starters comprised of stuffed mushrooms, green salads and papad.

I took a handful of salad tossing it with a little salt. I speared a piece of cucumber onto my fork, putting it inside my mouth.

I happened to glance at the uncomfortable look of Shalini, her eyes wide as she chewed her portion of salad. I liked the colour drain from her face as she watched the change in me. I knew the grooming classes were showing their result in my way of eating and talking. And I could make out a certain jealousy in her tone when she asked, "care for a little papad."

"No thanks." It amazed me how unsettled she felt.

But I could not ignore her attention towards me. It was a sign of victory for me. I was one up on her. Alas! I wished if Avinash could see this small transformation in me.

Soon dinner was served.

The table was laden with vegetarian seekh, mix veg platter, pudhina ghobi and bakherkhani naan. The dishes were mouth-watering and tempting.

What to eat first? I was not going to blow like a balloon if I would eat a little of everything? With this idea, I started taking small amounts of vegetables and half a naan.

I did not see how much the others took until Avinash spoke up, "Shalini you will just have a spoon of mixed vegetable and no naan."

Shalini giggled throwing her hand into the air, her bright painted red nails pointing at Avinash. "Oh, Avi dear, why do you think I tend to look like this?"

"Of course, very few have this tremendous will power like yours. After all the hard work you have put into the making of this beautiful Shalini. I have never seen you stuffing yourself unnecessarily."

How could Avinash only appreciate that bitch? Was he blind? Couldn't he see how sick I felt when he talked about this witch? This woman who was taken off guard by my dignity is now being charmed by my foolish husband.

I remained quiet, a frown creased on my forehead when he continued, "you are talented, capable, wise and above all smart really smart. Vipin you are lucky to have Shalini. Very few are lucky in the choice of their partners."

His words made her eyes light up.

I hated the word smart and all the other words that were fake and unfit for her kind of woman. Did Avinash really have such a low opinion of me? Was he unlucky in having me as his wife? I was hurt deeply wounded like a small child wanting to escape from here and go back to my house. Somewhere deep inside me, the last thread of self- control disappeared and my senses overtook my mind to control myself.

I started eating like a ravenous child. I managed to eat everything on my plate and still took another helping. Avinash squeezed my hand to stop me from hogging, but by his touch, I went very still as my anger slid under grief. I shrugged his hand off and decided to finish the second helping too.

I knew Shalini was loving every bit of humiliation offered to me by my husband. Indirectly everything was said to put me off. At least that's what I believed by the slimy, malicious wicked smile on Shalini's face. She was being pampered to the extent that she was flying high in the sky. Her friendly gestures, her moves and the extra niceness in her voice were despicable.

The desert was the lovely chocolate muffin with sauce. Shalini was having the last laugh so why not enjoy the whole of it? I thought.

I knew I was being stubborn as a mule, not waiting to stop myself.

With a touch of vehemence in my tone, I plunged ahead. "Oh Shalini, I am sure you would spare yourself from having extra calories. I will do justice to it instead."

I shoved my fork into the smooth, soft brownie fighting my tears from rolling down as I chewed and munched every morsel of it. But without enjoying the flavour of the chocolate that melted in my mouth, I pretended.

"It's delicious you are missing something Shalini. Avinash have it…You too Vipin, it's delicious."

This time Shalini was staring at me expressionless, but Vipin and Avinash continued finishing the piece of cake.

Finally, we departed, leaving Shalini with a satisfied look and me miserable.

I was waiting for Avinash to say something unkind. Maybe I needed that humiliation. The revulsion in his eyes clearly reflected his anger towards me, but silence enveloped the car. He did not even think that I was worth talking to. Reaching our house Avinash trotted upstairs towards his room, leaving me downstairs without uttering a word, and I went to the guest room.

I collapsed on the bed, sobbing. I had allowed myself to be a laughing stock.

I just blew the hard work I did. Just when I turned a new leaf in my life I retreated to my old ways. This just proved I had no will power, no spine. I had wasted my human life in wallowing in self-pity. I felt my legs crumble underneath me. I cried and cried. I did not know how much time passed.

A long time later, I struggled to my feet. My chin determined, eyes sharpened, I went out outside the room's balcony viewing the moon and a few glittering stars in the night sky. I didn't feel one bit better, but I was determined not to repeat this mistake again. Never ever would I do it again!

CHAPTER 22

The next day I rose early. My mind was racing; I had to tell about it to Guruji. The thought of wasting my effort was disturbing me. My mind was not at rest. I entered the washroom and turned on the water before stripping down so that I could avoid looking at the mirror. I knew I was a coward. However, I started counting the rolls of fat. Not even one had diminished. They were all there to remind me of being a buffalo. I turned off the tap and hastily dried my body with the towel, covering myself with comfortable track pants and a T -shirt. I drove my Honda at full speed to reach my yoga teacher before the other students arrived.

In a dreadful mood, I rushed, crossing the hall and entered his room. Guruji, as usual, was warm and welcoming. "Guruji." I took several deep breaths before I gathered the energy to speak. "I have made a terrible mistake. I… I spoilt my diet plan and like a hungry pig ate my heart out at dinner yesterday. Oh no, am I going to pull up all the fat that I had reduced? Am I going to blow even more? I'm so sorry about my foolishness. How will I make up for the sin, I have committed by not following your instructions."

I was getting hysterical, but Guruji instantly pulled me up. He was not anything, but positive.

He spoke in a calm demeanour persuading and comforting me. "It's all right. The light has not fallen from the sky upon you. Getting out of control once in a while is permissible. It may sound strange that it's a sign of being positively healthy."

My eyes flickered in surprise. "Positively healthy!"

"Yes. Why do we wish to eat particular kinds of food?"

"The most common answer is that people love its taste. It's a simple human sense desire Guruji."

He stopped me with an upraised hand. "The simple human phenomena has a scientific meaning too. It's how our brain 'decodes' the food item in question. Our brain has a lot of saved data in the form of memories, senses, reactions and much more. It also has stored information about tastes which are sweet and salty. They are pleasant, and the brain knows these are good to the tongue. Bitter gives a negative reaction. The brain knows it might be poisonous, and harmful. Sour, on the other hand, has a different story. The sour taste receptors on our tongue know that the stinging item is a source of irritant, and, as a reaction, our mouth will pucker, our eyes will narrow, and our nose will wrinkle. Our mouth secrets 'water', that's saliva, which is an attempt by the body to reduce the effect of the sourness. It's not just sourness but a similar thing can happen with very salty or spicy food! The extra saliva secreted not just alleviates the sour taste, it also aids in digestion."

His eyes shone with humour. "So Smita, you have actually digested the food you ate."

Blank I asked, "If this is the case, then why to follow any kind of diet."

"The reason is that extra amount of calories if not burnt will increase fat in our body. And that's the reason we exercise. Most importantly unhealthy snacking will not give your body any proteins or minerals. What will happen to the muscles and bones? "

I nodded my head acknowledging the facts. "You are right Guruji."

The friendly tone disappeared into a strict code of conduct. "I think you have understood the point. You need to go to the next level of the program. Along with yoga start going for evening walks to burn off extra calories. You can start with half an hour and then go in for a one hour brisk walk. That will help you to cut down fat faster."

My lips disappeared between my teeth, and I felt uncomfortable. "But, will I be able to do it?"

"I'm not here to make any judgment. Let me ask you a question. How long did it take you to put on that weight?"

The question took me aback and confusion clouded my mind.

Without waiting for my reply he continued, "It's you who have to decide the best for yourself. You have to be hard on yourself, but as I said just once in a month you can feast yourself. I have given you a menu, follow it. I suggest making a chart and post on it the time, the date what you binged on and why you did it. Ask yourself, has it really helped my health. Was it nutritious enough to bring good to me or was it another satisfying pleasure that I indulged in. One thing more, you are not disappointing me, but yourself. You are embarking on a change in your lifestyle. Food was at the top of the list. Conquer it and you are halfway up the road to achieving what you desire. You can do it and you will do it."

He ended with one sentence. "Every conquering temptation represents a new fund of moral energy. Every trial endured and weathered in the right spirit makes a soul nobler and stronger than it was before."

His words of assurance were full of impact.

Back home, I used up few minutes telling myself that I would work hard, follow the rules, not wanting to disappoint my teacher nor myself.

Again, I wanted to prove to myself that I was not weak to allow anyone to conquer me. Avinash had been doing it all the time and I had let him do it. I could not comprehend why I had let his words or thoughts rule me.

But as time passed, Avinash's behaviour towards me was upsetting and depressing. I decided to talk it out with my friends and we decided to meet on Sunday at the Oberoi coffee shop. Crossing the swimming pool, we entered the coffee house that was spacious, furnished properly with round tables and chairs. Its walls were painted white with antique paintings adorning one of the walls, complimented by the large chandelier on the ceiling that illuminated the hall. We took the four chaired side table, at the corner to keep our privacy.

Durga had become really close to Roshni and me. She was taking these classes to learn something new, she had a zest for life that was contagious and awe inspiring. She was also taking separate classes to improve her English. According to her, there was just one life and you should do all that you wanted to do with it, living it to the fullest.

Roshni and I both ordered sugar free coffee and Durga in no mood to compromise her taste bud savoured her hot chocolate.

Sipping on the chocolate drink she was observing me with the corner of her eye. "I am seeing for quite some time, that you are upset over something."

It had been ten days since the incident and it was eating me up. Since then Avinash had become ruder in his attitude towards me and I hated it!

The kind of friendship I shared with my friends was understood. It had little to do with blood, and everything to do with heart. We had hooked up the day we met. I wanted to ease my discomfort. I wanted to get rid of the burden of misery that I was carrying inside me.

"Family life is so tough. No enjoyment with serving only your husband and kids, especially a husband like mine." I sighed.

Durga who was now munching on her cheese sandwich mumbled, "What's your true soul mate like."

The words true soul mate punched me hard on my face and I smirked. "Ha! There is no word such as true in his dictionary. He's insensitive and rude and does not care for me. For him, I am just a slave who looks after his house, his children and him. Last week he kept on praising that woman in front of me at the restaurant. I felt every barb; every word hit me with a bang. It was demoralising and what happened next was atrocious… "

She told them how she stuffed herself with food, till she felt sick with the lasting look of revulsion on Avinash's face.

"Hmm." Durga stretched out her hand to offer me a sandwich and added with a flourishing gesture of her hands. "Cool kar baby. Take a bite."

I pushed the sandwich away. "This is serious Durga."

Roshni who was listening interrupted, "that's why she is here to prove her worth. She will show him what she is made of a strong, talented woman who cannot be taken for granted. You know it's a challenge for my best friend and I am supporting her."

'That's good." Durga now wiped her mouth and picked up her mug, enjoying her hot chocolate merrily. "And your m - in- law? Let me guess if I am not wrong, she is a full-fledged Hitler, after you all the time. Do this… do that, you don't know how to handle things properly in the house, you haven't been taught anything, you don't know how to take care of my baby boy Avuu… Blab la blaaa."

"'Avuu?..who? … ohhh!" The realisation hit me who else, she was calling my husband Avuu.

Roshni let out a snort. "He's her pet. The nick name suits him. Avuu.. Momma's boy. But for Smita, she is the famous Hitler of a rich Delhi man holding a stick in one hand to strike my friend whenever it suits her mood. It gives her immense pleasure to hurt her."

"Chalo a complete butcher's family with a stubborn headed mule at the top. Your hasne wala band.' Durga laughed heartily. "Well all goes well when you really know how to play the band."

"Play the band? How?" I mused rubbing my hands over my face.

"Let me make you aware of my filmy story. Ours was a love marriage and after our marriage, I came to know that my husband Manav Mooken was a unique gem, a rare diamond one of its own kind. He was aggressive and brutal. The verbal onslaught was just the cream over the cake when he chose to go even beyond. Add some chocolate icing over the cake. I mean, girls his abuses in small little matters were not enough and after I had two boys he went on to hit me mercilessly. Things had turned out to be so ugly that he started drinking and beating me every day. A point had come that I no longer could take this onslaught and chose to leave him."

Durga dumped a cookie into her chocolate drink and took a hefty bite. "And I reached out to my parents and family members for help, who were too feeble to go against the norms of our prestigious society. The girl once married had to live and die in her sasural, her husband's home. There was no help at all and one day I decided to give up my life. But, the very thought of my little babies did not allow me to go ahead with it. They needed me more than anyone else in the world. I knew that no sooner I die he would not waste a moment to marry again. So I had no option left. One fine day I happened to come across Bhagavad Gita that was kept in my home temple. And the very verse of Krishna who said, *"O Arjuna, surrendering all your works unto Me, with knowledge of Me, without desires for profit, with no claims to proprietorship, and free from lethargy, fight!"* Sparked a new hope in my life. I had to fight this injustice, but the question was how. My bones had become brittle by continuous beatings and my face and body had bruises all over that did not get time to heal because the new ones continued to cover them.

Then, as luck would have it, I met one of my college friends who had become a lawyer. I narrated my story to her and she encouraged me to go and join karate classes that would give me the strength to fight anyone who even tried to touch me. Then what else, I joined the classes silently without giving the slightest hint about it to anyone in my family. My husband's wrath was increasing day by day, but I kept learning new skills of defensive art. After a year of karate training one day my husband came drunk at night."

I wasn't about to miss out on hearing what would come next

and never realised that I was biting down the side of my tongue waiting for Durga's move. The coffee was left untouched I was so engrossed in what she had to say. Durga with her mouth full continued. "I was sitting comfortably on a chair next to the table in my bedroom. My husband was drunk, but he had enough senses to hurt me. He bolted the room's door and slowly approached me with a dirty smile on his face as if he was going to make me his bait once again, but I kept sitting. He looked like the boring, ugly husband, so ordinary, someone you'd pass on the street and label "loser," the tag seemed to fit this man. He had thinning hair, neither tall or short, nor fat or thin, a box of a man coming out of a T.V serial that pictured him perfectly as a gone case ready to be slaughtered..."

Her eyes took a faraway look. "Then he stood before me muttering, "I think darling, you are now used to my generosities."

He unbelted himself holding the black leather belt in his right hand with which he was about to attack me, but when I did not move at all he seemed to be a little disturbed. As soon as he raised his belt and spanked it at me, I caught hold of it and snatched it from his hand kicking him hard in his stomach. He fell down with a startled look. For a moment he was numb and I liked his look that was no longer amused or cool. He was horrified as if he had seen a ghost."

Durga stopped speaking a mischievous smile playing on her lips as if she was recalling her husband's face.

"Durga you are driving me crazy. You did what? Hit your husband!" The disbelief in my voice made Durga jump like a giddy schoolgirl.

"Oh yes, damn yes! And then he raised his volume trying to suppress me. "How dare you revolt back like this? Don't you know that good wives should be submissive?" He thundered.

In reply, I laughed and bowed down, staring hard at him, "oh yes, thank you my Parameswar for telling me my duty as an obedient wife but I am so sorry I am not so great. Hey, Bhagavan forgive me of my sin." Having said that, I yanked the belt hard at him, hitting him first on his chest and then thrashing him right and left for about twenty times all over his body.

He gasped and rolled backwards, his fat fingers stopping the blow of the belt. "You bitch. I'll call the police and have you locked up for the rest of your life," he then said his face bloating red.

I again laughed at him and moved a tad closer, kicking out his leg, catching him by the throat, I batted my eyelashes at him replying sweetly, "really Prannath first get out of my clutches then plan your next move. Ok, now let me treat you with some of my goodies. I want to see what kind of a man you are when the real wife has the edge. C'mon, hit me, pull up your hand."

He struggled to get up, but couldn't and then yanked his hand to hit back at me, but I was quick enough to twist his wrist and push his hand behind his back. He screamed at the top of his lungs, sweat rolling down his brown swollen cheeks. "Please leave me alone. Look, I'm sorry for using my hand on you." He pleaded and I just loved the strangled-sounding voice.

"So how does it feel when you bear the brunt my dearest? The pain that you inflicted on me thousand times had to come back at you. You should also have the taste of your own medicine," I said to which he cried, "please stop now. I am not able to move my left leg. It's jammed."

But I was not finished. I said in a singsong voice, looking absolutely horrified, "oh no what have I done. Darling Prannath I'm sorry, so sorry. I'll fix it!" I then moved a few steps backwards as my husband started to squeal like a stuck pig when I advanced him.

Scared, he blubbered, "what… what are you going to do now?"

My lips sure twisted into a slant when I heard that and was quick to reply, "patience, dear… have a little patience. Oh, I forgot you don't know its meaning at all. Marriage vows and virtues have no meaning for you. They are just meant to be recited for the ceremony's sake. For people like you, a woman is an object of lust, greed and desire who has to be beaten when desired and taken control of."

I then leapt into the air, landing on his left leg and rolling him onto his chest, I dragged him on the floor. Then I cuffed his hands tying them with my chunni. Within seconds, my combat training skills emerged from within and I smashed him in between his legs. Spinning backwards, I slashed hard at his lower back. He was almost blacked out.

I finished the beating session by shouting, "I love this moment. You look serene. I waited all these years and promised myself that for once I would show you the stars in broad daylight. And that's what, probably you deserved. I wanted to avenge what you kept doing to me. After all the years of love and care, I gave to you this is what I got in return and that's what you got back. Now if you ever in your wildest of imagination even try to lift your dirty fat finger at me I will screw you. You get that!"

"Yes…." He had croaked with a nod with his voice cracking with desperation."

Pausing Durga wiped a hand over her mouth.

I was silent, listening, feeling her pain her anguish and her victory.

Her eyes clouded. "Then I went to the door unbolted it to see both my sons standing shivering, waiting for their poor mother, whom they thought was again victimised crying, but they cheered up seeing my sparkling face. They asked me, "ma, why so much of noise again." To which I replied, "no beta nothing has happened to me. I am fine. Now your father has become alright. Do not worry and concentrate on your studies."

The first time I saw my sons opening up and they hugged me crying hysterically as if their mother had some transformation that gave them strength and happiness.

It was then when I realised that it was so important to be strong for my children because forget about me, they were suffering from inside and this mental trauma was robbing the joy from their life."

When Durga stopped Roshni and I sat there blinking at her, not fully comprehending what she'd just said.

Durga laughed at the look on my face. "This is not the end of the story friends. This game of supremacy continued for a few days. After a nights beating the next day my husband was all over rolled in bandages. Before I got up from the bed, my morning tea was ready for me. He entered limping into my bedroom and sat on the side of the bed being careful not to touch me. Then, with a soft squeaky voice, he said, "my darling... My sweetie pie... please get up."

I rubbed my eyes to see him sitting beside my feet shivering as he passed a weak smile.

I barked at him, kicking him at the bottom, "get off my bed you fool."

He'd immediately stood upright, every ounce of his flesh

shivering to death.

"Darling, you… you look so beautiful. I have made tea for you."

He picked up the cup and handed me the tea. With a disgusted look, I then took a small sip, knowing very well that he had not ever lifted a finger to help me in the kitchen or other household chores. Forget tea. I remembered the times he spat the tea on my face, had thrown the hot tea on my hands. It was my turn now. As soon as the hot liquid touched my mouth, I spat out the same on his face. "What have you made? Are you still drunk? It tastes like sewage water. You don't know even how to make a cup of tea. Useless, good for nothing. Now do not touch the breakfast, my children will fall ill with the sick food you'll cook."

After saying this I had jumped out of my bed and his head was hanging low. He gave me way helplessly looking at me from behind when I stormed out of the room. Since that day he remains quiet, does whatever I tell him to do, concentrates on his work and even takes care of the children."

With a flourish Durga brushed her palms together and took a bow.

It was outrageous! I held up my hand, my body heaving from racks of laughter.

"What the hell!" Roshni was hiding her face behind the paper napkin choking a hilarious sob. "That's it!"

Durga shifted her chair in front leaning forward. "No, no. You have to hear this. Then one fine day… after a week the soul of the macho man erupted once again. He'd thought wisely enough to again make me his humble prey. I was alone, standing on the balcony watering the potted plants when he came from behind. I whirled around with a disgruntled look sniffing his mouth to check whether he was drunk or not. Oh alas! He was stinking sparing himself enough energy to fight back. And then he started hopping like a mad frog showing off the big misfit boxing gloves in his hand. Such a fool I thought I married.

He had no brains at all. I tilted my chin sideways and snapped, "at least learn how to wear boxing gloves first." I could see the formation of the lump in his throat as if something had choked his vocal chords. Without wasting time he boxed at my face and I swung to the left twirling my leg onto his making him stumble hard on the floor. "You fool," I'd then pulled his hair and remarked, "this is enough for you. Do you want VIP treatment? I caught his leg and whirled him in circles till his head started spinning and he cried to stop. He folded his hands asking for forgiveness once again and I insulted him by throwing water on his head. "Stupid man this suits you well. Again, if you try any of your charming tactics on me, I will not waste a moment to throw you off the terrace. All clear or not?" I had barked at him. He'd then whined. "Yes… all clear… madam, my doll I am a fool, a dog, a brainless creature No more mistakes now master, No more."

"Stop whining like a puppy dog and get lost from my sight." I'd snapped back. Guys, you won't believe he sprang to his feet and ran like a mad bull, out of the balcony and then the house. Since then he keeps on prowling through the rooms to check for me stealing away even from my shadow. And what else he tries to impress me with his behaviour and actions satisfied with the idea of making me feel important. But it's nearly impossible to please the lady of the house. Above all, he has thrown all the liquor bottles down the drain and is scared to death at the sight of me. He has learnt to respect me out of love… you know true love?"

We all burst out in spills of laughter together, unable to stop ourselves till the other surrounding people started to stare at us.

My eyes watering I had to hold my stomach to stop myself from being looked at by others.

"Ssshh… ssshhh. Control girls. It's enough for now! Oh, Durga you are great! You are the real Bhavani." Laughing like a maniac Roshni blew her nose in the paper napkin.

I eased towards Durga's chair and rubbed her shoulder. "You have done what, seriously, I would not have been able to in your circumstances. You are wonderful and beyond imagination. But why didn't you leave him?"

"When I was in it, I didn't question it. But I had the choice to change my destiny. Aree darling, when a woman comes down to do something nothing can stop her. You are your own guide, friend and help. These men are cowards. When they see the real face of their wives, they hide in their small holes like rats! You are doing the correct thing by standing for yourself. Show him your guts." She jerked her fisted hand in the air.

Durga was truly a source of inspiration. I did not know that she had faced so much; my problem was like a stick in a stack of hay as compared to hers. My determination grew stronger. If she could change her destiny, I could also do it!

CHAPTER 23

The self-confidence and attitude improvement classes ended
with me becoming more positive, Durga becoming less
hesitant and Roshni…well what to say, she became cockier,
anymore and she would have been teaching self-confidence
herself.

Whenever I entered the building I didn't know why the
words spoken by Sophia Loren 'Beauty is how you feel
inside, and it reflects in your eyes. It is not something
physical' inspired me.

The next session was quite interesting on a woman's
favourite- tricks how to apply make-up. Our teacher Max
was also interesting. He was short and trim, in his late
twenties. His hair was long with bangs up to his nape and
then rod straight. It was highlighted with a light golden
colour giving an overall effect of shimmering streaks of light.
His face was clear and fair, but on closer look, I realised that
he had applied foundation on it. He was quite, how to put it
beautiful, with pink lips, straight nose and smoky eyes.
Dressed in fitting jeans and a black T- Shirt on which it was
written in silver 'I was born to be different, not perfect so

don't judge me!' He couldn't seem to be able to stand straight. Two tiny gold hoops glinted in his right earlobe. The angelic face that it framed would draw middle-aged and elderly ladies like the sirens' song drew sailors.

The room where we were seated was outfitted with a big, brawny desk and a couple of wide leather chairs that I thought felt as if you might sink into them. Max was perched delicately on the desk with his lifted leg swinging in the air. He was rummaging for something in his bag. A plastic chair was kept beside the desk on the podium.

"He is a twink," Durga murmured under her breath. She was sitting in the middle flanked by me on one side and Roshni on the other.

"What?" I asked. Roshni giggled. Durga wiggled her eyebrows.

"What?" I asked again confused.

Durga gave a pout and fluttered her eyelashes. Roshni was now choking with laughter.

"Darlings! Please give a moment before I start the class." Max, our make-up teacher said in a melodic voice busy fiddling with his bag, taking out all kinds of blush on, lipsticks, mascaras, bottles and creams.

"Darlings, ooh la la!" Durga muttered, giving an easy smile, one I thought might pass for innocent on a less wicked face. Roshni now laughed out loudly.

"Have you lost it?!" I rolled my eyes at Durga. "Why are you both laughing?"

Durga cocked her head. "You are such a babe Smita." Roshni looked at me over Durga's shoulder with just the faintest glimmer of humour in her eye. "God Smita, just look at his arms, they are waxed!"

"Waxed?!" I looked at Max who was now standing with one

hand on his hips. I peered closely at his arms. Well, hot damn! He had waxed his arms, then I got it. "He is not straight!"

Durga snorted. "Now she gets it!"

"Aw, Girls, stop talking." Max clapped his hands gaining our attention.

Girls! It was some time since I was called a girl, in fact, precisely seventeen years but who was counting? It made me feel like a school girl again.

"Now make-up is an art," Max said reverently flinging his arms around.

"Art!" Durga brushed the nape of her neck trying to hide her merriment.

Max rolled his eyes at her as if she was a dumb-wit asking a stupid question. "Yes! It beautifies you, hides your faults and brings out your best features."

"I think my knowledge is limited on the subject. Will learn more from you," Durga remarked.

You had to admire him. Whatever you had to say about his personality, but it was sure that Max knew his subject well. It took Max ten seconds to come up with one of his deep thought provoking lines.

"When you meet a person, what is the first feature in her face that you notice?"

"Eyes!" I instantly replied because that was the first thing that I noticed in a person.

"Bingo!" Max shot a finger in the air, as if to prove a point. "Your eyes are what people usually first notice about your appearance. Now…" He trailed off tracking his eyes from one person to another when he zeroed on in Durga.

"Now ladies here are beautiful eyes." He pointed at a pair of swan-like shaped black huge eyes. Durga did have beautiful eyes.

Durga blushed. It was obvious she was not accustomed to anyone calling her eyes beautiful.

"Thanks." She batted her eyelashes sweetly.

"You will be my apprentice." With a triumphant ring in his voice, he waved his arms in front of the chair.

"Come, darling, you need to sit on this chair." He patted the chair beside him and turned towards his metallic suitcase containing his ammunition.

"Apprent... means?" Durga turned to look helplessly at me. "What is he saying?"

"He is asking for your help, you just have to sit and he will apply make-up on you."

"No way!" Durga wiggled into the chair looking horrified. Roshni jerked her head in Max's direction and made clucking noises. "Look who is scared."

"Nonsense!" As if baffled with herself, she scooped a hand through her hair. "Scared of him!"

I handed it back to her. "Ah, ha spunky I like that. Now get up and go!"

"Fine!" Durga grumbled and wound her way through the chairs occupied by the other woman.

With a thump she sat on the plastic chair, her face screwed up. Roshni and I started giggling.

Max was now holding a liner in his hand as he came to stand beside the chair; his other hand was splayed on his chest. He gave her an up-and-down study. "Darling, I must say, you are pretty, but that scowl is definitely making you look old. Now relax and let my magic begin."

Before she could answer he pushed Durga on the chair, straightened her up as if she was a puppet and then went on, "now this, as you all know, is an eyeliner. There are two kinds' liquid and pencil. I will be using both. Instead of lining your eyelids with a liner, apply your liner right in between your lashes. This is a great way to appear as though you're not wearing any makeup at all, yet adding a little bit of colour and definition to your eyes, and making the base of your lashes appear thicker."

Like an artist painting a picture he made definite strokes. The results were startling, Durga's eyes looked even better.

"If you don't already own a white pencil, invest in one now just for this simple trick! Instead of lining your water line with dark eyeliner, use a white pencil to create the illusion of a bigger eye. Let me show you."

He lined Durga's one eye with black and the other with white. The results were obvious. They appeared bigger. "Fabulous isn't it?" He turned her face right and left to admire it.

Max was holding his next ammunition, a mascara. "Place the wand deep into the base of the lashes, wiggling it in left to right."

By now I noticed even Durga seemed to be enjoying herself. There was respect in her eyes as there was respect in mine for Max. He was just amazing.

The class went on, just concentrating on the eyes Max told us how you could change the shape of your eyes, how you could make them catty or Smokey or plain and simple.

The whole week was devoted to make-up. My mind and book were filled with information if you have Asian skin, you should choose a foundation with a yellow base, as opposed to a pink base….when it comes to picking out a shade, test colours by placing them on your jawline... For Angelina Jolie's lush lips line your lips just outside of your natural line.

"But sweethearts when I say *just outside of your natural line*, I mean slightly. You don't want to look like a clown by overdoing it!" Max said and had looked pointedly at Durga. Durga had become his favourite pupil, only God knew the reason because she was always grumbling and always the guinea pig on whom Max carried his *art*.

Plus, it seemed his mission to improve Durga's dressing sense. Max was also our specialist on dressing.

He was always behind Durga. "Lady you have one terrific figure, but horrible choice in clothes!" And Durga being Durga was always at odds with him.

He'd obviously caught her in the midst. "Mental! He is mad! I will dress the way I want to," and Durga was always yelling. But the whole scenario was highly entertaining.

I had already talked to Max regarding my weight. "I am doing yoga to become fitter. Please advise me on what will suit me a few months later, when my figure is more flattering."

Max had replied in his usual drawl, "sure sweetheart, whatever you are comfortable with. Right now you have a little more poundage on you that you should not have, but you're working on that. It will go off in a few months' time now and dear you are still pretty with it so think what a beauty you will become after you get rid of it!"

I had smiled, thinking yes, just a few months away.

CHAPTER 24

I may have borne two children, looked for my household, but I doubted that I'd ever worked harder or put in longer hours. There was the sheer physical demand of exercises which had upped my respect for anyone who did it. But slowly I was getting used to yoga classes, my evening walks and the grooming classes bringing me satisfaction. They had become a regular part of my life. In fact, after a time I started enjoying all my classes and my body got used to exercising, the sessions of grooming. I made sure to stick to the diet plan having my oats and banana in the morning followed by milk. In the afternoon I was given the choice of eating stuffed roti or a moong dal chilla with salad and oil free vegetables. So I ate them alternately and at night it was plain soup and salads. In between, I savoured myself with black sugar-free coffee to satisfy my hunger pang. I was entitled to a cup of hot cocoa, but I saved it for later when I sat down to read a good novel before going to bed.

The confidence in me had brought a remarkable change in my outlook towards others. I had stopped cribbing and whining about small little things. I even started to ignore

Avinash who as usual occupied in his own world, was still not aware of the change in me. It was my outer and inner transformation the efficient condition of a person's true progress.

Above all, how did it matter now? The company of Durga, Roshni and other women in the classes had changed my perspective of looking at myself. I felt happy, I felt occupied and I felt that I was one of them who was heard and listened to. They made me feel important and I gained respect amongst them whenever I voiced my opinion on various subjects starting from household activities to political arena all over the world. My entire demeanour from posture sitting to culinary skills to the art of talking and presenting myself, including my creative ability to dance was explored beautifully. All thanks to the grooming classes. A woman was a multi-tasker. And if she really wanted to bring out her talents she could do anything in the world. Only three months had passed and I had discovered this side of mine. I learned so many things that it was startling.

The next class was on table manners and etiquettes. Roshni had to go on an assignment and wasn't able to attend the class, but there was Durga. And in my opinion, there were a lot of things I could say about her. She was fun, smart, and after Max's session on clothes great to look at.

Today she was dressed in a sky blue kurti and white leggings that put a glow on her face. She could depending on her mood present a polished urbane image and then turn and become casual ready to fight on the street. There were just some things I loved about her.

Around ten people, including Durga and me, were seated at a round table, which was laden with food and all kinds of cutlery.

Our instructor was an aged woman called Chetna with dark, choppy hair that was grey in colour. She wore silver framed glasses over a pixie face that was intimidating because she must be around five feet and weighing not more than ninety pounds.

Chetna said with her jaw set, "now ladies you can see the napkin. Once seated, unfold your napkin and place it on your lap. Now use it for occasionally wiping your lips or fingers. At the end of dinner, you have to leave the napkin tidily on the place setting." We took are respective napkins and placed it over our laps. Durga picked up her napkin and gave it a good jerk as if after washing clothes she was shaking off excess water. I braced myself for Durga's antics; I already knew that she wouldn't be able to resist doing something or the other funny.

"Now, this is not the way to jerk your napkin. This is not a duster. Place it delicately." Chetna admonished Durga and then went on addressing everyone.

"Now see the cutlery you have to always start on the outside and work your way in. If you have any doubts regarding which cutlery to use the best is to observe your host."

Various shaped knives, spoons and forks were placed on the table. "As you can see serving utensils are placed on the right side of serveware. When a serving spoon and serving fork are presented together, the spoon or knife is laid on the right ready to cut and lift and the fork on the left to steady and hold. So now, please lift your fork in the left and knife in the right."

Everyone picked up their forks and knives with Chetna maneuvering, adjusting them properly in their hands. She stopped behind Durga who was holding the knife as if she was ready to attack the food. "Durga you are not supposed to kill someone. Hold the knife and fork with the handles in the palm of the hand, forefinger on top, and thumb underneath." She helped Durga hold them neatly in her hand.

 Chetna then sat at the head of the table playing host.

Next food was served and we started eating. Picking a piece of paneer with my fork, I popped it in my mouth and swallowed it wanting to eat a second one.

My eyes shifted when I heard Durga grumbling. "Durga?" Durga's jerked her shoulder and answered in mock disbelief. "Aree knife… fork, Bhagwan has given hands no then why don't we use them?"

"I agree." I shot her a quick, amused look before I took another bite. Durga was again in her element and there was no point arguing with her.

"Hold your fork like this… a knife like this." Durga eyes were bugged out and mouth slightly open as she heard more instructions from Chetna.

"The utensils are to be returned to the platter or serving bowl in the same position. You must consciously refrain from embarrassing yourself and your host." I gasped and swiped a hand under my nose chocking on seeing the expression on Durga's face.

Chetna was demonstrating taking dainty bites without the slightest of speech. When she opened her mouth to eat it seemed like a wide ocean and it looked like a tiny mole after it was cramped shut. A mechanical robot whose every movement was fixed and precise. "Take small bites; do not chew with your mouth open; do not talk with food in your mouth, and do not place elbows on the table."

Durga who was busy stuffing her mouth stopped munching

and scratched her head. "Great, thinking about this you will forget to eat only."

My hearty laugh caught everyone's attention; they stopped eating to look at me. I coughed slightly to hide my embarrassment.

Chetna asked in a no nonsense tone. "Are you fine dear?"

"Yes," I replied, my tone and gaze presumably all innocence.

"Are you fine dear?" Durga mimicked Chetna under her breath, her brilliant eyes twinkling with merriment.

My face broke into a smile and I realised that it was filled with joy. Durga could be charming and entertaining and with such friends, life could certainly not be dull.

CHAPTER 25

One Sunday my family decided to go for a picnic to our farmhouse in Chattarpur. It occurred to me that I was actually looking forward to the day. It had been months since I had taken a break from the exercises and classes. On reaching the farmhouse I could make out the long and stately rows of palm trees lining the winding driveway created a beautiful umbrella through which the sun rays made dancing patterns on the cobblestones.

The house was big, rectangular and diamond-shaped glass windows winked in the bright sunlight through which the garden presented a picturesque view of colourful circular flower- beds and a landscape covered with small marble statues emerging through the tiny bushy green plants. Avinash was particular of the grass that was thick and light green.

The interior was simple and comforting mainly comprising of wooden floors and planks.

Avinash went and sat in the lounge with children while I wanted to freshen up a bit.

I entered the room, its neatly laden bed and wooden chairs kept untouched behind a small table across which a decorated round dressing table was placed, caught my attention. After freshening up I took out a brush from my hand bag and started combing my hair admiring myself all the while. I wore my hair down, tied loosely at my nape, and the style offered me a softer gentler look. My hair felt soft and silky. The regular nutritious diet was helping them to flourish. Even I noticed my face had grown thinner and the dark circles had reduced. I felt heavenly. I applied a little kajal onto my eyes; a little blush and bounced outside. Avinash was not there, but both the children were seated talking amongst themselves. My tender heart warmed at the sight of them.

I approached my daughter Naina, leaning down at her I tried to catch her attention. "Hi what's up? Why don't we take a round outside?"

Naina spun her head darting a kind of suspicious look at me. "Mom your hair!" My daughter ran her fingers through the length of my hair and gaped at me. "It's lush, smooth and wonderful. You are looking pretty."

The compliment came as a surprise to me. Happiness seemed to leap into my eyes before I was aware the emotion was there. My daughter's compliment was the best I could ever have. It was something I had waited for a long time. "Thanks, sweetheart." I kissed her forehead, cupping her small shoulders with my hand and pulled her snugly against me.

"Mom!" She protested, obviously proving a point that she wasn't a baby anymore.

"C'mon both of you! Let us have some fun." I had carried with me badminton rackets and a basket of goodies. I steered both of them into the garden, first, we took a round of the garden chatting like friends and then placed a mat big enough to accommodate the basket and the three of us. I could see them feasting on the cheese, thousand –island-dressing sandwiches and chocolate chip cookies. The sandwiches were Samarth's favourite while Naina loved the baked chocolate cookies. They laughed gleefully adoring the goodies.

"Shall we play a bit of badminton?" I shifted my gaze from Naina to Samarth who appeared to be hopping with enthusiasm.

"Oh yeah, sure," both of them spoke ecstatically in unison. Then we three set off to the net to play badminton.

With children on one side and me on the other, I played with enthusiasm striking the cork every time it came in my direction barely missing a few shots. There was energy inside my body that made me play for a full one hour. I realised it was the work of the yoga, the regime of proper food and exercises, providing strength to my bones and muscles.

"C'mon, hit harder Naina. This is your chance to go one on one with me." I shifted to the right and left, managing to hit the shuttle at Naina's direction. After a few unsuccessful shots, Naina smashed harder this time not allowing me to counter the attack. The shuttle fell down and Naina counted it as her triumph. My encouragement had worked and her jubilance over her victory made me proud of her.

Samarth then came running to me giving a kiss on my right cheek. "That was fun! Mom, how did you do it? I mean you were very tired the last time we had come for a holiday." He acknowledged my effort of connecting with him as a friend. My goodness! Nothing more could have been better than this. I hugged both my children. I had never thought it would be easy, but had assumed on the basis of experience that when you become a mother, maternal skills blossomed naturally inside you. Then later with the passing time when your children grew up, they needed you more in a different role. It had been quite an interesting afternoon.

By this time, the sun had hidden behind a thick grey cloud. "Come, I'll prepare something for you both. So tell me what should I make?"

"Chinese!" They both reacted with excitement. "Fried rice, noodles and manchurian."

"Your wish shall be fulfilled. Give me half an hour and mom will prepare everything for you."

They became babies again demanding my attention. I realised one thing at the moment it was not only essential to give children love and attention but to be actually involved in the child's life you had to be active in every department. I realised because of lack of health and energy I was missing all the enjoyments of playing with my children. For the first time, I saw respect in their eyes. I decided that I would make it a point that over time I would no longer be the mom who only cooked and served their needs but someone with whom they could share their feelings.

The children were so happy. I was so happy to get their love and attention. I picked up my feet and took off to the kitchen preparing everything for them. To my surprise both my children helped me in chopping and getting the dishes made conveniently. Avinash was busy on the phone discussing some business deal. I sighed, what was the point in coming for a holiday if you couldn't enjoy it with your family?

The laced mattress on the wooden dining table on which white coral plates enhanced with blue and gold border surrounded by filled diet coke crystal glasses and bowls of three dishes were properly placed.

I placed a fork, knife and a spoon on matching blue-laced napkins beside the plates. A crystal bowl filled with water had red rose petals swimming at the top, spreading its sweet fragrance around. Voila! The culinary skills were a boon in disguise. The table was decorated beautifully.

I called out to my children and husband. They assembled around the table.

I caught Avinash's look of surprise as he stooped down to smell the fresh aroma of manchurian the dish being his favourite.

We all perched ourselves on the dining chairs, facing each other across the table. I sat beside Naina and Avinash by Samarth's side. I did not know why I did not eat anything; instead, my attention shuttled back and forth between children and Avinash who were relishing the food. This was how a family should be.

"Yummy mom." Both children took their turns to praise me munching onto the dishes one by one.

I watched Samarth as he painstakingly folded his napkin to clean his mouth. Every time I looked at my son I saw myself. In his eyes, his colouring, the adorable quirk of his smile, I saw the echoes of my youth.

"I love fried rice." I turned my gaze to Naina who resembled Avinash, in her complexion and features. She was busy digging a spoonful of rice from the bowl. I gave her a maternal squeeze and murmured, "try the noodles sweetheart."

I served the same to both my children who chided gently one by one. "Mom, this is delicious."

I probably did not know what to make of my children

passionate declarations. I came to know that they didn't shade their emotions. With equal fervour, even Naina loved her mother, her best friends and books.

Avinash's gaze travelled to the length and breadth of the table and he remarked, "I had no idea about this kind of creativity you possessed."

Avinash's words of appreciation after years of marriage sounded unbelievable to my ears.

"Ma, can I have some more coke."

At Samarth's request, I got up and moved to the fridge. Opening its door, I took out a can of diet coke.

Handing it over to my son, I noticed Avinash who ate in bemused silence, observing me with the corner of his eye.

"You are not eating anything?" He asked.

I smiled. "Not really hungry."

I simply didn't have much appetite. In fact, I didn't have the craving to eat after following the diet plan religiously. It had become imbibed in me to eat my regular meals. All these delicacies were not as tempting as the adorations giving to me by my family.

Avinash still hadn't left his gaze. My eyes caught the light and glint of it and I wondered he had something in his mind that he wanted to share with me. His eyes were reflecting a different emotion.

I waited with every appearance of calm. I wondered what he would say.

Then he said it in a low, husky voice, "your suit has loosened around your waist. You have reduced. You look better, younger."

He surprised me when my lips curved, almost affectionately. Yet I felt my chest puff out with pride at his words.

"Have I?" I asked warmly.

He nodded. After a period of about ten minutes, Samarth and Naina climbed down from their chairs carried their plates to the counter by the sink and fled the hall. Bidding both of us Goodnight they left the grown-ups lingering over their meal.

Avinash scanned the hall as if to make sure children weren't lurking nearby eavesdropping. I saw him get up, move towards the kitchen basin and wash his hands. He walked towards the deck near the glass window. Inserting a CD into it, he switched on the music. It was my favourite. "Pehla Nasha."

I kept smiling, picking up the dishes to keep them in the basin for cleaning, but Avinash outstretched his hand towards me taking mine into his. My heart fluttered, triggering the memories of our honeymoon. I had forgotten the strength of Avinash's hands, the shape of his fingers, their warmth and power.

"Will you dance with me?" I heard the edge in his voice, knew it as a sign of rising and reckless mood. He skimmed his fingers through my hair and then took me to the middle of the hall where he swayed me into his arms, dancing like a windmill.

"I always liked dancing with you. Remember the first time we danced together before marriage. I like the smell of your hair. When I get close enough, I can see myself in your eyes. Your eyes always did me in." He slid me into a slow swaying dance.

"No. My eyes..." I felt myself tremble and warning bells were lost under the thunder of my own heart.

"Yes, your eyes. And they still do. Sometimes when we spend the night together, I'd wake up early to watch you sleep. Just to see deep into your eyes when you opened them."

"It's not fair to tell me all this after such a long time." My voice shook.

"I know. I should have told you earlier. But it's never late than ever."

Suddenly he pushed me forward firming his arm on my back and swirled me around.

It was a wild dance, moving both of us in circles until Avinash's leg slipped on the slippery floor. I closed my mouth to fight my laughter and stretched out to help him up. But he pulled me down as I rolled.

I felt the echoes of that boundless, consuming love I once felt for him. My mouth found his, and I kissed him hard. When I came up for air, all I could see was Avinash's glazed eyes. A heartbeat later we both got up and though I hadn't lost that much weight that Avinash could lift me in his arms and carry me to the bedroom but we went there hand in hand. The night had never been so beautiful.

The next morning I woke with a start. I saw him in deep sleep and climbed out of the bed without making any noise I showered and dressed in slacks and a T-shirt. I couldn't remember ever feeling happier trotting down the stairs to make breakfast for my family.

Soon Avinash and the children accompanied me on the table and we enjoyed the hearty breakfast. It was time to go back home. It was a Monday and he had work, though the children took a day off from school.

Avinash left from the farmhouse directly for work, whereas I dropped the children to school and then drove home.

Back to the grind!

But before leaving he did kiss me lightly on my cheek and I was surprised. It was so rare that he was amorous with me and I saw a hint of the old Avinash in his eyes that were filled with tenderness and love for me. And I wondered if life would ever be the same again.

CHAPTER 26

On Thursday evening the class was on deportment and elegance through poise, expression and carriage. It was end of September and the evening was cool. I could already scent the end of summer, with the start of rains.

The trees were bright, their colour splashed across a dull grey sky layered with sulky clouds. Time was moving forwards, and only a few weeks were left for the contest. I ran through everything that came into my mind as I drove the last miles towards the class. In my wildest dreams, I had never thought I could have spent a night like this one. I had half hoped that it would be a romantic day, one whose memory I would always cherish, I still couldn't believe that Avinash could be seriously interested in me even now. Talk about shooting yourself in the foot. I grimaced at myself. But as the days had passed and it was as if nothing exceptional had happened between Avinash and me. He was back to his indifferent self. But this time it did not hurt because I had an objective in life, after glimpsing the old love between us I was greedy for more. I now wanted it back and had decided to try my best.

I skirted the Delhi traffic and reached the club. Unlatching the seat belt, I eased out of the car and into the building. On entering the hall I was surprised to see a stack of books kept on the table. Then I peeked out, blinked in automatic admiration. The woman who stood beside the table was a vision. She had a mass of dark brown hair that she had bounded in a bun at her nape. She wore a long blue dress over a body that any woman on earth would kill to have. She had a pretty face, and her long neck curved gracefully down to wide, strong shoulders, then small breasts atop a flat stomach with a tiny waist. Even the way the woman was standing was as though it had been choreographed with elegance and gracefulness.

As she noticed me she smiled and with a slight tilt of her head gestured me to come in.

Roshni was already seated and I took a seat beside her.

"Wow!" I exclaimed.

"Even I had the same reaction. The woman is astonishing!" Roshni agreed.

The words were barely out of her mouth when Durga entered and seeing her comical expression and dropped jaw, it was obvious that even she was experiencing the same emotions. After ogling at the woman for a few seconds, Durga shook her head and stomped towards us taking a chair to the left of Roshni.

"Wow!" she repeated my words.

Like me, she watched the woman with admiration. "She looks like poetry in motion. I wish I could be like her."

That was something we all wished for. As soon as all the students had come the class started.

The graceful creature moved forward to stand in the middle of the room. "Please line your chairs on one side of the room. We need space."

Even her voice was soft and melodious. There was scraping noises as everyone picked up their respective plastic chairs lining it to one side.

All of us stood in a circle around the woman.

"My name is Aneesha. In today's lesson, we are going to learn how to become a lady. Being a graceful woman is one of the hallmarks of being a lady, and as important as being a feminine, well poised and well-proportioned woman. Now I would like to see your walks please, one by one."

All of us took turns walking. Roshni strolled in her usual casual way; Durga stomped man-like and whereas me, there was no mirror in which I could see myself… so I really didn't know my gait. The others were not bad, the young girls were trying to imitate models. The swaying movement of their hips and the deliberate pout was a comic sight.

After observing all of us, Aneesha squirmed a little and cleared her throat. "Unfortunately for us, most of us learn how to walk by copying faulty and ungraceful models." There was a lilt in her voice, echoing those of foreign lands. "We should not waddle, as that suggests obesity, nor strut as fashion models do on the runway. As children who copy their parents, it is no doubt that we have been marred by examples of bad walking from generation to generation. We should walk in a manner that is characterised by grace and freedom. It should not be hasty or hurried, legato, not staccato, not aimless. Here watch me."

And watch we did, her walk was like a deliberate rhythmical movement of legs and feet in sync with gentle compensating movements of head and arms in a slow graceful swing.

With action and words, Aneesha demonstrated. "When we walk, our upper torso should remain as strong as possible; it should not be swaying back and forth. We should not be over-arching our back. Our heads while relaxed, should not distract others by bobbing, but should be slightly lifted, as though you have a confident expectation of life. I suppose that is where the training by placing a book on your head comes in. Why don't I see all of you now walk again with a book on your head?"

I think none of us covered the whole distance with the book intact on our heads.

"The rule is head up, back straight, shoulders back, chest out and abdomen in is to be obeyed." Aneesha paused a second for effect. "And smile."

We were made to walk again and again with the book on our heads, till we got it correct.

"Now you need to practice this every day and especially you Smita, you need to practice for fifteen minutes at least every day as in just two months you will be taking part in the Mrs Perfect competition. Now please get your chairs back and sit on them."

There were again scraping noises as the chairs were pushed and we sat down. Aneesha stood in the center with clear supervision. "You should not fall into the chair like Durga just did, throwing herself into it." Durga instantly straightened. "Nor should you sit cautiously like Smita as though you suspect that it is dirty or would break under your weight."

I blushed rosily.

Aneesha went on, "do not sit squarely on both feet, as that is too manly again, sorry Durga the way you are sitting." Durga again shifted uncomfortably asking sharply, "then how should I sit?"

Aneesha smiled. "Sit with your legs closed, but lean them at an angle to one side. Like this." She sat showing us how to do it.

"And last but not the least, dress your best, always give yourself the confidence that you already look great. There is a psychological effect that takes place. Your body responds to your thoughts and projects how you feel. Now, are there any questions?"

"Where did you get that body of yours? It doesn't seem real," Roshni blurted in a forthright style.

Aneesha's eyebrows rose, her eyes laughing. "I am a ballet dancer. So you can say it keeps me fit."

Roshni clucked her tongue over the revelation and there was chattering amongst the women admiring the reason for her perfect body.

Few more questions on posture were asked and then the class ended another lesson over and well learnt.

CHAPTER 27

As the time passed, I kept on practising my walk. It was somewhat exciting to try it at night when the house was quiet and everyone asleep. I practised it for half an hour every day and it started showing in the way I walked as one day Naina commented, her eyes round with curiosity. "Mom you are walking straighter, not slumping, somewhat like the way models walk."

I had just walked into the children's room.

I beamed wanting to give a long, heartfelt yell. "I am improving my walk, sweetheart."

"Yeah," Samarth agreed, his eyes growing wide as he bit into a big wafer that he pulled out of Lays family pack. "Mom is even looking prettier and younger."

I climbed on the bed where both were lounging trying to stand like a model with one hand raised to the right and the other on my hip. "Well thank you that means mom was not pretty earlier." I teased my son, unwilling to let the moment go.

"Mom, stop acting smart," Naina whined, "you know what we mean and you have lost so much weight. I know you are hiding something!"

I thought for a moment what was the harm in sharing my secret with them? "Ok, ok, I will tell you a secret, as you already know I am taking classes to reduce weight..." Both the children nodded.

I leant forward my tone conspiring, "l am grooming myself on how to walk, sit, talk and to become a complete lady. I am taking part in Mrs Perfect competition, but it is a secret and no sharing the same with dad. I want to give him a surprise." "Wow, mom!" Naina jumped on the bed, emotions of joy flooded onto her face. "Now my mom will become chic, hep and happening and no longer stay dull. All my friends will become jealous. I am so happy!" Naina hugged me, her cheeks burning bright with enthusiasm.

My daughter thought I was dull! Well, that was a rude shock.

One had to accept that in today's time children expected a tad too much from their parents, just as the parents expected a lot from their children. If you didn't change with the changing times you would lag behind and the world along with your children would move forward. It was hard to admit that I was forever crying over the fact that Avinash was busy; he did not give time to me. In fact, only today Avinash had left for one of his business trips for a month which had made me sad, but then I thought I wasn't counting my blessings, I had my children with me, I had my life. It had become embedded in my nature, I had clung on to that one incident and then it had become my excuse for poor self-esteem, bruised ego, a lack of belief in my own femininity and marital dissatisfaction But what was under all that? Really under it? I mused. Loss of happiness, loss of identity. I had lost myself somewhere along the line until whatever was left, whatever I had been able to recognise, had been unattractive, that I had escaped from it. Escaped from standing up and taking charge of my life, at that moment, that one word had summed my life perfectly till now. I had become dull, but no more though I was a slow bloomer, but never late than never. Letting out my breath, I closed my eyes and felt nothing but the sweetness of relief. Now my days, my nights would be filled with joy.

"Mom!" Samarth shook me, the Lays packet forgotten on the bed. "Mom you seem lost; I asked when is the competition?"

"In one and a half months," I took delight in informing him.

"Are you kidding… just forty -five days!"

"Surprise! Isn't it?"

Amazement, swiped his face, but he gave me a look of genuine pride.

  Then my eye fell on the pillow kept on the bed. A devil perched on my shoulder, with a mischievous grin I picked up the pillow and lightly hit Samarth on his shoulder who stumbled on the bed.

"Mom!" Both my children shouted surprised.

I hit Naina on her head.

"Now it's war mom," Naina brightened with exhilaration as she picked the pillow. "Samarth let's attack!"

Naina was now standing in the middle of the bed, waging a fierce, violent war with her pillow. Feathers flew everywhere. I was standing at the foot of the bed hitting my children lightly on their butts and heads.

We tore apart the room, with pillows tossing in the air like a bulldozer hitting each other. All the furniture was upturned, the bed sheet was ruined and the chips that the children were having blanketed the spotless marble floor. The feathers from the pillow flew in every direction and there were crunching noises each time someone took a step. Plus there was the melodious sound of laughter and giggles of my children.

"No, no, no!" I screamed in mock terror as they pushed me on the bed. There was only one way to win, I tickled Samarth, he rolled on the bed laughing.

"Mom, that's cheating!" Naina bellowed her eyes lucent with the notion of tug-of-war.

"Everything is fair in love and war!" I laughed and tugged Naina who went skidding down, managing one scream as she sailed belly first on the bed falling.

All three of us were now lying on the bed our breathing laboured. I puffed out my cheeks and slowly expelled air.

"Mom that was fun! What has happened to you? You never used to have fun," Samarth puffed out a huge breadth confused. He rolled over and wrapped his arms around my waist. Lying down in the middle I tossed aside the covers hooked my arms around both my children,

"Well, as Naina said. I had become dull, but no more!"

"Mom the Sunday vacation at the farmhouse, now the pillow fight. We love spending time with you." Samarth, snuggled closer.

I pressed my head down on the pillow closer to my children, savouring this feeling of belonging, of again being a part of my children's life. I was having the time of my life. I was finally in the middle of it, part of my children's lives and loving every moment of it!

"Thank you, my sweethearts." I gently swept aside Naina's hair and brushed my lips over the smooth skin of my son's cheek.

"Now I have to go for my class." I loved them with the brightest smile and unhooking my arm got up. Closing the room's door softly went out.

Before it shut completely I heard the children talking amongst themselves.

"Samarth mom is taking part in the Mrs Perfect contest. I cannot believe it. How did she do it? I mean it's great, she's wow, she's amazing. She behaves like a rock star and now will become one too. We both will tell our friends about her. Ooh! I cannot imagine the look on their faces when they will hear about mom. She's the coolest mom on earth."

Samarth was so excited that he was literary jumping on his toes. I knew for him only the thought of a competition was exciting.

I peeped through the opening to see Naina's reaction. She was standing looking upwards as if staring into an imaginative sky laden with stars uttering, "I am thrilled to see her on the ramp like a model."

I gently shut the door and leaning on it was absorbed in the thoughts of this new relationship between my children and me that was definitely better and different I loved the special brand of comfort and belonging with them that had increased over a few months simply by changing my attitude.

All I could say was that God was giving me happiness in short doses over the past few months.

CHAPTER 28

Two weeks later, it was ten in the morning and I was rummaging in my cupboard for my standard kurti and tights. My hand skimmed on the parallel and I grabbed it deciding to wear it. Pulling it on I was stunned at how big it was on my frame. The parallel actually slid on the floor. I knew I had lost weight, I knew my clothes had become really big on my frame, I was getting through by hemming them, but this was amazing. This was the same parallel I had worn for dinner with Shalini. It was boggling my mind, I hadn't realised how much I had lost, hiding my frame behind the huge clothes.

Putting the pant aside, I put my hands around my waist not believing that it had happened. I went to the drawer where an inch tape was kept and measured my waist. I felt a thrill when I saw my waist was twenty-nine inches. With my fingers crossed, I stood shakily on the scale after a full five months. I saw the needle stop at sixty-two kgs and I burst into tears. Just five more kgs till my ideal weight.

I felt an energy. I had this feeling now only good things would happen to me. But before that, I desperately needed new clothes. I couldn't roam about looking like a clown in clothes that were several sizes bigger than me. I dressed quickly in my oversize kurti that hung loosely on my frame and churidar, whose waist I had tightened into a knot.

I called Roshni irritated to wait for several seconds before she answered, "hello."

"Where were you? Why did it take you so long to answer the call?"

"Sorry, my cell was on mute."

"Roshni, I really need clothes. Nothing fits because I have dropped so many kilos. And it's been so long since I have brought anything pretty. I don't want to wear the old stuff; I want some bright colours, some clothes in which I look nice and young. Nothing serviceable...you know what I mean..."

She didn't even hesitate for a second. "Great idea! I'm game. You were definitely looking a little weird in those clothes. We will head to the mall right after the grooming class, just grab your credit cards and cash and let's go for it!"

We left the class a little early and entered the ambience mall skirting our way through the glass entrance into the wide spacious glistening area. I felt like a giddy schoolgirl. Taking the escalator, we reached the second floor, making our way through the crowd to reach the trendy shop. Durga wanted to see some kurtis for herself while Roshni and I decided to check out the counter for the latest trends in fashion.

We stopped to admire a clothing rack stuffed with clothes of every colour of the rainbow. There were skirts, blouses, dresses, slacks and scarves. The side one consisted of all kinds of parallels, pants and jeans.

Soon Durga came up to us with a yellow knee length kurti. It was plain with an embroidered V neck that made it look quite stylish.

"It's nice Durga," I murmured, genuinely liking it. Her dressing style had definitely improved all thanks to Max. All his gibes had worked.

"Ok, I'll buy this one then. What about both of you?"

"Just checking on the stuff right now," I replied.

I wandered off to the ethnic wear department when Roshni stopped me. "You're in the wrong department, dear."

"I don't think so. I have always dressed like this." What was wrong with Roshni?

"If you wanted to hide your figure, then this would be perfect for you, but the new Smita does not need to hide herself behind clothes," Roshni urged.

I glanced longingly over my shoulder. "But…"

"No buts," Durga insisted, dragging me into the other section. "Leave yourself in our capable hands now, darlings," Durga purred mimicking Max, "we want something sexy."

I gave myself up to the two women as I tried one outfit after another, listening to what matched with what, what jacket or blouse with pants or a skirt.

"Try this pink blouse." Roshni suggested pulling out a beige colour slacks with it. I did not like it much, though tried it after Roshni's stuttering protests who shoved me behind a dressing room curtain.

She was right about the pink, I thought as I slipped into the top and the slacks. The bright colour was an instant mood lifter. It felt so decadent to wear something so close fitting. And the back, I turned to look over my shoulder was low. Would Avinash allow me to wear something revealing and casually suggestive?

I came out wearing the outfit when I became delighted to see their mouth open. "Perfect. You are looking adorable."

Roshni assured me.

"Aree the girl next door is sexy chic yaar." Durga's comments made me laugh. I felt great. Unable to resist I again landed up inside the dressing room.

I scrutinized myself from every angle. Holding on to my hips, first, I turned left, then right, then again left and finally took an about turn.

Then facing the mirror, I was thrilled. "I look great."

The fitting was perfect. I was enjoying my figure that was now 36-29-39 and the pant added that extra edge of smartness to my thin waist. My slim, well- toned body reminded me of the new models who walked the ramp on fashion shows. I was also no better than a model now participating in the Mrs. Perfect.

I put my hands on my waist and smiled at the thought of cat walking on stage. The clothes that I used to only see and ignore adoring them in my dreams were now being picked and tried by me.

I enjoyed every minute of this unique shopping experience. Within minutes, I was buying everything. Everything was stunning. I was wearing it all in good health.

I was able to select from the variety and loved everything. Even Roshni picked up a crème coloured parallel with a matching fitting small black top and a blue dress.

"Wise choices." Both my friends approved of the two more tight fitting ones, a dress and a skirt with matching top that I chose.

I jumped up, held out my credit card and grinned from ear to ear.

Turning to Durga and Roshni, I said, "Let's roam about."

"Yeah, we have really pampered ourselves. Now let us enjoy something else."

I pocketed the charge receipt, slid my credit card back into my wallet.

Now we three exited the shop, laughing our way through yet another escalator on the upper half of the mall.

We were loaded with shopping bags. Somehow, within three hours I accumulated what seemed like an entire wardrobe with accessories.

"I can't carry anything else." I shook my head, exhausted.

Stopping Durga snatched some of the bags from her and shoved a few to Roshni whose hands were empty except a lone packet.

"Hey!" Roshni protested, her face screwed up.

Durga and I giggled as if we were twenty-year-old college students all over again.

We barrelled through the crowd gathered around a trio of men disguised as clowns to please the children and I stopped cold. I grabbed Durga's sleeve. "Do you see what I see?"

Durga stared in the same direction as me and then shook her head. "What?"

"Sandals," I whispered.

"Stop looking." Roshni wrapped her arm around my elbow. "Let's go. Do you have a free hand?"

The idea was appealing. I had a weakness for sandals. I had to buy them.

Durga gave an airy wave to the dress that she pulled out of the bag. "Free hands can be created sweetie. Matching sandals, why not?"

That was all the incentive I needed. We headed to the shoe shop.

All kinds of sandals adorned the shelves from top to bottom in all colours and sizes.

Durga tapped her lip with the finger of her free hand lifting the strappy black shoes with four-inch heels from the rack for herself. She tried them on asking for another pair of her size for herself.

"You'd have blisters and calf cramps before you'd walked a kilometre in those things." Roshni muttered.

"They are not for walking but flaunting at a party. Have some style."

Roshni's eyes danced as she commented, "ya ya make sure you don't fall head down in them."

Durga just ignored her trying on the pair.

It was some time and I was still trying to find something to match with my pink top and the blue dress.

Roshni was standing beside Durga and me continuously complaining, "I am feeling so hungry, and it's been hours since we are shopping. I'll die of starvation and dehydration and the pair of you won't even notice when I'll be buried under a mountain of shopping sacks."

"We are not supposed to hog darling. You know how the rules of the diet plan go." I rolled my eyes back on the shoes.

"But rules are supposed to be broken once in a while. That's why they are said to be rules." Roshni's voice was breathy. "I am hungry."

"We'll have something as soon as I pick mine…" I trailed off as my eyes fell on a plain gorgeous shiny pink pencil heels. I whisked them up wiggling my toes in my new sandals. Taking a few steps forward and backwards, I found them comfortable supporting my style of walk. I realised I was walking straight with a swing in my step. The catwalk imbibed in the strides I took. The lessons had polished me into becoming a lady of my own kind. The way I dressed and carried myself had made me generously confident.

Making the required payment, to Roshni's delight we three headed towards the food court that smelled gloriously of all kinds of food. South Indian, Chinese, Mughal, Thai and Italian.

"Oh God! I'm going to faint with hunger." Roshni reached the Chinese corner ordering mixed noodles.

"I'll go in for a dosa." I turned to look around for Durga who was reading the menu chart above the Pizza corner. After the payment, we three stood together with our trays of pizza, dosa and mixed noodles around a table.

Durga gave me a wicked devil of a grin over a slice of pizza. I chuckled, it was not only her, but I too was relishing every morsel of delicious food after a long time. 'Once in a while, it was ok to have what you wanted,' I remembered my yoga teacher's words.

After hours of spending quality time together, buying little stuff, window shopping we stepped out of the mall with our shopping bags.

Then enjoying a few minutes of city drive I dropped Durga and Roshni peeling off towards my home.

I returned, exhausted and flopped down on the bed, dropping my heavy shopping bags on the floor.

The unforgettable day had bought sunshine once again in my life.

CHAPTER29

A day with my best friends was a treat for me. A day for myself was the perfect antidote to the mother and wife's blahs. But though the frequent breaks were fun time I had the most adorable husband who always missed me. I fancied every moment I spent with him and with the passing years it was this man who had been the king of my life and I his queen.

As I was settling his cupboard my eyes fell on the T-shirt which I had brought for him years ago which I clearly remembered he cherished. And still, he kept it as a memory.

I was jolted out of my thoughts when a pair of hands enclosed my waist. I knew it was his loving touch.

"I caught you, Roshni." Kunal's voice was a smooth sonat breath.

I giggled when I turned and circled my arms around his neck. His deep almond eyes stirred all the memories inside me, churning them with fresh spurts of longing and love. The echoes of his words you are my inspiration, my everything, during our courtship were till date the same giving a feeling of warmth. We were together in all the ups and downs of life, in our struggles, in our childish fights but never was a time we were away from each other.

"I think I'll have to trap you in our house else I might lose my wife's sight in the blink of a second."

I knew I was spending more time away from home, but there were Smita's problems and she needed me.

"I'm already trapped by your love dear… but." I linked my hand with his and sighed. "It's Smita."

"Oh yes." He instantly watched me with speculative eyes knowing Smita's problem and in a way, he was a pillar of support in her matter.

"How are the classes going for the competition?"

"Good and Smita is doing well. Just a few weeks are left and she needs just a little more push. I'm sure she's going to make it."

"I trust your judgement. And what about Avinash?"

"He needs a good jolt to realise her worth. Her change is not affecting him much, but I know she will shake him up. It's just a matter of time. Anyways he is out of station."

"Certainly Smita is a friend of my wife and if I can revolve around this silly and naughty girls little finger I can see Avinash's future taking a major summersault." He winked at me.

"Really!" The sandwiched layers of his belly which overpowered his waist over the years teeter-tottered as I tickled him and he ran outside with me after him. I eyed him as a mini Hotei who was the cutest jolly.

For minutes bouts of hilarity kept us engaged. I told him about Durga as well and also about the plans of going out with my friends today. He always gave a supportive smile, but now it was time for him to go to the office.

"Have a great day," I told him as I kissed him on his way

out the door to work.

As an executive in a Multi National company he often worked for long hours.

I stood in the doorway and watched as my husband backed the car out of the garage. Kunal paused halfway down the driveway, rolled down his window, and called out, "what time will you be home?"

"I won't be late. Ten at the absolute latest. That okay?"

I felt a bit silly asking my husband the permission to stay out, but he often got anxious when I got late.

His worried look was perturbing and he deserved to be happy for all he did for me over the years and so I tried my best to do the needful.

His lips curved warmly. "My Rani, of course, and enjoy yourself."

I smiled at him and said, "I love you."

He confessed the same and I waved him goodbye as the gates enclosed behind his Scorpio.

Saturday offcourse and it was our hair that needed some treatment. We were to meet at the saloon I recollected.

I walked towards my garden to hear the coo-coo of the cuckoo bird that was a melodious sound of a harp to my ears. And as it semi- circled its way around the orange bush I saw a mother squirrel busily feeding bread crumbs to her baby and I supposed the father was lazily hanging his tail on the thin twig with legs parted as if he was surfing under the cosiness of the morning sun. I was careful not to disturb them, but I counted my blessing of having the same beautiful family

CHAPTER 30

I was given strict instructions to get my hair cut, in order to complete the makeover. Roshni, Durga and I took advantage of it being a Saturday and there being no classes today to pamper ourselves. I wore one of my new outfits, black Capri's with an elastic waist and a matching top whose neckline, armholes and hem was circled with checks. It was a more pleasant, if less atmospheric drive on a sunny morning through the Delhi traffic.

We had agreed to meet at the salon suggested by Aneesha. It was one of the classiest Indian salon in South Delhi operating since twenty years in the field of hair and beauty. The beauty salon offered a unique blend of Indian-Ethnic looks and Euro-American styles providing you with the most exquisite and exotic ambience and traditional warmth. Roshni and I arrived at the same time, whereas Durga arrived just a few minutes apart. Roshni was dressed in her usual pencil jeans and a T-shirt whereas Durga's dress caught my attention. A simple blue colour top that left her arms bare and black pants, it showed her toned gorgeous figure. Her flame tipped hair tumbled gloriously over her shoulders. It was obvious that she didn't need a haircut; the wild disarray suited her personality perfectly.

"God Durga, you are looking just amazing! That outfit is really looking good on new. It is a definite improvement from the outfit I saw you dressed in the first day." I remarked impressed.

"Same goes to you darling. You are looking like one hot chick with a slim waistline." Durga said with a smile on her face.

"If the mutual admiration society is over then let's go!" Roshni interrupted linking her arms with ours and pushing Durga and me inside.

The staff was efficient and as soon as we entered the reception area we were asked about our requirements.

"I have booked an appointment for three people in the name of Mrs Sharma." I peeped in the diary kept in front for appointments.

The woman checked it and nodded. "Yes, madam, please come this way."

I walked inside greeted by my reflection on the two huge mirrors on both sides of the salon, with a row of chairs that were filled with women of all age groups. Some were getting facials done, some haircuts and a few threading. We crossed the room into another room where more chairs were placed that were empty.

The staff offered elegance and warmth, making us comfortable in chairs.

A small, squat woman wearing a pink and white uniform stood behind my chair. I glanced at the name tag. Her name was Angela. "Madam, what would you like to get done?"

My mouth dry I looked at Angela through the tall mirror in front. "I want to get my hair cut… something trendier."

Angela removed the band from my hair; dividing sections of it, she studied the same. Finally, she responded, "Madam, your hair is long and silky, but it is sticking up at the end." She picked a book kept on the table, flipping it open she showed me a style that would look good on me. "Your best look depends on your hair texture and your face shape. This style works best with fine to thick straight hair like yours. Plus, you need to get your greys coloured."

I knew I had to colour my hair, but the model's hair was considerably shorter than mine. "I don't want to lose my length." I protested pressing my lips together. I didn't want to let go of my hair. What if they did not grow again?

"Ma'am the ends are damaged, you have split ends!" Angela insisted brushing a hand down my hair.

"Smita, your hair at the ends look like they have been attacked by a buzz saw. Let the woman do her job for God's sake!" Roshni declared her feet were submerged in water being cleaned by a woman, whereas another woman was scrubbing her hands.

Roshni liked to keep her hair short for convenience in work not liking the hassles of long hair. "Easy for you to say! You never had long hair! But me…"

"Even I want to add something," Durga butted in. She lounged in the chair beside me, her feet propped on another chair. Her face was covered with a yellow face mask, her eyes were closed with two cucumber slices placed on them. Without moving a facial muscle, she just moved her lips. "Your hair is long and silky but, they are dull! It needs to be cut sweetheart because it makes you look soooooo boring and old!"

I swivelled around and grabbed at her cucumber.

"Hey!" Durga jerked, shot up and gaped at me. "Watch it!"

The other cucumber slid down and got, stuck to her cheek.
"Give my cucumber back!" Durga shouted and grabbed the
cucumber from my hand.
Laughter bubbled from my throat and out of my mouth.
"Fine, as you say!"
Durga snickered, but her lips quirked. "Well, I always have
the last say!" She again flopped back on the chair and placed
the cucumber on her eyes.
Roshni reached over to squeeze my shoulder. "Smita just
relax and enjoy the experience."
I leant my head back and tried to relax as Angela started her
work.
I sat looking docile for the entire procedure as the
hairdresser washed my hair, snipped, tugged, brushed and
combed them. I closed my eyes as she snipped more, my
glorious hair, which I hadn't cut since years except for a trim
was gone! Woof! Next, she coloured the hair finally blow
drying it.
I looked at the mirror and then looked again. Was it me? Or
some younger woman?
It looked stylish and adorable when the dresser was through.
A side part enhanced my cheekbones. My hair was in long
layered wavy shag with a long, heavy, sexy side swept bang.
All of it framed my face setting of my features, somewhat
making my face look slimmer. And definitely no greys!
 "Wow!" Roshni gave me the once-over.
Durga whistled. "Who is this young lady?"
God, it was such a boost for my ego. "Do I really look okay?"
"You have been transformed into something magical. It
looks sexy and young like you are yourself." Roshni put in.
"It looks better than your long hair. You have been
converted from mother earth into a movie star in just an

hour at Angela's hands." Durga remarked.

I snorted with glee. Nobody had ever said that I looked like a movie star. Swept by affection, I leapt up and grabbed Durga's face in my hand planting a noisy kiss on her cheek.

"Well, look at this!" Roshni sounded amused.

"I've got one for you also." I turned towards Roshni and gave her the same treatment.

"Sweet God, what got you so emotional?" Durga chuckled.

"I never had anyone tell me I looked like a movie star," I replied happily.

"You can count on us, baby." Durga gave me a hard squeeze. "Now your new look calls for a celebration! An all-girls night!"

It was amazing what new clothes could do for a person. Of course, it didn't hurt to have a new body and hairdo to go with it. I was excited for the all-girls night, feeling just a tiny wit guilty of leaving my children for a night stay with Roshni's children at home with Kunal. That man was a gem of a person. Roshni was very lucky to have him. Durga's boys were grown up aged fifteen and thirteen so she didn't have a problem.

Going out behind Avinash's back because he was out of the station was making me a little jittery. But for the first time in years, I wanted to do things without a husband and children. Suddenly, I didn't want to be anyone's wife or anyone's mother. I wanted to get in the car and let my hair down with two women who were my friends.

With a last guilty glance at my house, I practically ran towards the waiting car in which Durga and Roshni were already seated. A minute later and I was in the car and leant back against the seat smiling. In front of me was a whole night of freedom where I could be that young girl again without any responsibilities of proving myself, of taking care of my household and twenty other things that I was supposed to do. For a moment I closed my eyes, realising that I had not been to a discotheque in ten years, in which world was I living? Suddenly a laugh escaped me. Startled, I opened my eyes to see Roshni grinning at me. Durga was driving.

"Glad to get away?" She asked, sensing my happiness.

"You can't imagine," I replied with feeling.

Roshni squeezed my hand in understanding. Roshni had found her place and so had Durga, only I was searching for mine and felt it was just in my reach. I worked up a smile at her, then leaned my head against the seat and closed my eyes, feeling the best I had felt in a long time.

CHAPTER 31

I entered the hotel's lobby and watched myself walk in an attire-nothing more than a long black velvet dress without a frill or flounce whose surface sparkled like gems from top till bottom that sent off an icy glitter. It dropped square at the bodice from thin straps and fell with just the most subtle of flares to the ankles. A single diamond pendant adorned my neck clearly visible above the boat neck of the dress. I wore a marvellous deep maroon lipstick fluffing my long curly hair sweeping them past my shoulders.

I pursed my lips, liking the radiant red dress over Roshni's thin waist. The rubies glittering in her ears were the deep colour of a pure red rose. Durga on the other side was dressed in a plain dress knee length which I must say she carried off quite well. Its colour a silvery blue echoed the hue of midsummer moonlight. She wore small pearl drops at her ears. Only dresses for tonight!

We moved into the expansive two-level space that came with state-of-the-art sound. With gigs and comedy events already lined up in their calendar, we were told to expect a lot.

My eyes fell on the bar area, a spot with a vast wall display of all their spirited offerings apart from the giant hanging bulbs lit stairway.

Soon all three of us came out in the opening, looking around marvelling the outdoor deck seating that seemed to be quite popular.

When I looked at the stage I saw it was clustered with all kinds of young men and women, a mix of fair and the bright with hands sassily on their hips and legs flying. The music was just one bond.

I could not be considered part of the crowd; the truth was I wondered why I had come here.

Then the peppy music, the vibrant crowd and the exuberance of the young blood hugged new inspiration in me and I let the music sweep me away. Wouldn't it be wonderful after all these years to once again have a body that could leap with ease?

Every morning when I woke, I had remembered my thin body and missed it. I missed able to bend and stretch with ease and grace while performing my steps in Kathak. But now gone were the thirteen years of damage caused by gaining weight and now I would just enjoy feeling young again.

With Durga and Roshni equally excited, they started shaking themselves in tune with the peppy beats.

The rhythm of the music that had me tapping my foot probably made me step back into my olden college days. The nice retro music that made us sway with its soft music soon gave way to the hard rock style that had us stomping on our feet.

I was immersed in the dance, jumping up and down like a spring and I could feel my pulse galloping with the loud beat. It was more fun than I thought. I had completely lost it.

No one bothered to snap at you or even look at you. Everyone seemed to be in a paradise of their own, including me, who had become one of them, fulfilling my joy of dancing like an angel in heaven. There was no Avinash with whom I had to behave in a certain decorum, no duties to follow, I was a free bird not caged behind bars.

This sense of freedom was bliss. By the time everyone waited for the next music to play I was exhausted. As usual, Durga wanted something to drink, but the case was same for Roshni and me too. My throat had dried of thirst.

"Enough girls. I want something to drink."

"Me too." Roshni took a moment to catch her breath catching a glimpse of Durga who seemed to scan the area for drinks.

"We have to go there." I pointed ahead to an opening from where I saw boys and girls carrying glasses in their hands. Crossing the short distance between the crowd, we entered a small place that was a nice surprise. It was quite shiny; well lit, which was a positive surprise compared to all those ultra modern, fully lit youngster places one could see nowadays everywhere.

Amongst cocktails, they had the regulars — Margarita, Pina Colada, Bloody Mary, Gimlet and Screwdriver.

Roshni and Durga on either side of me were leaning onto the single menu card in my hand. "Here are the mocktails." Fingering the drinks one by one we whispered into each other's ears, "the speciality is Cool Breeze, Full Time Lover, and Fruit Punch."

"What do you think we shall order? I'll go in for a fruit punch and you both."

They were still thinking when I called the bartender. "One fruit punch please." I ordered followed by Roshni who asked for a cool breeze and Durga a full-time lover, all three of us wanting to try the different drinks.

He handed us the drinks.

I sniffed it. "Good timing all around if this tastes as good as it smells."

"I'm sure you'll like it, ma'am." His smile stayed in place as I handed him the money.

I sipped into the lovely flavours of the fruits that were naturally sweet and a bit tangy.

"Hmm. ...Tastes good," I commented, examining the expression of both my friends who seemed to enjoy the exotic taste of the special drinks.

All around, people sat, chatted, and sipped enjoying each other's company. Comfortable and comforted.

I turned and saw a young man coming towards us, most probably for a drink. His looks, black glossy hair, high cheekbones, the sooty eyes and full appealingly wicked mouth made him, in my opinion, a dangerously handsome one. He was beautiful, with a dark beauty, the sharp bones sculpted under the white skin. He was tall, but not powerfully built with a graceful, elegant body. Any woman could have fallen in love with the fairytale look of him as I fantasised him coming from some white palace.

"Good evening, beautiful lady," he drawled, with a broad smile.

Excuse me! I had to untangle my tongue. His light brown eyes were so clear in the light. If I looked into them deeply enough, I could see myself reflected back. They were alluring.

"Can I have the pleasure of dancing with you?"

That was kind of offer he was making. My goodness, he was flirting with me. I tilted my head, running a hand through my hair looking at the mischievous grins of both Durga and

Roshni. I glared at them in utter shock as if to say what the hell is happening! But they kept silent, trying to cover their mirth behind their hands. Durga winked at me and shoved her head as an indication to look in front again.

The young man had already had his hand displayed before me.

"Listen, I'm not interested." I faced looking at the front sipping into the juice.

Roshni shrugged my arm with her elbow and spoke in a low whisper, "what's the harm in dancing with him? He's so handsome. He looks decent."

"Are you mad?" I snubbed her.

Again the man's head came up between us and his eyes met the brown ones of mine.

I was feeling weird. Odd… strange. Gosh, it was so embarrassing.

"Just one dance... please." He insisted in a tone sweeter than honey. His voice was beautiful as well.

Looking up at him under my lashes I broke into a half smile. "Ok."

"Ah… thank you." He took my hand in his. My hand trembled from his fingertips as he moved onto the dance floor.

I could see Durga moving closer to Roshni to get a better look, throwing back her head and laughing.

I laid a hand on his shoulder still hesitant while he laid his on my waist.

The slow movement of the steps in sync with the soft beats of music picked up and I became comfortable to move around on the floor.

"You are very beautiful."

I felt a small pleasure. I didn't know I needed to be told that or that it was what I always wanted from Avinash as he hadn't given me the part of me I wanted from him. He was flirting with me. I may have been out of practice and short on experience, but I knew when a man was flirting.

My voice crackled down, "thank you. Hmm... you come here often." I tried to change the topic.

"Not much. Just once in a while."

"Oh... I see."

A minute of silence, I felt his eyes were staring at me now-long speculative looks when he asked again, this time more softly, "are you married?"

Married Oh yes, unfortunately. A single word that would break the man's, heart. I did not realise he was thinking so far.

I did not answer as he circled me around in his arms.

"As soon as I saw you I knew it that you are a lovely soul. It's a gift you have."

Oh my God! Here was a man who had such gifts of words in one who understood what's inside a person sometimes before that person knows. It was just a little frightening.

He waited in patience for me to say something.

"I am just a tidy soul. This is my first time in a disco after a long span of time and it's just a simple outing. Not used to discos and stuff like that."

I thought the young man would find me a bore, but he seemed to like what I said. It seems I had more skill in flirtation than Avinash gave me credit for.

"I think like me you are working on getting to know yourself a little better. We are different than the rest. I like you." I pinked and fluttered at that.

He started to touch my hair, but I edged back and he simply retreated back. My left eye started twitching a sure sign that

I was nervous.

"I'm sorry. I can't. I have something important coming up." A knot formed in my belly.

"You do not have to hunt for excuses I can understand." He took my hand again kept his fingers light when mine jerked. "There's a line between making a woman nervous and scaring her. I will not cross that line. When you'll get to know me better you will believe in me. You are pure like an angel! You are like a flower!"

He said with such earnest intention that the ground seemed to slip away under my feet. Angel! Pure! Flower!! Oh God, was he normal? Who said such things to a woman on the first meeting? Worse, he was serious!

I was half angry, but more than anything else it was a funny thing that I mused, a young man falling for a woman about five years older. Some part of me was happy entitled to a time of pleasure, but the rest of it knew it was going too far. I stepped back, taking a firm stand. "I'm married with two children."

I bit down hard on my lip, studying his tragic expression. Everything went still, it seemed like a film stopped in a freeze-frame. His stillness was as if he had felt the slice through his heart.

Nothing I could have said would have stunned him more. It wasn't just shock. A few minutes ago, he stared at me as if he knew me since ages and now he stared at me as if I were a stranger.

I spun away from him and I caught the way he flinched at the move.

I rushed to Roshni and Durga whom I gave a shocked stare. "Let us leave this place right now," I demanded.

"Why? You have more courage than I gave you credit for.

You have become a heartthrob. A bold beauty." Durga
tapped her fingers on the glass in her hand with the music.
"I wish you'd shut up."
"What happened?" Durga's eyes went to slits.
"I said right now." I grabbed Roshni's hand, hauling her
outside.
Durga slammed the glass on the table and scrambled behind
us.

"Now tell us what went wrong. We could have stayed a little
longer." Roshni gave a measuring look as she fell in line with
me for a walk towards the car.
"Oh yes! We were enjoying the party, especially your
dance." Durga beamed a mischievous smile at me.
"This is no joke, friends! Enough of teasing! That man
embarrassed me. In fact, he scared the hell out of me. He got
attracted to an extent that he was on the verge of proposing
to me. He thought I was his soul mate!"
Roshni's mouth turned up and brought out a hint of
dimples. "A handsome and romantic supposedly a charmer
became dazzled and flattered by our young Smita."
I could feel my eyelashes curling upwards in
embarrassment. "No one has ever hit on me before like this.
When he hit on me… the first few words were a shock. I was
being so stupid or clumsy in dancing with him. Oh God if I
hadn't told him about my marriage, he was sure not to leave
me. He was really working on it, you know... He said he
liked me, but the seductive dizzy look in his eyes spoke more
than words. It was as if he was trying very hard to make me
fall in love with him."
Roshni and Durga blinked a couple of times before Roshni
said, "really! How did you knock him down?"

"I said I was married. As simple as that."

Durga looked disgusted waving a hand in the air as we moved to the side of the pavement. "You could have had a little fun. Well, it's not every day that a young man is interested in you and says nice words."

Nice words. Suddenly the hilarity of the situation hit me when I remembered his nice words. "He said I was pure like an angel!"

"What!" Roshni exclaimed, as her face lit up in merriment. Durga batted her lashes. "My pure angel! My... My seeker of pure love, he doesn't know what a devil you can be!"

"Angel landed right out of heaven," Roshni added and there were bursts of laughter.

Laughter rose into my throat as I remembered his expression. "He even said that I was a flower."

With a rumbling chortle, Durga hooted, "God! Can you beat that! A flower which one?"

Red rose, daffodil, carnations... The names of all kinds of flowers flashed in my mind. By now I had caught on the humour of the situation and was laughing so badly that there were tears in my eyes as we crossed over the tracks and climbed the walkway.

As we walked on, out of the blue Roshni said, "poor man. I feel sorry for him."

I could find nothing more constructive to do than huff out my breath on hearing that. "Really?!" My voice was high pitched, almost a squeal. "Sorry for him, but what about me for listening to all this crap!"

I punched Roshni on her arm, mimicking her. "You said he seems decent. There's no harm in dancing with a decent man." I rubbed the particle of sweat on my forehead with my palm. "But more likely he was a quack! And you know what the worst part we didn't even exchange names. How silly can it get?!"

There were fresh bursts of laughter at my comment. I laughed until my jaw ached. Durga doubled over, feigning pain. "My stomach is aching now stop it. How much fun will we make of him? I can't handle it anymore."

Roshni smirked, opening the car's door. "You must be hungry!"

"Mommy! How did you know?" Durga threw her arms around Roshni.

Snickering, Roshni shoved Durga aside and got into the car. They were at it again, like Tom and Jerry.

Both kept joking and making fun the entire way, till they dropped me and drove home.

I tiptoed to my room changed into my night clothes. I didn't expect to sleep but I slept as soon as my head hit the pillow. I closed my eyes and imagined myself once again in the disco with my friends. The music, the long shrill cries of the crowd made me turn into a little dance of my own. And then the image of the man materialised before my eyes, his way of seducing me, his innocent, charming look in the open on a moonlit night, stars spilling out the light like liquid silver. A handsome young man who thought I was beautiful. It looked like something off the pages of a fairy tale.

Instantly I jerked upwards. God, I ran my fingers through my hair. I could almost convince myself that what I'd seen in the moonlight had been nothing more than a wild dream. I hadn't wanted to admit, but the idea of someone liking you was vastly appealing.

The first rays of dawn banked the horizon as I sat on the edge of the mattress, smiling to myself. I had deflected an overture from an attractive man, me Smita who was fat and ugly. I was amused and delighted remembering how Roshni had made me feel so important. The way Durga had held her aching stomach rolling into peals of laughter. The entertainment that all three of us had done so discreetly was an experience of a lifetime.

It had been the best night of my life. I didn't care how pathetic it sounded, I thought as I ducked my head through the nightgown. It had been wonderful, the talk and the laughter and the foolishness. The two very interesting women in my life enjoyed with me and made me feel part of what we had together.

A friendship just as easy as that. It was all about how I felt. I really liked it.

I climbed out of my bed, wincing, then grinning when my legs pounded. It was my very first late night party with friends after marriage. It was marvellous!

I tiptoed out, took my shower under the nice water that felt awesome soothing my nerves, enjoying the after effects of the nightlife.

Humming and singing a melodious tune I stepped out to dry off. I wrapped a towel around myself figuring something good to wear by cruising my wardrobe. Finally, I dressed myself in a flowered spring dress and a matching jacket.

My clothes were a reflection of who I was. At least of how I saw myself. And why shouldn't I be flattered that a young handsome man admired my clothes and my looks?

I smiled, then with my hair a dripping mass of curls, I looked at my face.

Though a little guilty that I was not thinking about Avinash, after all, I was legally married and loved my husband, but still, the thought made me giddy. I walked into my room, glancing at the bedside clock. "Oh shit, it was seven am. I am running late!"

I was embarrassed at having been in such a deep thought that I lost track of time, but there was something, I decided, very comfortable about feeling female again.

CHAPTER 32

The last weeks of summer passed in a blur just two weeks were left for the competition. Durga's and Roshni's classes were over, but because I was taking part in Mrs Perfect competition I was given extra classes on public speaking, improving my walk and how to handle myself in public. The sessions were gruelling and I missed my friends terribly. I was instructed to read the newspaper regularly plus I was given topics to speak on. This was the worst because I would be overcome with bouts of nervousness.

The first time when I was told to speak in front of an audience of fifty, as I stood in front of them sweat ran cold and clammy on my skin. I gave a single look of fear and shot out of the room's door, nausea hitting me and I stumbled to the bathroom, hideously ill.

The next time was a little better, I did not run, but stood grounded my legs quaking unable to speak. The third time Roshni and Durga decided to stay with me. They sat in the audience to bolster my courage. After four or five times, I became better and after ten sessions I was a pro.

Avinash was still not back from his business trip, it had been more than a month since he was gone and would be coming back next week. I was sure, even he would be surprised to see me. I was losing weight steadily and if I continued to lose more I would either have to go shopping again or get the new clothes altered. The life I had always looked for was around me and more. I felt a confidence inside me that ran like silver. Only a few months before I had taken a risk and for months following I was working hard.

Now that only a few days were left, it was now that mattered and I was giving it all I could. I had even stopped dwelling on the past. The past was the past and it could not be changed. And I didn't even want to change it because it had made me the person I was today. A better person and a better mother.

My children were my biggest support, the darlings ate their lunch and dinner without a fuss, completed their homework and would be always there to help. They loved to listen to what I did and the things I learnt. Those times in the night when we sat together and discussed our day were precious and unforgettable. A new bond was forged I was not only a mother, but also a friend and guide. I just loved the respect my children showed me.

The next session was an all important counselling one with Karen where she would be deciding further classes for me. I just prayed I would pass her test.

CHAPTER 33

I was sitting waiting for Smita to come inside. I had to decide whether more grooming was required and adequate confidence had been instilled in Smita. According to my staff and Karen Verghese staff was the best there was a remarkable change in Smita and more sessions were not needed, but I had to see for myself.

There was a knock and as soon as Smita entered the room, I stood up and circled my desk towards her. Her head held high she walked towards me. I stepped back to get a better look at her. I watched wide-eyed because it was as though I was seeing movie special effect take place in front of me. Smita was dressed in a classy black shirt that was tucked into her dark blue jeans. A belt completed the outfit emphasizing her tiny waist. She had scored high points by matching her belt's colour with the colour of her shoes. Standing in front of me in her plain black blouse and blue jeans, with her glowing skin, she looked like a perfect pearl beside a bed of aquarium grave. Her hair was open, lightly streaked in rich mahogany hiding her greys and highlighting her features. They were cut in the latest style chic, bouncy and seemed to be glistening under the LED lights. Her makeup was so flawless; it looked like she wasn't wearing any. A black bag completed the picture. Years seemed to be sliding of Smita, along with the extra weight.

This was definitely not the same woman who had first appeared in my office. This woman was a man-eater all confident dragoness. I was pleased with the thought until I wondered what would now happen to her husband. I gave a secretive little smile liking the thought.

"Smita may I see that walk again," I requested aloud.

Smita walked back towards the door and then again walked towards me. Her gait was steady, confident with a little swish in her hips making her look sexy. Now I was looking at her, comparing the woman who had come to me earlier. She had become beautiful inside and out.

"Take a seat dear."

Smita took the seat, sitting with her back straight, her legs tucked daintily.

"Well, I really don't know is this Smita? Or someone else?" I could see her visibly relax when I asked the question.

"The one who had come earlier was not Smita, but who has come today is Smita."

Smita's voice had also become firm and confident. I gave her a one-sided grin, this woman was no longer beat up with life, and she could take life head on now. There was light in Smita's eyes and the light seemed to illuminate her skin from beneath it.

Reaching out, I put my hand over hers that were kept on the desk. "So now how are you feeling?"

She clasped mine lightly. "I can't describe it. I never thought I could look like this or take charge of my life. It seems all of a sudden I have so much."

"Why shouldn't you have all that and more?"

For a moment Smita blinked at me. "I never felt smart enough, attractive enough, clever enough, beautiful enough or confident enough." Her eyes clouded. "Looking back I can't see why I felt so inadequate. I believe that it was not Avinash who made me feel that way but myself. But you know I think I was meant to be that way, feel that way so that step by step my life would lead me right here. I regret nothing now."

I disengaged my hand and settled back on the chair. "Then my work has been done, dear."

Smita looked surprised.

"I have managed to help you in finding yourself. The Smita who was lost beneath layers of fat, inferiority and doubts no longer exist. You are ready."

"You mean now my classes are over," Smita said so softly that I could just barely hear her.

"Yes!" I extended my arm again for a handshake. "It's over."

Smita shook hands with me. Then she did something that surprised me, she got up and circled the desk to stand in front of me. I stood up and was instantly enveloped in a warm hug. Smita whispered in my ear, "thanks for everything."

Emotion seemed to overcome me and it took me a moment to calm myself as I took Smita's hand in mine. "You're welcome and trust me the pleasure was all mine."

She nodded and turned, walking towards the door.

"Oh, and Smita." I stopped her, who then looked at me questionably. I couldn't prevent myself from uttering, "After winning Mrs. Perfect, the first autograph is mine."

Her eyes were sparkling. "It's a deal, Karen!"

CHAPTER 34

Tomorrow was the big night. I still hadn't told Avinash about it. I didn't know what was holding me, maybe I was a coward, but it wasn't a very comfortable feeling. I had never hidden anything from my husband. Avinash was back today. I decided to tell him after the dinner that we were hosting for his friend Sanjiv.

The sound of the car pulling into the driveway diverted everyone's attention.

"Uncle has come," Samarth announced, peeling back the curtain and looking out of the window.

In a moment, the bell rang and as the door was opened, a man with a friendly, open face stepped inside over the tile floor with its colourful mosaics. "Hey, it's me."

Sanjiv was full of life and boyish humour. The children crossed the room greeting him filled with excitement at seeing the basket of chocolates in his hand.

In no time the same was out of his hand and the children rushed into their room to savour them.

Sanjiv Singh was Avinash's school friend who had come to meet us after a long time. He was about the same height, but thinner than Avinash. Being a successful businessman and a bachelor, his fair and charming ways attracted every single woman in town. He was garbed in an elegant dark suit. His mane of black hair swept back from a strong face.

Avinash stared at his lifelong friend, a smile stretching across his face; he greeted him with a warm hug. "How have you been yaar? It's been a long time since we had spent time together. Come make yourself comfortable."

Avinash guided him towards the sofa closest to where they stood.

I came down the rest of the stairs from where I was observing them, adjusting my right earring. I had worn a fitting black kurti and pencil blue jeans, letting my hair hanging loose in soft glistening curls. This was the first time I had dressed after Avinash had come back. I was desperately waiting for his reaction.

Suddenly Sanjiv's gaze flickered towards me with undisguised curiosity.

He said with a ready smile, "my goodness Smita. I must say you look gorgeous."

I did not know what to say and felt shy. Actually, a compliment from a man other than my husband was surprising. I flushed with a pleasure and found myself smiling as well. I acknowledged him. "Thank you."

Soon I found myself being studied by Avinash who came to stand beside me. He was looking at me from the top of my head to my toe. Like a woman! By heaven, he was looking at me as if he had seen me for the first time. The single-minded intensity with which I was being studied was rapidly stripping me of all my composure.

"Yes, actually dear, you have become a model. You are looking younger. Heavenly, I mean lovely. With the gold winking in your ears and around your throat, you look like rich honey."

Surprisingly, I seemed to have heightened Sanjiv's senses. I stood speechless for a moment and cleared my throat. "Care for some snacks."

Avinash merely nodded, a slight inclination of his head, and I took a step towards the kitchen, only to stop nervously when he made no move to let me pass. Raising my eyes, I opened my mouth to speak only to find my mind a vacuum. He gazed down at me for another unnerving moment and then moved away.

My mind fidgeted to ease the sudden tension and I walked into the kitchen. Carrying a tray of stuffed corn potatoes, I offered it to Sanjiv first.

Sanjiv's ready smile warmed me as he picked up a piece. Plopping it into his mouth, he immediately offered his appreciation. "Delicious Smita."

"Smita has turned out to be a wonderful cook and a smart beauty," Sanjiv said companionably making himself at home, as he took the tray from my hand, offering the snack to Avinash.

"I know better, after all, she is my wife." Avinash's words were precise and hard.

I couldn't be sure, but I thought I heard a note of reproach in his voice and wondered at its cause.

"So when did you come back from Bangaluru?" I asked Sanjiv to change the topic.

"Just a day ago. A business trip to Mumbai, to Goa and finally Bangaluru was a hectic one. However, I couldn't get a better deal. I managed to get a contract."

"That's exceptional. I always knew you were good at your work, but I hope you pay the taxes on time," I asked tongue in cheek.

Sanjiv laughed. "A smart one! You know how to hit a punch. I like your sense of humour."

I couldn't help being flattered by Sanjiv. Soon the helper got a tray of drinks accepted graciously by Sanjiv and the rest.

Sanjiv's black eyes danced as he turned and chatted with me, "I can't say when I enjoyed anything more."

He picked up another snack.

"Thank you." I nodded appreciatively.

Sanjiv glanced at Avinash. "This is the best part of being married Avinash. A wife who knows the way to a man's heart. Dignified and talented."

Avinash did not respond, but slightly tilted his head in agreement or disagreement. I again couldn't be sure, but nevertheless, his gesture was cold now.

Again Sanjiv's gaze returned to me and I felt the blush infuse my cheeks with colour. It seemed both men were studying me and uncomfortable, I returned to the kitchen to pay attention to the evening meal.

With my departure, the two men spoke easily for several minutes, then stood and wandered outside into the open. It was an hour or so later when they strolled back into the house.

Peering out the swinging kitchen door, I invited everyone into the formal dining room. "Dinner is ready. To the table, gentlemen. C'mon kids come to the table." I did my best to sound cheerful.

With everyone accumulated around the dining table, I gestured Sanjiv to sit down and begin.

"I'd be honoured to join you. As it is food smells awesome. Definitely, it's going to be delicious as well." Sanjiv sounded almost gleeful, staring at the huge bowls of food kept on the table.

I knew I'd made a mistake when I looked at Avinash. He was frowning and seemed withdrawn throughout the meal, which turned out to be something of an uncomfortable ordeal. But the children helped to carry the dinnertime conversation, Samarth plying Sanjiv with a variety of questions, especially regarding their favourite game Cricket. "Home food is the best and if Smita makes such scrumptious dishes I would land up coming here almost every day."

It made matters worse when Avinash started to cough with the gulp of water locked down his throat. Sanjiv instantly stroked his chest, making him drink more water, but Avinash shrugged him off by saying, "leave me. I am fine." But I knew he wasn't fine. He was cranky and restless.

The dinner was over in five minutes from then. Sanjiv gushed his final compliment of me being a wonderful host leaving my husband emotionally disturbed.

I obliged with a half-smile taken over by Avinash who escorted him out of the main door. I saw both friends laughing at something and shaking hands. Usually, Avinash sat for a longer time after dinner with Sanjiv but on the pretext of waking up early to go for some important work, he got rid of his school friend at the earliest.

By the time, I finished assembling the crockery in the kitchen with the help of the maid and bidding my children goodnight, who dispersed from the hall to their room the back door opened and Avinash stepped inside the kitchen. "I want to talk to you." He spit out the words stormily. "I hope you have not forgotten that you are a married woman with two children. And someone's wife who happens to be me! Married woman do not flirt with other men. I would appreciate that you stay away from Sanjiv."

"You mean flirting with Sanjiv. Me!" I was so aghast it took a moment for me to believe my ears. "Perhaps speaking to you on this subject now isn't a good idea," I said, waving my hand in a dismissive gesture.

"Why not?"

"Because I do not want to say something that goes against my dignity as a woman that I shall regret later."

"Like what, if I may ask?"

"As if you can bear to hear."

"I can bear to hear anything except see my wife behaving so vulnerably in front of my best friend. If you think that's so objectionable then we can clear the air right now."

My heart was broken into pieces. We stood half a kitchen apart physically. No, we were half a universe emotionally. Avinash was more than unreasonable, he was insulting.

"Sanjiv was gawking at you, and you were ready to eat it up." Avinash cleared the distance between both of us piercing into my eyes.

"What...what is wrong with your brains. I was ready to eat up...gawking...?" I was so furious even to speak coherently. Mentally, I became blank for a few seconds before I regained my senses, attempting to make sense of his accusations.

"You are nothing more than domineering, pig-headed and unreasonable. After all these years of being with me and knowing me, this is what you give me. Sometimes I feel how I stayed married to a man like you have? You have not only insulted me, but you do not even trust me."

"Trust you when you are going agog over Sanjiv."

"Agog? I did nothing. You invited him to dinner and me as your wife acted as any other host."

"And you got attracted to him."

I flashed an angry look at him, suspecting whether he was

drunk. I smelled him by coming closer, but he was hard and immobile. He wasn't drunk. I might have deemed this a sick joke if his eyes hadn't been so intense.

I froze in disbelief. Avinash honestly believed his friend was captivated by me. I who had never talked to men was being accused of being a woman of shallow character. What enthralled Sanjiv more than the stimulating conversation was the home cooked food, but Avinash took it in the wrong sense.

"He was charming you and the same was oozing out of you. Honey was pouring out of your mouth ready to flow into his hands." Each word hit me like an iron rod into my chest hard and painful.

"You make me sound like a slut," I whispered on the verge of tears pressing my fingertips to my temple. It was impossible to reason with a man who was bitter and revengeful. He had already put me on a trial and judged me finding me guilty and nothing I could do to defend myself.

"You are horrible." I broke into tears, turned and walked out of the kitchen into the bedroom.

I cried and cried tears flowing continuously. My heart sank to the pit of my stomach. He was jealous, pure and simple. It was all right if he complimented Shalini but another man could not compliment me. It all started when Sanjiv complimented me on my looks followed by the same for the snacks. It was not me, but his friend to whom he should have said all that.

Avinash had never realised my worth, but when anyone did, he was being sarcastic and jealous about the whole affair, making a mountain out of a molehill.

I lay to the farthest corner of the bed with closed eyes. It was the sound of a loud bang that woke me up. Startled, I reached for the lamp switch on the nightstand. I saw the interesting entry of my dear husband who went inside the bathroom and came out in his night suit banging the door of the bathroom even louder. I immediately got down from the bed, picking up my pillow and as I moved in the other direction, I happened to bang into Avinash who was crossing me.

"Damn you, woman now you are trying to hit me. First mentally and now physically."

I blinked. A slow, angry resentment festered within me. One time after a particularly bitter quarrel with Avinash, I had told about the same to Linda, who had said something to me which I never forgot. She'd said, never fight with a husband or boyfriend if you don't look good. Looking good gives you confidence. She'd also said stand tall and don't slouch and do not ever let someone tower over you while they are talking to you. Linda said that allowing something like that was gross intimidation. Something my husband excelled in. Well, but not today or any other day now. This wasn't the old Smita. This was the new confident Smita.

"If you hadn't come in my way you wouldn't be harmed. Anyways, you should have been careful unless your eyes have weakened. I think you should get your eyes checked. You are no longer that young now."

"Really! My eyesight is good enough to see right and wrong. By the way, loosing those pounds does make you wiser that you tell me what to do."

So he had noticed. I watched him rubbing his hands in anger. He made an interesting sight standing there in his blue and red polka dot night suit. If I hadn't been furious with him I might have laughed. I should put some dressing sense into his empty brains that tended to malfunction at times.

Avinash continued to glare at me and I couldn't help remarking, "what kind of night clothes have you worn? You are looking like a clown. A clown with no head accusing a woman for something so stupid."

"A clown! You called your husband a clown. I never knew you had such a long tongue. Since when have you started speaking in an uncultured manner? Oh, now I see you want to punish me for what I said to you regarding Sanjiv." He wagged his finger at me.

I was getting irritated with the way his finger was moving. "Stop wagging your finger at my nose. Since you have forgotten how to behave in a cultured way. You need some grooming sessions to teach you a few basic manners. And yes, very wisely said you had no right to link me with your friend the way you did."

He stopped wagging his finger and folded his arms across his chest. "You don't know the outside world. You have stayed in a cocoon, how would you know how men see women. If protecting my wife from a man is wrong then I am wrong. I was merely being considerate."

"Protecting…considerate." I echoed as if the words were a source of amusement. "Right, I could see the way you proved your consideration towards me."

Avinash muttered something I couldn't hear, but from the snatches, I caught it was better I not know what he said. He marched across the room limping slightly. It was then I realised I had stamped on his little foot finger. But before I raised my hand for his help he was already on the bed.

I lay back on the bed and turned onto my right so that my back was to him. Anger boiled within me and I took out my frustration by hitting the pillow many times, punching it as if to stuff the down farther into its case.

"I don't want you to move or make noise. I want to sleep," he demanded.

I had never thought myself sarcastic, but he was bent upon bringing the worst in me. So I laughed loudly.

"Quiet," he snapped harder this time.

At my laughter that was louder, Avinash peeled back the covers with enough force to lift them away from my shoulders. I sat up, reached for the blanket and jerked it back. Avinash yanked it toward him and for one mild moment, the two of us were immersed in a furious tug of war.

"Do you mind?" I shouted, pulling it with all my might.

"Yes, I do!"

I released the grip and the blanket went slack toppling him on the floor. He took a moment to compose himself and struggling to his feet, he toppled once again on the floor in rage.

He remained silent consuming his anger and rushed to the bedside couch. He shut his eyes and turned to the other side determined to ignore me.

I switched off the light. The bedroom was bathed in a blanket of darkness, but the tension between us crackled like static electricity.

I ignored his shifting, but my chest burned with righteous indignation. My temper was frayed, to say nothing of my nerves and I was still so angry that I didn't know if I could bear to be in the same room with him and not explode.

The silence was so uncomfortable that with every passing minute I turned from side to side, then rolled onto my stomach before dozing in sleep.

I woke up with the noise of the utensils that came from the

kitchen. Wearily I got up tying my hair into a pony seeing the empty couch. I went into the washroom splashed some water on my face. Pale face and two puffy red eyes poked at me.

"Oh God, I am looking so messy."

I dried my face with a soft towel and slumbered out of the bathroom. Sitting on the bed, I looked up at the ceiling and closed my eyes. I decided if I did not do anything wrong, why should I feel guilty or sad. I stood up and took quick steps to move out of the room towards the kitchen. I drank a cup of hot tea and then prepared sandwiches for the children.

The settlement on the dining table made me uneasy; I knew Avinash was sitting there. I felt a lump in my stomach.

I did not go out instead directed the maid to serve sandwiches to children and cornflakes and milk to Anivash. Soon Naina called me out and I stiffly entered the hall. I noticed the children staring at both of us with an anxious look; they must have heard us shouting last night. I did not like their sad expression. So I ruffled Samarth's hair and pecked Naina's cheek promising them to talk about it later. After they left, I banged the glass of juice on the table without offering it to Avinash and stamped my feet. My chin came up now, a gesture of pride. I swiftly turned and ran head on heels over the stairs into my room.

In a few minutes, I showered and changed, storming down into the hall where Avinash sat hooked on to the newspaper. I knew he was at fault and it was harder for him to admit it. He was upset and angry casting furious glances at me. But I didn't take kindly to orders anymore. A few minutes later without even looking back at me he banged the main door behind him and left.

I started to tingle when I thought about talking about Avinash's behaviour to Roshni. Roshni had a good head on her shoulders. May be my friend would feel or see something I was missing. Then again, she would think I am a total nutcase taking all this nonsense for so long.

CHAPTER 35

I sat in my hot car until the air conditioning finally cooled it down. I turned the key and drove away, aimlessly driving up one street and down another. Where should I go? What should I do? Damn, what had gone wrong with Smita? In thirteen years we had never fought like this, Smita had never spoken to me like this. What had gotten into her?

Maybe I should just go back and apologise. Apologise no way! It wasn't my fault that my friend was ogling at my wife. Damn! When had my wife turn so... beautiful? How did she become so gorgeous in the last month and a half? Her words were ringing in my ears. I knew I was wrong and I hated it. As I drove I saw the tennis academy and I steered the car into the parking lot.

I walked inside; to my left was the burnt-yellow roof of the café and the smell of coffee wafted over. I turned right; to see the joggers moving around the court, while the players stood their ground, knowing the odds favour a quick blow over. I made my way to the empty tennis court where I met my second cousin Raman.

"Hi Bhai, how are you? Long time no see." He was in shorts

and white T-shirt holding a Tennis racket in his hand.
Raman was a few years younger than me blessed with a
clear skin and a sharp nose.

Raman glanced through the spectacles. "We can have a set of
tennis. I hardly get to see you these days."

I started to refuse, but reconsidered quickly willing to
change my mind from the unpleasant events.

I picked up the racket from the chair and said, "a game is on
hand."

"Absolutely perfect! Prepare yourself. I've been working on
my backhand."

I bulleted one over the net returned by a firm hit by Raman.
Sweat dampened his face, ran down his neck. His mouth
peeled in a snarl as he raced over the court. He was good at
striking, but broke his serve again while prancing around in
his designer shorts.

"You have missed the serve again Raman."

"Ya bro, you are good at it. Have to practise its putting."

"But your backhand is lethal."

Raman laughed. With his time of serving that he managed, I
blew the next return as well. The game continued, both of us
racing back and forth with the movement of the ball.

"Bhai by the way Nishi is also taking part in the Mrs Perfect
contest." Raman smashed a hit returning it to me.

With yet another strong blow, I barely was able to register
what he was trying to say.

"What contest?"

"The same contest in which Bhabhi is also taking part. The
Mrs Perfect contest for married women organised by the
ladies club. It's today. I'll be there on time to support Nishi.
So we will meet again at the club Bhai."

My expression changed almost instantly. Burying my

competitive spirit, I took a dive surrendering the game and missed my turn losing the movement of the ball that flung my left.

"So brother you've lost your chance. I've won this one."

I sent Raman an indulgent smile, as he bid me goodbye and wished me good luck. I threw the racket feeling loose and weak. Yes, I had lost my chance. There emerged a bubble of annoyance in my throat that I automatically swallowed. A storm of cold bitterness ripped my heart whose pain was unbearable. After all, Smita had made me a stranger in her life. She had taken such a major decision, not even thinking the least bit of informing me about it. She was participating in the contest. What contest! And it was today. I did not know anything about it. Maybe Raman mistook someone else for Smita. Yes, that's it! I had to go home.

As I walked on towards my car, I seemed to withdraw into my own thoughts again.

My mind raced, I stopped dead on the walkway. But she had been losing weight and yes, she had trimmed down and she was looking amazing. Was all that effort for some stupid contest or was she having an affair? Was that the reason she booted me out of her decisions. Smita having an affair! It was almost too ridiculous for words. Still, it explained her attitude towards me. After a long thirteen years of marriage with two children and a husband like me, how could she betray all of us? I had given her everything she wanted, then where did I go wrong in understanding her?

It was hard to accept disloyalty from a woman who had such warmth. Well then, maybe I should just let bad enough alone. So I decided not to talk to her anymore and let her live the way she wanted.

Damn! A clattering racket behind startled me, but it was only a street car. In a few seconds, it trundled past me and stopped.

I picked up my pace, fighting my anger and slipped into my car. The force with which I pushed hard at the accelerator set the car racing along the main road. I did not realise when I reached the house in fifteen minutes.

I just wanted to go in and have a cup of tea. But, as soon as I pulled open the house's door, I saw Smita standing alone. I could not control my emotions and clearing off the distance between her and myself, I said from behind her back, "So you do not think that I have any more value in your life Smita."

Suddenly, she turned around giving me a blank stare as if I was some dumb wit who was talking to her.

She did not seem bothered and saying nothing walked to the marble showcase to keep the cut glass inside one of its blocks.

Here she was swallowing my pride, risking my peace of mind and well-being and all I could do was give her a single icy look.

Temper was rising inside me like a tremendous wave at her arrogance desperate to flow out. "I want some answers from you and I mean it. Do you understand? I am not barking like a mad dog."

She moved like lightning towards me glaring with wide eyes. "You sure are barking like one. And what answers do you want?"

"I had met Raman at the club and it was from him that I came to know that my dear wife is taking part in the Mrs Perfect contest. My wife who was supposed to share everything with me now feels nothing for me. I am nobody for you now."

"Really? Did you have time for me? Suddenly, what has cropped up that is making you howl once again. Anyways how does my life matter to you? For you, I am only a menial servant. I am struggling for respect all the time. You do not give me time, respect or your love. You do not involve me in any of your decisions and life. I am constantly looking for it. As if now, I care. When was the last time you actually spent time with me? Hmmm… let me think. Oh yes, now I remember. It was ten years ago and later it was me alone. And you did not care for me, my emotions, then why should I involve you in my decisions?"

"Yes of course, especially when you have found someone else to replace me."

"What!" She put the back of her hand over her mouth, staring at me with wide-open eyes that were now wet and shiny.

"Speak up tell me the truth."

"The truth. You want to know the truth. The truth is that you are a sick-minded male chauvinistic pig. You have not and will never understand me or my love for you. I am not a traitor like you. You can get involved in extramarital affairs, but it is not in my blood to do such wonderful things. I do not think I owe you any explanation. Yes, I am taking part in the contest for myself and I am proud of it. Stop me if you can."

I was caught off guard by her bitter response. Before I could say anything Smita walked out on me going into the children's room.

CHAPTER 36

As soon as I entered into my children's room, both Samarth and Naina who were studying looked up towards me with a smile.

They stood, sensing my tension.

"What happened, mom?" Naina rushed at my side holding my arm, giving me a solemn look.

"Nothing." I made a valiant effort to swallow the pain Avinash had inflicted. Knowing my anxiety would alarm the children I moved away from them to the side window.

Both my children came up to me holding me tightly from both sides. My nerves were stretched taut, I did my utmost to disguise my pain from them. But I knew they had grown up and heard the tears in my voice. They noticed the traces of moisture that ran down my ashen cheeks and both of them became adamant, trying to wipe them from my face and asking me who had made their mother cry.

They forced me towards the bed, made me sit down and sat down beside my feet. With his hands on my lap, Samarth pleaded, "Mom, why are you crying? Did dad say something to you?"

My cheeks had flushed, and my eyes sought relief from Samarth's steady gaze, but I chose to be tight-lipped.

Naina was pushy in asking me all kinds of questions. "Tell us, Mom. I know something is wrong. You cannot hide it from me."

After a few minutes of their continuous questions with sincere pleadings, tears burned down my face and I opened up to them. My heart sank and I bit my bottom lip when I lost control of myself pouring my heart out. "I was taking part in the Mrs Perfect contest, but now I won't because your father does not want me to. I think I have made a terrible mistake. I wanted it to do it for myself."

I lowered my head and covered my eyes with my palms. "Ma..no ..you have done nothing wrong." Naina wiped my tears with her fingers that were soft as a feather over my skin.

I was still crying when Samarth broke into silent sobs that shook his shoulders. I felt my throat thicken when he raised his arms and hugged my middle. "Mom I cannot bear to see you cry. I love you. I am saying you will take part. That means you will take part because you want to. I am going to talk to dad. How can he say no?"

"Yes, mom. It's your life and you know what, it's a wonderful idea. I will also talk to dad about it. Mummy, we are proud of you. You are great. We both are with you and will always be. We will also surely come to support you no matter what. We don't care what dad thinks and it does not matter to us if he comes or not."

I sniffed in a dainty manner, touching my nose with a lacy handkerchief that was Naina's favourite. It was the best piece she possessed and I remembered she could not bear a spot in it, but now she parted with the same for her mother.

A memory of a stubborn girl who was her father's pet popped out of my mind. My heart had but now pronounced with such assurance and belief that she did care for her mother. Though she did not reveal her love, many times rude and mean in her mannerisms, often challenging in her approach towards me, today I saw a different girl altogether. Wise and thoughtful.

My fingers soothed her head as I tucked her against my chest and draped my arms around my son tilting my head first to kiss Samarth and then Naina. A caress, a hug even a moment of close contact like this it was becoming so blissful between us, and my heart rejoiced as Naina's hand patted with sisterly affection against Samarth's hand that surrounded me. And she pulled him in heat and annoyance. "Come let's go to dad right now." But I reached out to their arms to hold them back. "Just stay with me, my angels. I don't want you to talk to your dad. Be with me right now. Don't go anywhere."

"No mom." His chin lifted in a determined gesture.

"Please, Samarth you are my good boy. You will listen to your mother."

Samarth gave a solemn nod. "Fine." I gripped his hand, the warmth of that tender hand cradling my own with such heated comfort that I relaxed my fingers within his grip and unfurled it.

"C'mon mom, pack up everything. Make a move. Do not waste time. Let's go. We want to see you all dressed." Eager to banish the chill of the situation Naina in a thrill of anticipation of what her mother would look or do jumped around. Joined in was Samarth in this beautiful ride of excitement that was contagious, making me laugh and rejoice.

With a deeply drawn breath thoughts penetrated the agile workings of my brain effectively enveloping my mind with a satisfactory peace. My children were bright and logical. This was the first time in my life that they had crossed important ground together forged a bond that wouldn't easily be broken. Life's lesson didn't come cheap. After a period of struggle, I learnt that one could learn a lot from young ones. No one could be a better teacher than them to give hope and enthusiasm to the parents lacking in it. I thanked my children with a smile so grateful to God for making them a part of my life without whom my life had no meaning. Children were the best gift any woman could have and my children proved the saying correct when they supported me, loved me so, so much their spirit lifted me up. Their pure unconditional love was surprisingly so effective that once again I treasured their being with me. They were my true angels. No, my guardian angels!

Both grabbed my hands, bickering back and forth as they hauled me to my room.

The empty room, fortunately, showed no signs of him, in which case my attention went back to Naina who was powerfully active in her move. "Mom tell me what all is there you need. I'll gather all the stuff." She slid open the cupboard frantically skimming through the outfits.

Samath checked for my bag, zipped it open.

"Wait ..we have to go to Roshni auntie's house. My stuff is there."

"Then why are we wasting time sitting? Let's go out kick some butt!"

I nodded with a laugh and sauntered out behind my children, feeling like the queen of the world, hoping in my hearts of hearts that I would never lose this feel ever.

After Smita left I slumped on the sofa. My body felt heavy and tender and my stomach raw. The image of Smita's face floated back into my mind time and again. The episode had been one hell of a harrowing experience. Did I go far? Was I correct in accusing her of having an affair? I loved her, but she was in love with idea of love and I sure as hell didn't measure up to the white knight she imagined she married. I'd tried my best to do everything for my family, but where did I go wrong.

Was I ruthless, was I being selfish, was I inconsiderate? Did I hold on to her so tightly that she could not breathe in her life? Had I ever stopped her from doing anything, or was I insensitive to her needs. I should have been the one telling her the snack at the dinner was as scrumptious I had ever tasted and it was light and fluffy. I should have told her that it should be me and not anybody else flirting with her and it should be me with whom she could share all her secrets. Many thoughts kept coming into my mind making me confused. Did she break my heart or was it I who broke her trust into pieces. The effort of trying to figure out how to sort out the confusion exhausted me. I pushed myself up to my feet, dragged on my shoes. I needed to go out; I needed peace and so left the house without looking back.

Walking slowly along the walkway my mind was still restless. I was at fault, but admitting it was harder than I realised. If I felt more comfortable, I'd go to her now. But Smita was upset and angry and frankly, I feared I'd willingly say or do something more to infuriate her. It was better to wait, settle down and then approach her.

After several minutes, I walked back and entered into my

house. Smita and the children were ready to go somewhere. I moved towards Smita and she looked into my eyes drilling into them. They were filled with open hostility. Samarth was standing to her left carrying his mother's handbag over his left shoulder while Naina was on her right as if guarding her from…me? Their own father?

The stand-off lasted only a matter of seconds before Smita sighed. "I do not want to cause you any trouble. I am going to pick up Roshni and go to the club with my children." She glared at me belligerence simmering in her eyes and then maybe not to antagonise the situation she shifted her gaze towards the table.

"There are the other two passes for mummy and you. If you have the time or feel the need to come join us at the club." She spoke stiffly.

I was again beginning to experience a healthy dose of anxiety myself. She was growing darker and colder by the minute. I wanted to talk things out with her. I knew I had been harsh, but wanted to mend my ways. I wanted things to become right between us.

I took another step forward and I started to speak when Smita sent me a scathing look that silenced me. I saw her storming out of the house with the children and I did not have the courage to stop her. The knot in my throat felt as though someone had stuck a fist down my oesophagus.

I gathered strength and walked slowly towards the table. I picked up the two passes as sadness crept onto my face that read

We welcome you to the Mrs Perfect contest.
Please be seated by seven pm, at the Sunshine Club.
While I read the invitation, mixed emotions played inside me.

Was she really going in for some silly contest? I had to admit it hurt to know she had functioned without me? Which then brought up a nasty thought? Did I subconsciously want her to fail without me? The fact that I even thought such a terrible thought bothered me. Knowing and hearing it aloud from her that she didn't need me or cared about what I felt was a sad reality and I had to deal with it. I told myself I just needed patience.

I could see it all clearly, may be more clearly I thought amused at myself. I was older and should have been stone-cold sober and I had- admittedly added a few flourishes to the memory. Even now touching my forty with none of the naïveté of the boy left in me, I believed it.

The beautiful memory of Smita before marriage flashed in my mind. I remembered her walking along the parapet, under the hard white moon sliding in and out of shadows like a fairy with her hair flying and her gown billowing. She owned the night at least I thought so.

As I'd wondered to the iron gates, she had looked down straight into my eyes. I'd felt the punch of it, the power like a blow meant to awaken my soul. My mind had sizzled from it, and nothing- not my youth, not even the shock had been able to dull the thrill. By the time my mind had clicked back into gear Smita's mother had shouted her over, and she was gone.

I blinked as I recollected many such precious moments with her not only before but after marriage as well. Maybe it did not occur to me that I had changed.

Through these years she had been with me being part of me and I realised I had treated my wife like a puppy, that's what I had expected of her that she would always be happy to see me, that she would rush forward eager for my attention, but what about her happiness and attention. I was busy, not giving her the time and attention she deserved. A grim line of restrained fury crossed my lips, leaving me disheartened and dejected. Yet the other side of me felt a tingle of happiness at the prospect of my wife's participation in the contest. This bold step of hers was an eye opener. It was her decision rather her way of getting rid of her frustration of being ignored and insulted. She was not having an affair; I realised that was an unfair accusation. I was wrong and I deserved the harsh punishment. She had the right to treat me like this. I kept the passes back on the table. It was time to humble myself. It was the hardest thing for me. It was a word that had always stuck in my throat and it was called compromise.

And I still wanted her. I realied with a slow dawning smile. I wanted every bit of her; I wanted her in my house with me and my children. I wanted my family back. I was a part of her past- present and surely one way or another of her future as well. The decision was quick to make. There was no confusion, no misunderstanding. I would support her. I had to get ready and rushed upstairs towards my room. Obviously, I had to wear the best outfit, to match my wife.

CHAPTER 37

Roshni's room was classic. Bright geometric- patterned rugs over dark wood floors, framed photographs clicked by her of her family crowded the pine mantel, a set of antique spurs, and a pretty hunk of turquoise on a shelf where books leaned against each other drunkenly. Lovely dried-flower crowded in brass urns-that would be Roshni's touch, I assumed.

The furniture was wide and deeply cushioned and feminine. Dark colours to contrast with light walls and bright rugs. An interesting mix, I decided. Simple, feminine and pleasing to the eye.

Roshni reached for my hand and gave it a gentle squeeze after I narrated the entire incident to her. The atmosphere was almost... intimate. His arm across the back of an empty chair, Samarth was leaning back, speaking animatedly about one thing or another. Whatever he was saying obviously amused Naina and Roshni's children, who laughed more than once. For a moment I looked relaxed and at ease.

The thought was broken returning to the subject at hand. "Perhaps you misunderstood." Roshni looked concerned offering me tea. Having a rare temper, Roshni recognised the danger signs when they were stuck on my face.

"No, I didn't." Temper leapt into my throat. When I couldn't choke it down I shoved away the cup and got to my feet. "Where does a man get that kind of nerve, that much arrogance?"

"Most are born with it and yours is a specialist. He became worse because you encouraged him."

"I know what Avinash is up to." I got up whirling away to stock around the room unable to sit in one place. "He needs a wife who obviously has no backbone. Well, he is wrong about it. I have got one. Maybe I have not used it much, but it's there. I am never going to be told what to do again, or where to live or how to live. Not ever, ever again."

Roshni studied my flushed face, the fisted hands and nodded slowly. "Good for you. Why don't you take a bit of breath now and sit down? I will call Durga and then we will leave for the venue. Till then you just relax and lie down for some time. Everything will become all right. Now just concentrate on the competition."

The children had fled out of the room and Roshni made me comfortable on the bed. Giving me pats, hugs and again congratulating me on my stand against a bully, left, tucking a throw over my legs, she generally did all the things women instinctively knew how to do to offer comfort.

It helped a great deal to vent to a friend. It took the sharpest edge off my temper, strengthened my resolve and gave me the satisfaction of having another woman outraged at Avinash's behaviour.

As my temper finally faded away, I became restless. I soothed my throat with tea brewed again by Roshni and this time it felt good. Only two hours were left to reach the club and another hour to finally bring out the performer in me. I wanted to change my mind. I stood up still a little jittery. I felt like taking a shower. So I went inside the bathroom, locked the door, I tied my hair into a pony. I stripped off my clothes and stepped into the shower tub. The spewing water from the vent felt so good. A balm to the weary body and soul. I felt the cramps inside my body ease out, but my mind whirled.

Why was I making this a life and death event? It's me. I worked so hard for it. Is there some flaw in me? I didn't weaken. I stayed through the entire course of bringing myself out. I did the best I could. I gave my hundred percent to everything. I don't have any more in me to give.

Why couldn't I believe what Roshni, Durga and my children were saying? Should I believe what Avinash once said that I wasn't smart enough to handle things myself? Once words were spoken aloud they couldn't be taken back. So I had started to believe him. Had I got it ingrained in me? No! Did it really matter? I had to rise above all this.

My slumped shoulders squared imperceptibly as I tilted my head to feel the cool water sprinkle over my face. *I do not want to fail.*

Then a niggling voice in my head attacked me. *C'mon Smita what if you fail? What would be the worst scenario? C'mon, take the courage and spit it out. No one is going to hear you in the shower. Be a sport come out with it.*

I raised my voice, "damn you if I fail what will Avinash say? Will he laugh at me? He will be proved right and I wrong. No, I won't get a second chance. This is not for me. I get one shot at proving him wrong."

You don't have to prove anything to anyone but yourself. Why are you even wasting time in thinking about it? Avinash is not some

*God that you would have to appease or prove anything to. He is a
sorry excuse for a man. You encouraged him Roshni had said. Had
I changed him? Had my behaviour made his attitude insufferable?
Because all the years of my marriage, I had been burdened by this
dreadful belief that because of my stubbornness I would have lost
Naina. I remembered his humility, then the slow change as I bowed
down to his every wish. But I still loved him, always had and
always would, but my attitude had made him bossy, controlling
and a prig. I realised that if I failed or won as long as I kept
thinking about Avinash with all the feelings and thoughts about
him it would keep on affecting me.*

"No! It won't," I snapped at myself. "I will not let him
trouble me." I came out of the tub looking at myself in the
foggy mirror. "Am I feeling as bad as you say I am Avinash,
maybe I need to straighten myself up?" I cleared the mist
over the mirror from my hand and belted the robe I had
slipped into.

*Let the past go. It's gone. You have to move on Smita. You cannot
let anything, especially your husband come in your way. It's not
about winning a contest, it's about making yourself feel better, feel
satisfied. Show yourself who you are? You are Smita an individual
having your own identity. You do not have to see yourself as a
victim. A victim was helpless against a situation and you are not
helpless.*

Throwing the towel after drying my hair and dressing I
marched out of the bathroom to see Roshni and Durga
before me. Durga came running towards me hugging me
with the usual affectionate animosity that we both shared
with each other. She tucked her hand in mine walking to the
side sofa.

"Baby come just sit down. Relax you are looking tense."
I blew out a breath as I obeyed her, but I didn't feel

completely relieved. Roshni slid onto the sofa on my right and Durga on my left squeezing me like a rat between two cats.

"Listen there is nothing to worry. Forget everything your husband, your duties, your fights...everything. You have just one target and that is now to get into action. There is no need to hide away from yourself bring it out... show to the world what you are! On second thoughts forget the damn world, pamper yourself with the idea of the real you. We both are with you."

Durga tried her best to boost my ego, as always she was a person who could bring in a lot of comfort and strength in one's life. And so she exactly spread her magic.

Roshni cajoled me. "She's right. Make a move."

"You both are sweethearts. I love you. I love both of you."

"And anyone who doesn't love you is a moron." Roshni kissed my cheek and Durga nodded in confirmation with her remark.

"For that, you both get a hug." I gave them a squeeze. "Whatever the hell happens, I'm glad I've got the two of you."

"And we both have you." Durga swung an arm around each of us. On a bray of laughter, I gave them both a little nudge when the three of us angled our eyes towards the door that thrust open and all the children came bubbling inside.

"Mom, it's time!" Naina said excitedly. "We have packed the necessary accessories. Let us make for the club."

"Durga what about your children?" I asked. I wanted them to also come.

"My younger one has an exam tomorrow and the elder did not want to come."

"But, then who is taking care of them?" Roshni eyed her

concerned.

Durga's rolled her eyes. "Who else? My darling husband is babysitting!"

That instantly eased the tension as the room erupted with laughter.

Roshni's three children were delighted at the prospect of some kind of fancy event taking place and were ready to go with us. Roshni's eight year old son Vivek remarked, "come, aunty, why are you wasting time laughing?" He leapt up and down and clapped his hands.

"Ok, Ok." I pulled his cheek planting a tiny kiss on it. I felt secretly delighted to enjoy the children's attention and their innocent curiosity to enjoy the event.

I watched them and my friends and then flashed them a grin. Finally standing on my toes their trust empowered me. I had to do it for them too. There was no cowardly retreat now.

I spoke in the strongest voice ever. "Let's rock it guys."

For a moment, all of them stared at me in complete silence as if some devil had entered inside me. The children took a long swallow and the silence immediately broke into peels, of laughter when the three of us guffawed followed by the little ones.

The back of the car was filled with boxes, bags and garments. It took us three trips to carry everything outside with the children doing most of the work.

We sat down in two cars, one Roshni was driving and another Durga.

"Let's rock and roll!" Durga screamed at the top of her lungs.

CHAPTER 38

I was clad in the latest designer saree, its side pinned
properly by Max, over my shoulder. It was a chiffon and silk
mixed cloth whose fall fell in perfect pleats over my waist
and legs. He fussed for a few minutes, pinning, folding
fussing over me like a mother hen. I touched my stomach
feeling that actually, it had flattened. I let out a long, long
breath. I was at least twenty-five kilos lighter than I had been
a few months ago.

Before the realisation of my body could materialise before
my eyes, I was made to quickly sit down on a stool before
the mirror.

"Smita, dear sit." Max's tone was gentle, yet somewhat
urgent. His smooth fingers were thoroughly applying
foundation on my face. There was no moment to look at the
mirror as he started decorating my eyes with tender coats of
eye shadow and kajal.

Finally, after ten minutes I opened my eyes to look how
beautiful they looked. Eyelashes that looked thick and long
shaped like a swan's till their tip and the blue golden eye
shadow that made them look huge and glowing.

It was said that the eyes were the door to the soul, and it really made my soul alive. They were looking amazing. Then final touches of light pink blush on, on my cheeks and a subtle rose colour lipstick was applied on my lips toning well with my complexion.

Max flopped back, splaying a hand over his chest. "Transformation! Just look at yourself."

The subtle highlights accented my dusky skin tone and dark eyes. As a result, whatever Max's magic fingers had done it really was a transformation. Was it him who gave me a finesse of a beauty or was it naturally glowing from inside. It was the work of both.

"Thank you, Max you are a genius. I think I have never ever looked so good in my whole life. It is all because of you. Your makeup has given me the confidence to face the audience. Thank you!"

"Sweetheart!" Max dabbed his eyes a little. "You are looking like a vision. I am so proud of you." With a sentimental smile, he threw an arm around my shoulders and hugged me from the back. He then did something that was even more unexpected. He rubbed a little kajal from his eyes and marked the same behind my ear. I didn't know whether to be embarrassed or grateful for his affection.

Flushed I swivelled the chair and took his delicate hand in mine. "Thank you, Max. You are a gem."

"Gosh, sweetie, don't you dare cry. It will spoil my hard work." His lips folded into a thin, smile. "Now, on your feet! Go on, look at yourself in the long mirror and give the other women a run for their money. My bet is on you," he said with a triumphant ring in his voice.

I moved towards the wall near the stack of outfits hanging over the stands to look at myself all over before a long mirror.

Walking like a model picking up my saree a little being careful not to trip, I kept smiling at the women who passed by me. Emerald earrings dangled from my ears complementing the attire.

Then crossing the stand I stood before the long pier mirror. I was hit by a sight of myself and even though I didn't believe what I was seeing and feeling, it seemed to be real.

Staring back at me was Smita that I hadn't seen in a long, long time. A body that had a lifetime of fat and dullness had been now made into a beautiful machine of a twenty-five year old. I loved its flatness and tightness.

What surprised me as I looked in the mirror was the look of confidence on the face of a thirty-five –year- old woman. Correction, I did not look thirty-five –years- old now. I felt and looked like a twenty-five –year- old.

This wasn't the woman who would bow down to the wishes of her husband and get humiliated by him. This was the woman who believed in herself and sure would go far in this world to make her name.

I leant closer towards the mirror and turned my face to the left and right. O my God, it is pure skin. No lines nor wrinkles just pure, smooth glowing skin. Over the years, I had not taken care of my skin, but these six months of healthy, nutritious food and exercise had done wonders to my skin. It made it bright, clear and healthy. Anyone could mistake me for a preferably younger woman.

What I did this moment would determine how the rest of my life would go. The truth was that I didn't know what was waiting for me in the next moment.

Soon the announcement was made for the Mrs Perfect show to begin. The staff was ushering the contestants to stand on the stage. We were given instructions to stand on the crosses with our numbers that would be marked on the stage. And then we were supposed to take a round of the stage, according to our names that would be announced.

I started feeling jittery. I sidled closer to Roshni who could make out the nervousness in me. Roshni had breezed inside the backstage claiming that she would be taking pictures of the event, which worked because of her name. A camera was hung around her neck and from time to time she was clicking pictures of the activity around. But I knew she was there to support me.

"Roshni," I was stumbling. Panic was an icy poker jabbing through my belly. "What if I fail… what if I disappointed myself? Worse yet, what if I make a fool out of myself. What if…. huhh what if?"

Roshni reached for my shoulder, comforting me by stroking them. "Sssh…calm down…You have to shift into neutral, Smita. You're way too tense. Relax."

Roshni's voice dropped down even lower as she whispered into my ears. "Today is no different than any other day be it yesterday or the day before yesterday. You were ready then and ready now. Mind over matter. This isn't the end of the world. You are not going for some war, it's a simple contest. Chill out."

I clutched out to my stomach. *Easier said than done.*

Emotions storming across her face, Roshni, laid her hands on my arms. "I know it's not easy, but it's not impossible. Nothing is impossible till it's done." She could read my mind and continued in a low whisper, "I want you to go and kiss some ass. You can do it, my dear, just stay focused. I am betting on you. You cannot let me down. And finally, do it for yourself! You are the one who is important and no one else."

She could really make me feel good. I knew I had been given a second chance in my life, and I'd chosen this life and these people because I loved them. But I also learned that I needed to love myself. I knew I could do it and win the contest. I wasn't a failure, a doormat, but a woman of substance who had a mind of her own. I spent the entire life with Avinash for him and my children, so now the impulse to tell him what happened to me was wrong.

"Everything you want in life is waiting for you, outside your comfort zone and inside your effort zone." Roshni gave me a little nudge to send me along.

I heaved a mighty sigh straightened my spine, pushed my shoulders back and with the air of confidence moved out with the other women on the stage. I was in awe at what I was seeing- throngs of people, all men, other women and children cheering and supporting the women of their families. I felt self- conscious as I stood on the pink stage, dazzling with bright yellow light surrounded by people. I had never been this visible, in fact, I couldn't remember being in such a crowd of people. A table was kept right in front where five people were seated. From their haughty expressions and carriage, it was obvious that they were the judges.

The host was a handsome young man, dressed in an immaculate black suit. With a smile, he announced dramatically, "please welcome your host for the evening Kapil." He gave a dignified bow. "Now I welcome these ladies to this arena in the hope of being Mrs Perfect, the beauty with a purpose." He paused gesturing towards us. "Heading to the start of the show I would request these beautiful ladies to walk to the tune of this lovely song played

by our live band. C'mon ladies show them your sexy walk!"
A blue spotlight illuminated the band at the corner of the
stage which started playing pretty woman.

As the names were announced one by one the twenty -five
contestants walked forward, took a round on the stage and
then took their place, I was number ten. Moments before
starting my walk I was super excited but nervous. At a
glance, I saw my children giving me thumbs up on a side
table and my mother-in-law gazing in my direction trying to
comprehend the magnanimity of the contest. Beside them,
Durga was hooting, "Smita! Smita!" Roshni was busy
clicking pictures.

The moment I saw their cheerful faces waving at me, I
picked up myself and made my move like a lady, following
the line the other ladies had taken. Automatically the
training ingrained in me took over back straight, shoulders
back, chest out and abdomen in.

With a beautiful smile on my face, I glanced at the audience
gathered all around the area where families sat in groups
gliding forward. Before I turned my gaze fell on my husband
who was gawking at me. I was stunned he had come. His
presence slid through like hope. I caught the feeling, held it
to myself and turned around walking my way beside the
row of women who stood in a semi -circle.

My heart was beating so hard that it seemed to drown the
sound around.

Kapil's high pitched voice resonated across the hall. "That
was an unbelievable opening. Don't you agree guys?" There
were loud claps and more hooting. "Before heading to the
next round that is the…." He trailed off looking
mischievously here and there. "Hold your hearts ladies;
there is a change in plans. As usual, we have introduced

something new and this year the surprise element is the special talent round. The contestants will be judged on self-confidence, physical fitness, capability and creativity they show in this phase of the competition. So ladies roll up your sleeves, you have just an hour to prepare something fantastic to show to our judges. Till then let me introduce the ghungaroo group who have been gracious enough to sing and play for us."

Oh shit! Talent round! Why did it have to happen to me?

CHAPTER 39

The contestants scrambled backstage. The atmosphere backstage was electric with tension. All were rushing towards their suitcases, clothes were thrown, tempers snapped and in general there was chaos where nobody knew what to do.

God, you have lost! Roshni, Durga, your children will be so disappointed in you, said a niggling voice inside my head. I came down hard on my heels, my head in my hands. I mumbled something that encouraged the niggling voice to vent again.

What happened to all that self-confidence? You said you were going to win. It doesn't look like you are going to win. You are a loser! Loser! Smita the loser! Loser!

"Oh keep quiet!"

You can't tell me to shut up. I'm you. That's like telling yourself to shut up. Will you move! Get up!

"Get out of my head! I am getting crazy!"

I felt a push. "Smita what are you doing? Have you gone crazy talking to yourself on the floor?" Roshni was beside me.

"I have lost Roshni, I have no talent! What will I show to the judges?" I heard my voice, oddly flat and calm, but a part of me was shuddering.

"Well, God almighty after all the gruelling sessions in grooming. You can just cry, you silly girl." Roshni pulled me.

"Get up!" she thundered.

Panic tickled my throat. "I can't!"

"If you don't get up this moment I swear I will beat you black and blue. You idiot!"

"Wait a minute here! Are you calling me an idiot?" I gasped, when had Roshni turned so abusive?

"Yes and fool!"

"Fool!" I sprang up, how could she use such language with me, her friend?

"Well, that got you moving!"

We sent each other mutual looks of heat and annoyance. Then she gave a lopsided grin.

"How could you forget that you are a dancer?" Roshni's voice rang out loud and clear.

I was horrified! I opened my mouth and then closed it a couple of times before finally blurting, "are you kidding! That was ages ago!" I was barely fifteen then and now after twenty years how could anyone even expect that I perform?

"I am not kidding. You can do it!" There was so much passion in Roshni's voice that it set me thinking.

Impatient Roshni laid a hand on my shoulder, gave it a little shake. "You have precisely fifty minutes to practice your steps. You couldn't have forgotten it all!"

"I don't know." I rubbed a fist between my breasts as if something ached a little.

"Oh, honey…" Roshni broke off, there was suddenly a

ruckus and I saw Durga plowing in followed by more family members who were heading towards the other contestants giving Durga grateful glances and thanks.

"How did you get inside?" I asked surprised.

"Planted one on the bouncer's ears, will set it ringing for some time!" Durga replied easily as if she didn't have a care in the world fussing with her hair in a timeless female gesture.

"You are just too much!" Roshni snorted letting off a pained sigh. "What else can be expected from madam? Except for wham bam!"

"It got the word done no," Durga said in a dismissive tone as if brushing aside an irritating mosquito. "Ok forget this, what are you going to do now?"

Roshni beat me in answering, "she will be dancing. She has learnt Kathak." Roshni then flicked her glance at me. "You already have an extra pair of clothes, that white suit, you can wear that. Just tell me the song on which you will perform, I will tell the band to play that for you."

Song? I tapped a finger on the side of my nose a faraway look in my eyes. I wasn't sure why I didn't protest that I would not dance, but somehow I could hear the strains of music from the past, Tak Tak thai, Digda dig dig thai... Madhuban mei Radhika nache re, Madhuban mei Radhika... I was twirling... hands straight, shoulders stiff, feet moving. I still had it in me; maybe I could do it!

"Madhuban mei Radhika nache re," I said softly, very softly. At least I knew I would be able to display my skill comfortably on this one.

"It is time for the talent round to begin. The contestants will be called randomly to perform. The first performer is..."

And so it went on... "And now the next performer will be Mrs. Smita Sharma, she will be dancing on Madhuban mein Radhika nache re. A classic choice. So please put your hands together for our next gorgeous lady Smita!" Kapil's voice rang in the auditorium and in my head. I was next!

I was frozen. Fear fluttered at the base of my throat.

It took me a few seconds to recover from the feeling demanding my mind to obey the strength hidden inside me. No! I admonished myself there was no reason to be afraid. I had to do it.

Enough dawdling, enough introspection, I thought and no longer shaking like a leaf I quickened my pace towards the centre of the stage.

The soft music came in whispers towards me and I stretched up my arms and turned. In a way, it had been fifteen years since I had danced this way, but in another way, it seemed just like yesterday. I put my hands forward, then up above my head and began to twirl my body in a tight little circle. With the music, I stomped my feet in a perfect alaap as taught by my guru, the taal and beats playing in my head. The audience began to clap to the rhythm of the music while I twirled and performed graceful Kathak steps never losing my balance or my momentum. Like a river glazing in white smooth waves of the suit flew in sync with my steps and I was the merging water flowing smoothly besides the passage of crowded trees who were silently absorbing the depth of its beauty.

And at last, when my feet halted into a defined posture, my eyes closed, the single moment of silence broke. The audience burst into applause. I opened my eyes that fell on the enthralled face of Durga who was generously whistling, then Roshni giving me a victory sign.

At their side, my mother-in-law was smiling and my children were jumping madly. I was afraid to look at Avinash, but could not resist myself; he was clapping like a man gone crazy! Oh, my!

Kapil emerged again waving his hand before the audience. "Thank you Smita. It was wonderful. Wasn't it?"

The crowd hooted again as I folded my hands in a namaste. I bowed gracefully and retired out of the stage, the grinning face of Avinash and his enthusiastic applause lifting my spirits and my heart. There was pride, enough satisfaction of knowing that I could rely on myself to do the impossible.

One by one the other performers appeared in chronological order meticulously performing their bit till the talent round finally ended. "That was something! All the contestants were marvellous!" Kapil announced after the last contestant had given a sterling singing performance. "The results of this segment will be announced after the next round which is…any guesses?" There were shouts of the evening gown round from the audience.

Kapil chirped happily, "you have guessed it correct. The evening gown round! The contestants will select the evening gown of their choice, but, there is another twist," he paused for effect. "The husbands will also participate they will escort their wives on stage during this segment of the competition. Evening gown will be scored on self-confidence, poise, and grace that the contestant show in this phase of the competition. So men, it's time to stand up for your ladies!"

I had changed into my evening gown. I had Max to thank for the change in my hairstyle. I was leaning towards the mirror sliding murderous red on my lips when I heard the announcement. I dropped the tube of lipstick in my purse. I didn't want to face Avinash now! But it was something that couldn't be avoided. The only choice left was to go and to go fully armed. I would drive him mad while I was at it. I dabbed perfume at my collarbone, in the valley between my breasts, at my wrist. I slid on my shoes, delighted the stiletto added inches to my height.

Next, I picked up the diamond earrings and slipped them in my ear lobes. The earrings made the column of my neck look seductive as the slightest movement brushed the diamonds against them. I checked myself in the mirror front, back sides. Then tossed my head. I pressed my lips together, opened them with a cocky little pop. "Beware, my husband." When Avinash entered backstage his eyes widened, blurred. I actually saw the pulse in his throat jump. I couldn't have scripted his reaction any more better.

CHAPTER 40

This was the first time I had seen my wife dressed in an evening gown. It was hypnotic, the way she looked at me fully, directly and little defiantly. It surprised me, her confidence, and the change in her. She wore a dress of deep forest green, the sort that covered a woman from neck to toe and still managed to tell a man that everything under it was perfect. She'd done her hair sleek and loose, with a little-jewelled clip anchored between the crown and the tip of her left ear. It was just another tease; it didn't do anything but sit there and made her sparkle. My wife looked fascinating. I just wanted to pick up a shawl and cover her up, so that other men would not see her like this. This possessiveness and jealousy shook me.

Diamonds glittered in her ears and I recognised them to be the same that I had gifted her on our anniversary. It meant a lot to me that she had worn them on one of the important days of her life. Her neck was seductively bare.

Slightly dazed, I walked towards her, having no eyes for

anyone except Smita, I did not even feel the jolt of women brushing past me or hurrying towards the stage. I stepped in behind her, leant down and sniffed. The air smelled of lilacs and of her.

Even a dead man, I imagined would have felt his blood warming. Smita stood close and let her fingertips rest lightly on my arm. I wondered if the room was over warm or if my wife simply radiated heat. I felt like a giddy young boy leading his first date for a dance. My tongue was tied into knots and my knees had turned to jelly.

"We need to go," Smita said coldly, her lips pursed in a thin line.

Oh boy, my wife was still really angry at me! Was my only clear thought.

I couldn't believe Avinash was looking at me like this, as if I was a woman…a desirable woman. It had been years since he had given me that look as if I was something to be cherished. I felt warm all over. Now standing beside him waiting for my turn I curled and uncurled my fingers on his arms. He suddenly gripped my hand hard enough to rub bone against bone as if scared of letting me go.

I looked into his eyes, surprised but there was no time for speculation, from both sides women on the arms of their husbands flowed like mermaids taking few steps one by one as introduced by their names. Avinash and I moved in perfect sync, but this time I was not walking behind him like a stray puppy on a leash but beside him as a wife should. The round ended with the contestants standing in an arc on the stage.

On cue, Kapil sprang forward. "Husbands are requested to please take their seats."

The men took leave of the stage. Avinash gave me a lingering look, but I ignored it. His look, the way he was watching me was making me nervous.

Kapil went on, "the gorgeous Miss Padma, famous supermodel and actress will announce the top three contestants out of these beautiful twenty-five women."

Miss Padma stepped forward; she had her own distinctive style of walk that was a gift of natural elegance. She was dressed in an electric blue sequenced gown that highlighted her curves and features to perfection. It had a long slit that parted with the slightest movement, revealing the length of her leg. She looked like someone out of a very sexy faerie tale.

She stood beside Kapil in a perfect posture and said in her soft melodious sexy voice, "girls this year are sensational, gorgeous and sparkling.

We the judges were supposed to choose three, but it was nearly impossible as all are perfect. So after a lot of deliberation here are the top three!" She opened the envelope that revealed the names. "Not in any particular order the first contestant who is in the top three…" she trailed off, her bright purple lips curving as the audience screamed out names. "The woman with the melodious voice Mrs Sakshi Jain!"

There were loud claps as I recognised the woman who had performed last in the talent round and her voice was really amazing.

I was silently praying, please let my name be next, please, please, please God. I knew in my heart, I had performed well and deserved to be in the top three.

Mrs Sakshi Jain came forward all smiles; she had straight black hair that spilled around a pale face of perfect angles and curves. She was tall and slim, garbed in a long gown of fluid silver.

"Congratulations Ma'am because you are also the winner of the talent round." There were more cheers as she received a bouquet of flowers from Miss. Padma. Photographs were clicked while the cameras installed recorded the fantastic live show.

"Now the next contestant is…" there were more shouts. I could literally hear my children screaming my name. Roshni and Durga's eyes were closed in prayer. I almost laughed when I saw even my mother-in-law's eyes were closed, her lips moving in chant. Avinash was looking at me intensely as if his eyes were telling me that it was not the only thing that mattered. The unexpected thought surprised me.

"Mrs Avantika Batra!"

My thoughts took me in another direction; I was by now thinking that that's it. I would not make it. All the training and hard work, my friends support, my children's support gone down the drain.

Avantika took her place beside Sakshi. Another stunning woman she was dressed in a shocking pink net gown regency style that showed off her tiny waist. She looked tall, willowy and a perfect candidate to win the competition.

"And now the last and final contestant," the same was said in a hushed whisper by Padma.

I drew in my breath, released it. My stomach gave a mighty pitch. It was now or never. I struggled to gather myself and find my core of strength. I knew I was afraid. I was more afraid than I'd ever been in my life and determined not to give in.

"Mrs Smita Sharma!"

I heard the blood rush and roar in my head, pulsing in time

with the gallop of my heart. Oh God! Oh God! I couldn't believe it. I had made it to the top three!

I glided towards the centre of the stage and stood beside Avantika.

My family by now had gone crazy. The children were standing on the seats clapping. Roshni and Durga were literally dancing, my mother-in-law was smiling warmly and Avinash looked kind of smug as if he already knew the result.

"The top three!" Kapil trilled. The other women discreetly left the stage.

"Now the last and final round," Kapil said ominously. "The top three finalists will be asked questions on stage. The scores will be added to their previous tally to decide the winner!"

A woman came on the stage with a glass bowl containing chits.

I was nervous. The carrot that was Mrs Perfect crown dangled at the end of a very long, very thorny stick of question answer round.

"In numerical order, the first one to answer the questions put up by the judges will be Mrs Smita Sharma."

I felt a tremble run through my body. Because my first reaction was gut wrenching fear. I willed it aside and tried to work up an easy smile.

Kapil walked towards me and spoke in a consonantal tone, "you need to pick up a chit to choose your judge who will put a question before you."

Panic leaked through my shield of will; mentally I slapped it aside and pulled out a chit. My pulse raging I spoke aloud, "Mr Habib."

"The famous makeup professional and hair stylist who has

worked his magic on many film stars. Let's see what he has in store for Smita," Kapil bellowed on the mike.

Habib was a short, squat wiry man whose hair was coloured with streaks of blue. On any other person, it would have looked terrible, but he carried it with an ease as if he was born with blue hair.

"Good evening, sir," I said in a voice which sounded calm to my ears despite my heart beating erratically.

"Good Evening Smita. First of all, congratulations on making it to the top three. My question is very simple. How will you describe beauty?"

I let out a little breath to ease the pressure on my chest.

"Thank you for the question." I racked my brain a little; the picture of Sophia Loren and her words instantly came into my mind. "As Sophia Loren once said, Beauty is how you feel inside, and it reflects in your eyes. It is not something physical." I paused for a few seconds. "Believing that you are beautiful is the first step to understanding your worth as a woman."

My eyes darkened. "Once self -confidence and self- esteem are chipped off, it's not easy to rebuild those things. But there is beauty in a woman whose confidence comes from experiences. For me, coming here, just walking on the stage took everything I've managed to store up. I am a beautifully confident woman who knows she can fall, pick herself and move on. She can achieve all she desires. This feeling of achievement is beauty for me. This self-confidence is beauty for me. This is how I will describe beauty."

The auditorium broke into the sound of thousands of hands clapping. The sound was like music to my ears. Music of Joy. Whatever it was in that second, I gave up the fear of losing. That knowledge left me breathless. Whatever the problem had been between my husband and me, right now as I stood on the stage while the function went on with the other contestants answering, I knew that inside I was a different woman. The loss or win could not change me. It felt as though a huge weight had been lifted off my chest, I suddenly felt like flying. I could move on and still live. Finally, the round was over and we were ushered backstage. The judges were taking time to choose the winner. The total scores of the three rounds had to be tallied in order to find Mrs Perfect.

Backstage Durga and Roshni were waiting for me.

"You did well sister," Roshni reached out for my hand. "Courage and beauty will surely make you the winner." Durga squeezed my other hand. We stood like that for some time, a circle of three. I drew strength from them. The moment of silence shattered as my children rushed into my arms literally making me fall on the floor. I gave a full-throated joyous sound. "You are going to throttle your mother!"

"You were just great mom!" Naina hollered.

"I know you will win!" Samarth was bursting with excitement.

"Ok, ok," I replied happily. I looked up and saw Avinash standing just a distance away, silent and brooding.

I looked away, what was there to say?

"Smita, Smita." The impatient look in Durga's eyes tipped her off. "The top three are being called on the stage. You need to go."

I blew out a breath and readjusted my gown.

The top three huddled again together on the stage, trying to provide comfort to each other with their touch.

"The winner will be announced by the organiser of the show

Mrs Tisha Wadia. She was crowned Miss World in 1980 and has been a part of many such shows. Being a part of organising Mrs India she has decided that the winner of the competition will be given direct entry into the Mrs India contest!" Kapil's voice ended on a high note. There were more claps. "Let me invite Mrs Wadia on the stage."
Mrs Trisha Wadia was a beautiful woman. She moved with grace and athleticism, the lines, the curves, the shape all beautiful strength. Dressed in an elegant black saree, she looked every inch the Miss World that she was.
She spoke in the rosiest of voice, "thank you Kapil for hosting the show so well. For years the sunshine club has been hosting Mrs Perfect competition and this year has been one of the best. Mrs Perfect is an effort to thank homemakers for the many roles they play effortlessly in our lives. This is not just a beauty pageant for women, but to show that womanhood is much more than external beauty. Today's competition was not only among beautiful women, but between most beautiful hearts and incredible intelligence. All the contestants were precious and all are winners for taking the step towards change. So after careful consideration and adding the scores of the top three we came to the conclusion that the second runner up is…" She waited a beat or two, "Mrs Avantika Batra."
Striving hard to hide her disappointment, I could see Avantika accepting the beautiful bouquet of white roses. She took a round of the pink stage and then stood a step aside.
I curled my fingers and because the tingling did not stop I rubbed them on the skirt of my gown. Balance, I told myself.
"Now the first runner up is…"
My legs trembled, my hands shook.
"Sakshi Jain!"

My body stilled. I just stood there struggling to catch my breath. The confetti, flowers falling all around me. The cameras were clicking furiously. I'd have sworn the world stopped. For one rushing moment, there was no sound, no movement. There was nothing but the sensation of warmth. And then Kapil's voice was echoing in my ear. "The beautiful, gorgeous, talented Mrs Smita Sharma is the winner!"

The muscles around my heart seemed to clench, leaving me breathless. My heart lifted. The magnitude of the joy was almost unbearable; I was ready to burst from it. I had won! Mrs Wadia took my hand and guided me towards the center of the stage. She then plucked the beautiful ruby and diamond tiara out of the lush pillow where it was placed. With steady hands, she placed the same on my head.

The feeling was heavenly. Next, I was presented with a bouquet of purple and pink orchids that were absolutely gorgeous.

After thanking Mrs Wadia I took a round of the stage waving and blowing kisses amidst sounds of clapping and cheers. There were roars of Smita! Smita! Smita!....

The next hour passed in a blur for me. My television and print interview over, I settled next to my children and friends. Roshni bought me a plate of food, which I devoured. I basked in contentment as the other contestants and their family stopped by to congratulate me. Everyone congratulated me except the person whom I was searching for? Where was Avinash?

It was midnight by the time the program ended.

Finally alone in the washroom, I could let my thoughts run. I changed into a long top and tights, brushing the tangles out of my hair; I tied it in a pony. I still hadn't seen him. Now I was getting angry. Was he so jealous, that he wouldn't even congratulate me? Male chauvinistic pig! I couldn't believe I had married him.

EPILOGUE

We all walked towards the car and it was there I saw him, leaning casually on the car. I didn't notice the nod that passed between my mother-in-law, my friends and my husband. They discreetly left with the children in the other car without me being even aware of it till I heard the roar of the engine. Wait, I wanted to scream, but no sound came out of my mouth. I was alone with Avinash. The parking was deserted; all had left because there were no cars except one. I could hear my own heart beating, could feel the blood pumping to and from it. In the shadowy light, he looked mysterious with his hair mussed from the wind that was blowing and his own restless fingers.

He waited with every appearance of calm as I walked towards the car. It annoyed me to get my bearings, seek my balance on seeing the look of adoration on his face when I reached him.

The wind was picking up and Avinash moved closer to me as if wanting to shield me.

"Congratulations. I am proud of you, my dear…dear…" He repeated dear twice and my heart ached with the lone word.

"Excuse me," I said and then stepped past him when I could feel the grip of his hand on my wrist.

"I'm sorry honey; I didn't mean whatever I said."
That threw me off; his saying sorry but I didn't soften my expression. It might have taken me years to learn to use my spine, but I knew now. Keeping the rigid smile on my face, I shoved his hands away. I turned to face his back and could feel my heart start to sink in my chest when he stood right at my back.
"It's so simple for you men to say sorry and get away with it. After so many years of marriage, you haven't had any feelings for me." I crossed my arms making no movement at all.
"Darling nearing forty is hard on a woman, but... "
"Age has nothing to do with this! And I am just thirty-five!" I half yelled at him whirling to dart my anger at him. "What is it you men want? For the first half of our lives we serve you and fulfil all your wishes and on the second half, you do not want us anymore. You think I am mad or I am undergoing some change."
He started forward, stopped short as if warned by the flash in my eyes. "I didn't say anything like that baby."
"No, but you meant it". In all these years of marriage, it was guaranteed that if Avinash shouted at me, accused me of something I didn't do I would cringe but not now. I confronted him. "What's the matter Avinash. Are you jealous of my success? Do you fear you would not be able to control me any longer? Or are you scared that I will leave you? You are insecure."
I had all this rage inside me, building and festering in me for a long time. In the last few days, I made a decision to not allow my happiness to be tied to a man. It was only what I had and looked up to. In the months I had spent with all the trainers and my friends I realised, that if I kept on staying

like this with him I would in twenty years time, be just as I was before. I was infuriated and shamed to realise that I had always obeyed. But there was more to me now. More that I had realised. I was making something of myself and by God, I intended to finish it. Without being guided along because I was so inept at finding my way. I didn't need a man to tell me what to do and when and how to do it. Once again the fearless, the bold and confident Smita who was buried, emerged.

"No! I mean I agree that I was jealous, but that was out of something else. You are a strong woman, but not a hard one. So I am asking you to put aside your anger for just a moment so you can see. It was…" He said.

I advanced on him. "No, you don't seem to understand. You don't see me. You see a woman who feeds you, buys clothes for you, arrange your parties and bear your tantrums. But, you don't see me as a person separate from you who needs to live. I've given all my life to you and children and now when they're grown I need time for myself. I can't take this anymore. I have certainly tried to make it up for you over the years but cannot take this humiliation any longer. I won't be anyone's convenience, the belonging has to be on both sides and complete. If you want to leave me, leave. I'll be off the hook."

"What the hell are you saying? Leave you." For the first time over the years of marriage, I had his full and undivided attention. He grabbed my hand, squeezed hard enough to widen my eyes in surprise.

"Hell, I was wrong in judging you. Not because I didn't trust you but because I was… you were right I didn't like the idea of any other man approaching you because I love you. You're as beautiful as the day I married you. There was always a part of you that I couldn't reach, especially after that incident. I had loved you for your boldness, but it became somewhat lost on the way. I know that you have been handling everything so beautifully. The house, the kids and me… but the Smita I married was lost somewhere. I have realised my mistake I was throwing you into a vision of my making. The Smita I am seeing now full of spunk and brightness, not someone who is always sad and just obeys. All these years I wanted to make you need me, but you were occupied I guess, in sulking, it became a part of our lives, and I agree I too was lost in this world of mine."

"But it's insulting and infuriating that you simply assume I'll fall in line with your plans. And that I'm too stupid to know what I want for myself."

It felt like my heart was sinking when Avinash met my eyes. "I didn't think you were stupid at all. I just wanted you to be the way I thought right and maybe I was a bit stubborn in my approach towards you. "

I saw his eyes change, and wariness come into them. "I was wrong in taking you for granted, in not understanding your feelings, not giving you time… But I needed you then and I need you to be with me now. There isn't anything you can't do perfectly my love."

There were tears in my throat and for the first time in my life, I found the taste of them lovely.

Avinash dragged a hand through his hair and came nearer. "All right. What I'm trying to say is that because you matter to me because what's between us matters to me the rest of it's a little bit complicated may be because of me. You might think you matter to me only because of your success, but that's not true. You just matter."

Until a minute ago, I thought everything had finished

between us and now the things were taking a U-turn. I
didn't know, but felt the same overwhelming love for
Avinash that had been in my heart since I had met him first.
I didn't know this man would feel so deeply for me. In all
these years, he had never uttered a word of romance or
depth that stirred emotions of depth inside me.

Then all of a sudden, Avinash placed his hand on mine, his
touch being so soft and tender as he lifted it up and kissed it.
Oh my God! I thought what was he up to? I saw him fishing
his pants pocket. He withdrew a small jeweller's box.

"You were angry with me because I came late. It was
because I wanted to buy something for my beautiful wife. I
saw it… hmm and bought it. I wanted to gift it to you."

For once Avinash was not asking me to be what he wanted,
what he expected, he found me perfect. He needed me just as
I was.

Avinash opened the box. Nestled in a small bed of maroon
velvet was the most exquisite Belgium-cut diamond ring I
had ever seen in my life.

My eyes started to burn from what I was seeing and feeling.
Avinash lifted my right hand and carefully scooping the ring
out of the box delicately removed the engagement ring
slipping this new one on my middle finger.

"This is for our new beginning. Do you like it?"

I was shocked. Everything smoothed out inside me like silk
brushed with a loving hand. There was a little buzz of heat,
then a lovely spread of warmth where the gold circled my
finger. This was the most wonderful moment in my life. The
man I loved was offering me everything.

"Are you still angry my dear?" He asked solemnly. "You
will never leave me. Promise."

I knew my eyes were wet, but I didn't care. I felt a warm

flush flood in my entire body. I had never been as happy as I was at that moment.

The sudden fury of the wind streamed through my hair. I longed to put my arm around his and tell him I was also wrong, but the words stuck in my throat.

And then Avinash pulled me into his arms shielding me from it gusts. I suddenly felt protective in his arms. This is what I wanted.

"I missed you. I love you so much. I always have and I would continue to do so."

He kissed me on my forehead and took my hand in his and then his kiss on my palm sent a long slow ripple sliding from my toes to my throat.

"Avinash..." I whispered in a slow hum.

"Let's go for a long drive. Only you and me," he said softly with romance shining in his eyes.

"But children?"

"Mom is there."

His hand in mine, he squeezed it warmly confirming his right over me walking ahead.

He looked so handsome in his suit, holding my hand, his eyes soft and deep as anything I had ever seen.

I looked above the moonlit night sky where the breeze had settled gently over his shoulders and the stars simmered their blessings of love over us.

I closed my eyes issuing a silent prayer of gratitude.

Thank you God for my perfect marriage!

JYOTI & VARUNA

Ms.JYOTI GUPTA
Graduate from Lady Sri Ram, Delhi University, she is MA in English and multimedia and web page designing.

Ms.VARUNA GUPTA,
Graduate from University of Delhi, she is a Chartered Accountant and M.Com.

Being sisters they are surrounded by a loving family and share their South Delhi bungalow with their naughty pet Tony.
Passionate about reading and writing they decided to pen down their thoughts and feel it's a wonder how ideas crowded their mind till they completed their book through sheer hard work.
They have even written a fictional novel Tatpurush- secret

of the illumined soul and are working on the other one. They love writing about families and strong women who are struggling to find their niche in life as well as action packed thrillers.

Finally their dream of publishing after a long struggle is coming true and they would continue to charm their readers with further work as well.

Hearing from their readers is one of their many pleasures as an author. You can reach them through their email jyotiandvaruna@gmail.com or facebook page https://www.facebook.com/jyotivaruna1/